THE PILOT

By ROBERT P. DAVIS

THE PILOT

ROBERT P. DAVIS

GOLDEN APPLE PUBLISHERS

THE PILOT

A Golden Apple Publication / published by arrangement with
William Morrow and Company, Inc.

Golden Apple edition / January 1984

Golden Apple is a trademark of Golden Apple Publishers

ISBN 0-553-19747-9

Published simultaneously in the United States and Canada

PRINTED IN THE UNITED STATES OF AMERICA

For Eloise

The author is appreciative of the assistance of the F.A.A., the National Transportation Safety Board, the New York Port Authority, and, especially, the contributions of Captain Emil J. Smith, Flight Manager of Operations, retired, major carrier.

Author's Note

Many will ask, even pilots: Could there possibly be an alcoholic airline captain? Unfortunately, the answer is yes, there have been some. This one flew for a major international carrier and, of course, his name was not Mike Hagen. Readers might infer that there are many "Mike Hagens" sitting in the cockpits of commercial airliners.

This is not true.

The chances of finding another Hagen on the flight deck are infinitesimal. All carriers—large and small—have the highest and strictest standards for pilot proficiency and conduct. Every day of his life, on and off the job, the pilot's career is on the line—unlike most other professions. But pilots, like anyone else, have certain weaknesses and emotions. Mike Hagen's story is not one of defeat, but an ultimate victory over a devastating problem, because in coming to terms with himself, he discovered a new identity, a truer one.

Although the main incidents in this book are based upon fact, the characters and the airline for which Mike flew are fictitious, and if the carrier bears any resemblance to an existing airline, it is just coincidental.

This is the story of a pilot, *not* an airline.

Palm Beach, Fla.
December, 1975

One

In winter it was always dark when he got up, but Mike Hagen hadn't been asleep very long. He didn't remember whether he passed out when the late movie started or finished, but the booze had gotten to his head and he woke up at 3:00 A.M. looking straight at a TV test pattern, hearing the buzz from the set. He glanced around the small study on the first floor of his Ridgefield, Connecticut, house, trying to see the clock as he eased his feet to the cold floor. He always slept downstairs when he was going out early. He brought his stocky frame upright, feeling the stiffness in his neck and the hot dryness of his mouth. Padding across the scatter rug to the small bathroom off the kitchen, he hit a roller skate and bumped hard against the door jamb. He stopped for a moment to listen for Jean to open her door or one of his two children to awaken, but the stillness remained, so he continued to the bathroom where he flicked on the light and looked at himself in the mirror.

He did not look forty-two, he thought. Although his eyes were puffy and there were dark circles under them, he didn't appear as old as other men his age. The hair was still abundant and amber brown, not dull or streaked with gray. Mike studied himself in the mirror for a while; he thought he looked a little like a

1

young John Wayne, but there was a bit more of the
Irish in his face, a ruddiness criss-crossed by rivulets
of minute blood vessels, the tiny, damning evidences
of a man who has drunk too much for too many years.

Decision time.

Usually when he awoke prematurely, Mike would
come to the mirror of this same bathroom, take a
drink of water, and think about what he should do.
There were three choices: take a couple of sleeping
pills; take a drink—but never both—he knew that
much; or just go back to bed and roll around for an
hour or so until it was time to prepare for his trip. He
hated this extra hour. Booze always put him to sleep,
but it awakened him as its effect wore off.

He heard hard rain hitting the roof. On mornings
like this he would allow himself one drink, and the
closer to 7:00 he could take his "spooker," the better
it was, but if he started at three in the morning, he
would need another by 7:00. He also needed a couple
of pills to go to sleep, but then he would have to get
up in an hour with a barbiturate hangover and drive
the sixty-one miles to JFK. He decided to do nothing
and he went back to his room, tried to read for a
while, then he put down the book and listened to an
all-night radio show. Finally, just before 5:00, he got
up again and made himself coffee and started the bacon. Plenty of hot bacon and eggs eased the empty
feeling in his stomach and grease, lots of it, made a
large slippery coating. His father, a hearty Irish drinker
who had worked as a carpenter in Florida, always
told him to "butter up before the sauce." He never forgot that because his father escaped liver problems and
died at seventy, sitting in the shade of the front porch,
still pouring down the Paddys'.

After breakfast Mike dressed, putting on his dark
blue pants, white shirt, and his mechanic's jacket
marked "El Al." He took his bags shortly after 5:00
and went to the small desk in the living room and
wrote:

Dear Jean, Please see that the bills on the right pile
are paid. I think we're behind—there's some
dunning letters. See you soon. Kiss the girls for
me. Mike.

He stepped outside and looked up into the black
sky. A slashing, windblown rain cut through the leaf-
less trees that were visible in the dim glow from the
outside light. He opened the door and ice slid from the
underside and fell to the cement. As the door cranked
up on its rails he walked around the Nova and put his
bags in, then his uniform jacket, finally the black
raincoat. Mike suddenly remembered his cream and
he returned to the house, slipping the half-pint of
heavy cream he had bought the night before into the
side pocket of his jacket. Then he returned to the Nova
and began his long drive to Kennedy International
Airport.

At 5:00 on this December morning passengers
intending to catch Intercontinental Airways flight 467,
DC-8 nonstop service to Houston—the popular first
flight out in the morning—were also getting up. One
of the men taking 467 was Peter Hanscom, Executive
Vice-President of IA's Marketing Division, who was
going down to Houston for a meeting with the southwest sales chief. Peter Hanscom had been in the airlines business for twenty-two years and he didn't like
flying. He couldn't explain it, nor did he ever tell anyone. Pete lived in Patchogue and he, too, would drive
to JFK, park his car in the employees' lot to the side of
IA's terminal, enter through the Operations door,
and board the plane. He had three children, a marriage that worked, and a good job. He was an ordinary
man; he had graduated in the upper half of his class at
Colgate, spent some time in Korea, married, and entered the airline business because he thought that was
the future in 1952. It really wasn't then, and he never
went too far financially until air travel gained in popu-

larity and marketing became a key management function.

Pete's wife Gail was up and she prepared him a breakfast. Just after 6:00 he got into a small Buick and started toward JFK.

As he drove down Route 7 toward the New England Thruway, Mike's thoughts drifted back to his wife: the way she squandered their money; her room littered with every cosmetic on the market and expensive dresses tossed aside unworn. Everything that had once been beautiful and gay about this woman was now gone. The love they had shared had evaporated long before they regressed to separate bedrooms. Mike kept asking himself why the hell he was putting up with the situation. It was getting worse; the gap between them widened every day.

They had never discussed divorce, though at times he could think of nothing else. He was a quiet brooder, prone to holding things in, and every time he thought of confronting Jean with those four well-rubbed words "I want a divorce" he would look at his daughters and something would stop him. It might have been his sense of family or maybe it was the feeling about divorce that an older Catholic, even if in name only, still clings to.

He felt like hell this morning, but then it was always the same: the first part of the drive was the worst with the alcoholic fatigue, the dull hangover one gets after years and years of constant drinking; that feeling eased and was replaced by blankness; finally came that slight sense of uneasiness, the out-of-sorts sensation that could at times lead to a minor panic when he felt his head was coming off. This wasn't too often and Mike tried not to drink too much before a working day. The third part of the trip, usually the last five miles, was the time the empty feeling returned to his stomach, when the greasy bacon and eggs finally let the pains through. Mike didn't mind the last miles because he started counting the minutes to Ellen's

Place, and he pressed down on the accelerator a bit so the car picked up speed as it cut a furrow through the slush, spewing the melting snow upward in a large "V" spume.

Ellen's Place was a drab, half-hidden Jamaica, Queens, bar and grill about nine blocks from JFK. Mike had selected Ellen's carefully. It was far enough away from the airport so the cargo handlers, mechanics, and other airline people wouldn't use it, and most of Ellen's early-morning customers were from the milk distribution plant on the next street or the commercial laundry three blocks away. To the front of the squalid, gray-shingled place was a short-order counter; to the rear, a bar with booths on one side and a few tables in the middle. In the back were the restrooms and a small kitchen where Ellen, a buxom, light-hearted widow, made her own potato salad and coleslaw and pressed together the cheap hamburger patties.

Mike had been coming to Ellen's for two years. Once he realized that he needed the morning spooker Mike went on the search for the shabby bar, his launching pad. On afternoons after work he would get into his Nova and drive around Queens; finally, one hot summer day he walked into Ellen's and had a drink. He told her he was an El Al mechanic and she laughed at an Irishman working for the Jewish carrier. Now when he walked in for that first morning spooker, he hated himself because he knew he was over the line. Ellen knew too, but she didn't care and there were a few others from the laundry and milk plant that nipped before going to work.

Mike made a whole false life for himself with Ellen and Charlie and Lou and the other men who sat at the bar in the early-morning hours. One day Ellen asked, "Mike, you only come around once in a while. What do you do all those other mornings?"

"Well, I'm usually up in Boston—at Logan—only down here when they need me."

"Yuh mean, all this time yuh was really from Boston?"

"I told you, didn't I?"

"Yuh rattled everything else off—yuh didn't say Boston."

Mike made Ellen listen to a whole existence he didn't have in Boston; a wife who taught school, sons he wished he had; how he went to Mass and Communion, which he wanted to be true; how he worked in the Little League and took vacations with his sons out west. She never asked too many questions that Mike couldn't answer.

He liked his fantasy life.

The rain seemed to be letting up a bit as he pulled into Ellen's back driveway. Mike took his miniature thermos, stuffed it into a pocket, drank his half-pint of cream, and moved toward the rear door. The place opened at 6:00 and once he reached the spooker stage, he never got there later than 6:30 in the morning.

He ordered coffee and Ellen made him the large cold drink from a bottle of one hundred-proof Old Grand-Dad in a special glass with his initials. He watched her every second, looking lovingly at the amber liquid flowing over the three cubes of ice she had put in the glass, and he could already taste the bourbon. She slid the drink over and Mike brought it up to his parched lips, and his world changed. During those first seconds his mind and stomach seemed to ease. The edge was off. He knew there were twenty-three sips to a four-ounce drink the way he took it. One time he ordered a second, but it was too much and he was afraid of the smell, even though he could pack five away by this time without visual effects. Mike had cleverly devised a much better way: he gave Ellen his very small thermos, which she filled with Old Grand-Dad, and then she packed tiny ice cubes in a plastic bag and slid the pouch into the thermos, where it bobbed on a small sea of bourbon.

"Damned smart," she told him. "They could knock you for drinkin' on the job."

"They sure could," Mike laughed, thinking what Ellen would say if she really knew.

He said good-bye to her, hello to one of the laundry workers, and came out again to the back of the bar. Ten minutes later he reached the Intercontinental Airways building where he changed into the deep blue jacket with the four gold stripes ringing each sleeve. Over this went the raincoat. He put the thermos in his flight bag. Mike's eyes were slightly glazed; he saw this in the car mirror, but he had a solution for that also; his captain's hat was one-eighth of a size too large so that it slipped down deep on his forehead, the visor casting a shadow across his eyes.

As a precaution, he got back into the car again and took a small pouch from his flight bag—his "survival kit"—which contained a very sharp men's cologne; Sen-Sen, which he knew worked better than the breath sprays or gargles; Visine for his eyes; and a bit of women's cover stick that he applied to the left side of his cheek where the blood vessels were beginning to appear like lazy red rivers.

This furtive deception was necessary before he entered "Operations," for in those garish lights the telltale signs might come out. Mike loathed the room as much as he loathed the sterile, matter-of-fact quality that characterized modern flying: buttons, numbers, procedures, cockpit challenges and responses, checklists and rules written by small people in small offices who, according to Mike, neither understood the finer points of aircraft operation or, more important, human nature.

Mike started flying as a crop duster and he thought he could outfly anyone on IA payroll except, perhaps, for a few of the senior captains who had flown by the seats of their pants in DC-3 days before the Second World War. They were rapidly disappearing from the business. In Mike's mind one needed the sense, the feel of flying to be really good. He had it. When a guy can twist an "Ag" ship in and out of tree-lined fields, he thought, and not break it up, that's flying, a special perception one learns when wires hold the wings together and the pilot sits in the open and feels the hot clay dust of an Alabama cotton field. That was *his* kind of flying.

Now he sat in a small, complicated office that went up in the air. Shit, he thought, the plane could fly itself, almost land itself; it all came down to numbers and procedures, not skill, for any fool could read numbers. Judgment was something else. Mike knew he shouldn't be drinking, but he figured his ability wasn't impaired; he still had air instinct, perception of the skies; a copilot; and a big, well-designed plane that flew on a Fairchild autopilot which, on IA equipment, was backed up by another autopilot. When he thought of the autopilot's autopilot, he laughed. For him it summed up the magnificent sophistication of modern commercial flying: the autopilot that didn't trust its autopilot.

But what about the human pilot, that tiny speck? Where was he? Right now it wasn't the equipment that was bothering Mike. He had to get in and out of Operations without detection, and the harsh lights, the shrill clatter of phones and machines, the zealous little people working on weather and scheduling were all repugnant to the pilot. Operations was truncated from the world above the clouds, he felt; most of the meteorologists' experiences were confined to data interpretation; probably none of them had ever felt severe turbulence or the terror of a plane cutting through an aggravated cold front, trying to twist between towering cumulus.

Intercontinental had the same regulations as most of the other carriers: flight personnel had to sign in at Operations one hour before departure. As Mike opened the heavy, unmarked door, he looked at his watch—7:20. He was ten minutes early. To the left as one entered was a rack where the crews put down their flight kits and overnight bags; further on to the right, a sagging leather couch and a bulletin board. The cork board was supposed to be for official company directives, F.A.A. or C.A.B., but it was usually filled with "Apartment to Rent" and "Roommate Wanted" notices, and notices of discounts to airline employees. Opposite the sign-in-counter were the offices of the stewardess supervisors, themselves ex-stewardesses, who sat in front of big glass windows and scrutinized the girls' appearances when they checked in.

The last office in the corridor was occupied by the Chief of Operations whose responsibility was the scheduling of personnel and weather operations. He reported to the airlines' Third Avenue executive offices, to the Vice-President of Operations, a Mr. Fitzsimmons, an old-time company man who was feared by almost everyone in the JFK operations division. The name "Operations" was actually a misnomer because most of the route planning, overhaul and maintenance, traffic and other procedures of running the giant carrier were handled from the New York City office, and the green and white room at JFK, like all operational rooms, was merely a weather dissemination, flight plan, and crew-scheduling center.

At La Guardia the airline maintained personnel and payroll records, additional stewardess supervisory and credit union offices, plus the offices of the chief pilot, Joe Barnes, and his five check pilots. Joe Barnes reported to Cliff McCullen, Vice President of the Flight Department.

In the center of the JFK Operations area was a large wraparound counter; inside the counter, banks of teletypes, desks, and computer terminals. On the left side of the counter were row upon row of terminal and area forecasts for every U.S. and foreign station served by IA and cities used as alternate airports. Around the other side were clusters of winds aloft charts, the "progs," storm warnings, and other weather data.

When Mike entered the room, he immediately signed in for the flight. The sign-in sheets were constantly monitored by a member of crew schedule who made sure that every flight had a full crew reported in

an hour before departure; if a crew member was
more than ten minutes late, a reserve pilot or stewardess would be immediately called out, or perhaps
yanked off another flight to cover the trip, if that happened to be more expedient.

After signing in, the flight personnel were supposed to check their mailboxes located on the floor below to answer any company mail that might have accumulated since the last trip. Actually the only time
anyone ever showed any alacrity in running to the
mailbox was when the monthly bid sheets were due
out. Mike went down to get the "garbage" as he called
it: updates on procedures, F.A.A. safety directives,
union notices, Third Avenue junk. Today he walked
to the wastebasket and threw everything in except one
envelope marked from the office of the chief pilot. He
opened it and tugged at the mimeographed sheet:

FROM: JOE BARNES
TO: ALL FLIGHT DECK PERSONNEL
I have been informed that some flight deck
personnel are loosening their ties or taking them
off when in the cockpit. This, obviously, is not seen
by passengers when you are airborne but some
flight deck personnel have been observed standing
or leaning against the open cockpit door when the
aircraft is deplaning passengers, especially on our
shorter routes. We permit the operation of the
aircraft without coats, but rules require that ties be
adjusted and all shirts be buttoned to convey an
impression of efficiency and neatness.

Mike laughed and folded the paper carefully as
he went back upstairs. He would add it to his "chicken
shit" scrapbook. He knew Joe Barnes, a damned fine,
high-time captain. Mike realized how hard it must be
for Joe to write such a memo because all the pilots
would laugh at it; the younger ones would button up
their shirts and many senior men would ignore the
whole thing. It was that simple.

Technically, Mike's crew was supposed to introduce themselves in Operations; the head stewardess, according to regulations, should identify herself and ask about any special problems or bad weather enroute in order to plan the food and beverage service. Actually, very few bothered. Mike already knew the senior stewardess on today's flight, Nancy Halloway, a tall, slim blonde, about thirty-seven, who came back to her flying job when the retirement age for stewardesses was removed following the Eloise Soots civil rights case against American in 1966. Once years ago Mike had gotten Nancy out of a jam with the company and the stewardess never forgot it; she always had a special, warm smile for Captain Hagen.

Today they chatted for a few minutes and Mike had just stepped over to the weather counter when his copilot, Jim Cochran, approached. He was a short, wiry man in his early thirties who had flown carrier-based jets in Vietnam. Jim knew about his captain and Mike realized that Jim also drank within the twenty-four-hour limit. The copilot was far from being an alcoholic, limiting himself to one or sometimes two drinks on a layover. They found out about each other in Houston one night, and it was a small joke at first because they said they had to *protect* themselves. They bid all their flights together, and scheduling never called this to anyone's attention since it was within normal practice. Their routes were always the same, woven around Mike's special need: 467, JFK-HOU, a three-hour, fifteen-minute layover in Houston; then, 221, HOU-SAN, overnight; and 602, DC-8 nonstop service, SAN-JFK the following morning. It was not considered a senior flight and Mike—having been with the line for fifteen years—could have flown copilot, perhaps captain, on the overseas routes that were operated with 747 equipment. But he had the Houston routine worked out with Jim Cochran and they always received their first-bid preference.

In addition to Mike's special problem Jim knew he had a girl friend in San Diego. The scheduling desk or flight operations never asked why one of their moderately senior men did not bid for the overseas routes even though Mike had "opted" for check-out on the carrier's newer equipment: the eight DC-10's and nine 747's that IA had on service. The equipment usually flown on the Houston-San Diego route was the stretch DC-8-61, a long-bodied plane being configured by IA with 28 first-class passengers sitting four abreast in the forward section and 175 in coach class section.

"What's it look like today?" Mike asked Jim.

"Sort of wild."

"This front you mean?"

"No, down over Kentucky there's an aggravated cold front towering six zero. A lot of wind moving up there."

"Shear?"

"Yeah, on the return side."

Mike was always interested in the weather because he had begun in an open cockpit plane, but many captains, knowing they could work above or around severe weather, took their advisories in a cursory manner, preferring to believe that the computerized flight plan was right. Mike walked over to the counter and looked at the Houston terminal and area forecasts disseminated through the "A" wire of the Federal Aviation Weather Service, FAWS. The terminal forecast was okay: scattered at ten thousand, visibility eight miles in haze, temperature and dew point well separated. But the real story that December morning was high above 30,000 and Mike studied the winds aloft chart; as he did, the second officer/flight engineer, a youngish, black man, came up and introduced himself. The third occupant of the cockpit was different each trip and he was the one Mike had to guard against, the reason for the thermos.

There was a deep aggravated low pressure centered at 6:00 A.M. that day just north of Nashville, moving fast with severe thunderstorms and icing conditions associated with a cold front running on line between Nashville, Birmingham, and Joplin with one associated, but less aggravated, front pushing off into

Pennsylvania. The flight would divert north of the weather, as they could not top the vertical development, which that morning was eating up the sky and pushing into the sixty thousand level.

There were weather advisories out for light aircraft and special notices—sigmets—for all aircraft operating in the area of polar-originated lows. Mike moved around to the far side of the multi-decked weather board and flipped through the pile of storm warnings: company advisory 39 caught his eye, so did Sigmet Charlie 4. They indicated light to moderate CAT (Clear Air Turbulence) in a rectangle running around Shreveport, Louisiana.

Returning to the far side of the counter, he again studied the various winds aloft charts, comparing them with the pressure gradients at various altitudes. The wind shear was there. Small arrows registered tangential wind directions present along the sharply defined frontal surface which, combined with the location of the jet stream, seemed to set up a much stronger genesis for CAT than the advisories indicated.

Mike's route would take him directly into the Shreveport core and he thought there must have been an update not yet posted. He walked over to the dispatcher.

"Any updates on turbulence 39 or Sigmet Charlie 4?"

The dispatcher moved to his machine, shuffling the information about to be posted. He looked at the print-out still clicking on the machine.

"No, nothing new. Check again in about fifteen minutes."

"Do you have my whoopee?" Mike asked.

The dispatcher smiled grudgingly. Mike always referred to the Machine Flight Plan as his "whoopee" from "Big Fucking Mommy."

"Here it is, Captain Hagen," he said, handing Mike the little print-out.

While the crisp, sterilized exactitude of Flight Operations was first on Mike's list of things obnoxious, the MFP was certainly next.

"How dare some machine tell me what to do!" he had said four years earlier when he was sent a directive from the chief of the flight department indicating that the flight plans would henceforth be handled via the IA computer, a most complicated contraption that seemed to arrive on the airline scene just as the cockpit autopilot, and the flight director began to chip away at the pilot's traditional role of flying the plane.

The ultimate assault, Mike thought, was the MFP because it took over much of the captain's preflight work. In the beginning many of the IA crew members disliked and distrusted the MFP's, but as the quasi-science improved, most of the pilots began to rely on the machine flight plans because they cut down preparation time and, for the most part, were quite accurate. Mike was different. He disliked the MFP from the beginning, and he would often refile his own flight plan in defiance, as if he were waging a secret war of attrition against a far-off enemy.

The MFP, which came in from the IA operations center in Kansas City via a Detroit-based computer, indicated the best route from JFK to Houston, taking into consideration meteorological conditions, load factor, and other data. The IA computer held as many as twelve routes designed to keep schedule and conserve fuel within the existing weather pattern, although the pilot could reject the MFP and ask for route testing. Mike realized it would take him, perhaps, thirty minutes to work up the same output the machine could provide in a matter of seconds, so he succumbed with his usual hidden scoffing and filed the whoopee.

The pilot moved back to the winds aloft chart, still concerned that the turbulence in the Shreveport area would be more acute than forecasted. Returning to the desk, he requested a routing around the Louisiana sector.

"We'll get you around it, but it'll take you quite a way east."

"Forget it."

Turbulence comes in several varieties: clear air

(CAT); convective, usually associated with severe thunderstorms or squall lines; and mountain wave, linked to wind systems traveling over rugged terrain. Mike first learned about turbulence in his open cockpit plane; he respected its power. There have been bizarre accidents where modern radar-equipped jets guided by highly qualified pilots with correct turbulence warnings clipped to their dispatch papers somehow got themselves tangled up with convective turbulence and had their planes torn apart in midair by the shearing winds. A government report issued in December, 1971, confirmed Mike's suspicions: The National Transportation Safety Board records for United States air carriers during the past eleven years showed a total of 755 accidents, 147 of which involved turbulence.

Mike Hagen knew them all. He sat at home with his bourbon and read the reports over and over, trying to establish a pattern of what to do, what not to do. The facts were shocking in this day of sophisticated forecasting and highly developed airborne radar.

For instance, in 1968, a pilot with almost 11,000 hours flew a Braniff Lockheed L-188 into convective turbulence near Dawson, Texas, pulled off a wing and killed himself, his crew, and eighty passengers; in 1966 another Braniff airliner of British manufacture hit turbulence near Fall City, Nebraska; the right wing failed in flight and thirty-eight passengers died along with the four crewmen. No one lives through these calamities. An Eastern Airlines DC-8 entered turbulence near New Orleans in 1964; the aircraft was equipped with airborne radar, the weather forecasts were correct, the pilot had 19,160 hours in his book, 916 in type. Yet, the jet was upset and dove into Lake Pontchartrain, killing the fifty-eight aboard. But of all the planes destroyed by turbulence, Mike remembered most vividly the one that crashed in the southern Everglades not far from where he was born.

She was the Northwest Airlines Boeing 720-B which was clawed apart by excessive vertical wind forces shortly after takeoff from Miami enroute to Portland, Oregon. Mike couldn't understand how it happened and it remained one of the mysteries of the air. But he knew the names of all those in the cockpit who saw the verdant Everglades coming up at them that day in a wild blur.

There was Captain Roy Almquist, 47, with total logged flight time of 17,835 hours; First Officer Bob Feller, 38, with 11,799 in his book and, even more interesting to Mike Hagen, the flight engineer, Allen Friesen, 29, who held an Air Transport Rating, having logged 4,852 hours as a pilot. There were 34,486 total hours of piloting on the flight deck of a well-equipped and maintained aircraft, and the Sigmet, a message designed primarily for aircraft in flight, warning of weather conditions potentially hazardous, was substantially correct.

Sigmet 3 prepared by the weather bureau in Miami indicated severe turbulence in thunderstorms with a chance of "extreme turbulence." This advisory was called to the attention of the crew of Northwest's flight 705 and it was appended to their dispatch papers. The flight departed Miami at 1:35 on the afternoon of February 12, 1963; she climbed to 17,500 feet and reported, and that was the end; turbulence grabbed her, the aircraft disintegrated in flight, and all thirty-five passengers and crew of eight perished. The report of the Civil Aeronautics Board issued June 4, 1965, was summarized in their usual crisp language:

The Board determines that the probable cause of this accident was the unfavorable interaction of severe vertical air drafts and large longitudinal control displacements resulting in a longitudinal upset from which a successful recovery was not made.

In plain language that meant the pilot was in the wrong place for some reason; he flew into a thunderstorm area when cautioned against it. The aircraft experienced an upset, a nose over, and while Almquist and probably Feller were trying to pull her out, the 720-B came apart, raining wreckage over a two-mile area of coral rock, marshy water, and hummocks of cypress trees.

Mike went back to Miami to see his few remaining relatives and he visited the crash site some thirty-seven miles west-southwest of Miami International Airport, and later he saw the mock-up in the hangar. He read and reread the accident report. What happened? It was a jet upset, that's all. Although the investigation conducted by Northwest Airlines suggested a possible control failure, Mike learned something from the Miami disaster: don't go near that shit and it won't get you. But you could see a well-developed thunderstorm cell on the airborne radar; CAT was different: the radar didn't pick it up and it could lead to a structural breakup or fling passengers about.

Mike walked along the jetway to his plane, a DC-8-61, the familiar "Stretch 8," license number N-8907C. He needed a drink, but it wasn't time yet. As always, he stopped by gate six—where IA's nonstop service to Paris was making up—and thumbed his nose at the 747, her outsized, shark-like nose pressed to the loading tunnel.

Mike started in open cockpits, made his transition to DC-3's, DC-6-B's, 727's, and finally the DC-8-61, which he thought was about the largest aircraft should ever be. But then Boeing came up with the 747, bringing financial hardship to more than one carrier because of high capital costs combined with a fall-off in passenger revenues and the sharp rise of distillate fuel costs. If the DC-8 was the "office" that went up in the air, the 747 was the flying "executive suite," but Mike had to qualify in the 710,000-pound monster and he did so reluctantly. What rankled him most was the 747 itself; when he first read about the design in the aircraft technical magazines, Mike told himself and a few others that it was "too fucking big to fly right."

He was wrong. Not only was the 747's control system most responsive, all the problems associated with size and inertia had been overcome by design and the power of the primary flight-control surfaces. She was just a damned good plane, they said, with high speed, high mach number handling, good stall characteristics, and good controllability with engine(s) out—among other favorable points—which the pilots who flew these Goliaths of the air recognized and appreciated.

But Mike was illogically mad at the plane. How could it turn out so well? Mike preferred the DC-8-61; the plane he trusted was 44 feet 5 inches shorter from her nose to the farthest extremity of the horizontal stabilizers, and her wing span was 148 feet 5 inches compared with the 747's 195 feet 8 inches. His archaic little DC-3 would perch under the mammoth wing of the 747 like a newborn bird in the protection of its mother, he thought.

He continued down to the next gate and entered his own office, and sat down at his desk. It was a special kind, set up vertically before him and jammed with instruments, knobs to push and pull, switches to click on and off, and all sorts of other things that went this way and that, according to a thick book that told the cockpit workers what to do—aided, of course, by voices in the earphones sputtering more directions.

At that moment, 467's MFP requesting routes north of the low pressure center was on the wire to New York Center, the traffic control headquarters located at Islip, Long Island. The flight would be slotted and given an altitude and heading that would not conflict with other outbound flights from New York's three airports. The weather along the frontal line was forecast to improve by 10:00, but the early outbound flights toward the south and southwest were all requesting a more northerly diversion bunching up over the Pennsylvania and Ohio airways.

Captain Hagen had his thermos routine down to a finely practiced art. Jim Cochran made a special effort to look down to the right side of the plane when the pilot opened his black flight bag, slipped out the thermos, and then lifted his heavy frame from the cockpit. On the DC-8-61, as IA configured the equipment, there were two forward lavatories just aft of the cockpit, a coat closet, and the forward galley serving first-class passengers. A service door opened on the right side of the galley and Mike could hear the clatter of catering equipment being loaded, so his move to the lavatory was not seen by Nancy Halloway or the second stewardess.

Once inside the lavatory, he slipped the thermos from his coat pocket and slid the spooker inside the small flap door marked "Disposables." (Figuring out how to hide his spooker had been a long process. In the beginning Mike thought he could solder four magnets to the thermos which would grab onto the underside of the counter top. It didn't work because the entire aircraft had to be demagnetized so as not to inhibit the compass and other navigational instruments. Then the search started. He needed a binder, some kind of industrial glue or tape to hold the spooker to the underside of the bin. He finally found a jellied gum adhesive used in the plastics industry, and the hunks of glue did the job: the spooker never came loose.) Mike reached up and pressed the gum hunks against the stainless steel sheet forming the upper side of the bin. The top was coated in Formica and this formed the vanity area, which was backed with a mirror and the usual small courtesy containers of tissue, soap, and towels.

When he was sure the thermos was fast, Mike removed his hand from the disposal door and looked at his face in the mirror. He was amazed how well the Visine worked. The glassy, reddish look around his eyes was almost gone and when he smiled, his fleshy face seemed to blend evenly into the bags under his eyes, creating an overall semi-furrowed impression. He put Sen-Sen in his mouth, splashed on a small bit of after shave lotion, then returned to the cockpit where he took off his coat, hung it up, and slid into the left seat fastening the belt lightly around his thick stomach. The flight engineer was outside walking around the DC-8's undercarriage for his visual flight check and the rain continued to fall, creating small beads that padded against the front windshield.

Jim Cochran had flown N8907C many times and liked the Stretch-8-61; Mike had 4,878 hours in type and 26,756 hours overall. For his age, this was hightime but many of his hours, over 9,000, were logged in Ag flying where a ten-hour day seven days a week was usual in the dusting season. As Jim was going through his paper work, Mike picked up the phone and pressed the stewardess call button a couple of times.

"Nancy, could I see you for a moment when you get a chance?"

"Sure thing. Be right up."

A minute later the first stewardess appeared at the open cockpit door. "Yes sir, what can I do for you?"

"Tell the other stewardesses we're going through rough weather this morning. There's a bad low pressure down near Nashville. They're diverting us north to an intersection near St. Louis, so delay your food service until we find some reasonably smooth air. I'll make a PA."

"Okay. Anybody want coffee now?"

"In a little while," Mike replied.

Jim shook his head and Nancy left the cockpit.

The flight engineer returned to the cockpit and sat down. He told Mike that the extra Jet 1-A—kerosene —was taken on and they were still 42,000 pounds under the maximum allowable takeoff weight.

Peter Hanscom arrived at the employees' parking lot just before 8:00 and he went directly to the station manager's office. They had coffee together and talked mostly about new gate security measures and the weather, but the station manager did not know about the deep low pressure that morning; it was not his job. He had enough to do handling the routine of boarding and discharging the fifty-six daily operations at the carrier's JFK station. A few minutes after 8:00, Pete walked along the clean, half-empty corridors to gate nine where the small block-lettered sign read:

FLIGHT 467—
NONSTOP HOUSTON
DEPARTS 8:30 A.M.

He handed his "Class C" ticket to one of the gate attendants.

"They told me first is pretty empty this morning," Pete said.

"That's right, Mr. Hanscom," the agent said, glancing at the ticket. "I guess the rain kept a lot of people home. We'll be boarding in just a few minutes."

Pete sat down with his attaché case and opened a *Wall Street Journal*. The agent walked out to the plane and handed the "non-rev" card to Nancy.

"The V.P. of Marketing is coming aboard."

"Who?"

"Hanscom."

"Good guy—bad guy?"

"Don't know. He'll be up front. Lot of no-shows today, all right if we preboard now? I've got a wheelchair case waiting."

She nodded and he went back out to get his passengers.

Jim was going through his checklist when Peter entered the plane.

"Are we boarding already?" Jim asked, glancing up.

Mike motioned to Nancy standing just outside the cockpit door. "Who's he?"

"Company official—marketing," she replied. "There's also an elderly lady, partly crippled—that's for openers."

Mike turned back around in his seat. "Shit, what a day," he said to his copilot. "Weather, invalids, company brass . . ."

At 8:14 catering was completed and the rest of the passengers began boarding. The invalid was taken to seat 29-A in the aft section and Pete Hanscom sat in 6-D on the right side of the aircraft four rows behind the forward galley. The agent hurriedly thrust the final papers at the stewardess, the door was closed, and 467 was signed off on time.

In the cockpit the crew began their "pre-flight" checklist which, according to the manual, had to be read aloud—the captain, first officer, and flight engineer/second officer each reciting the procedures from a prepared page in IA's DC-8 handbook. This, too, brought a small grimace to Mike's lips because in the old DC-3 days the checklist was a routine—mostly common sense—lodged in the pilot's head. But now many years later the script had been written for them and was staged. On the left side of the page was the heading, "Challenge-the readoff"; on the right side, the response, and the three men started the life-or-death playlet, with Jim Cochran taking the part of the challenging protagonist.

"Windshield heat," Jim cracked.

"Warm up," Mike answered.

"Cabin signs," Jim continued.

"On," Mike answered crisply.

"Parking brake," Jim called.

"Set pressure normal."

They went down the eighteen items on the list, the flight engineer reading back some of the responses, and when it was completed, Mike began his "engine start." Even this was not arbitrary because there was a sequence: number three was usually first, followed by four, the outboard turbine; then on the other wing, number two, and finally, number one.

(The only tenuous link between the Stretch 8 and the first plane Mike soloed in, a Waco biplane, was the starting procedure; neither could be started from the cockpit without assistance. The older jets require ground support, a DC power input, and compressed air to start the turbines to a satisfactory RPM where ignition was possible. The Waco needed somebody to swing the prop by hand; like many of the old crop-dusting ships, she was not equipped with an electrical starter.)

The DC-8 was pushed from the gate. Mike waved at the lineman below his window, then he started the engines and they rolled. Mike was feeling better; the pains in his stomach had eased, and his head, although slightly light, felt as if it were attached to his neck for a change. On bad mornings he would sometimes ask the flight engineer to check a rear strobe light, and when he was out of the cockpit, Mike would turn on the oxygen and suck in deep breaths to ease his head pains.

"467, we have your clearance," came the voice from clearance delivery.

"Ready to copy," Jim said.

He read back the clearance and ground control cleared 467 to 31-Left and Mike taxied out to the active runway. The ceiling at 8:40 A.M. was nine hundred feet overcast with two miles visibility in light freezing rain. There was a line-up of planes, and Mike pressed his PA button and began his customary announcement.

"Good morning, ladies and gentlemen, this is Captain Hagen. Welcome to Intercontinental's early-bird service to Houston. We're about eighth in line for takeoff. Things are a little slow this morning because of the weather. I'll turn off the No Smoking sign now, but just before we go I'll turn it on again and please then extinguish all cigarettes. The weather we're having here today is associated with a deep depression down over Nashville. We're going to divert the flight north of our usual route taking us over Pittsburgh, south of Columbus, over Cincinnati, and then along the Mississippi to Little Rock, Shreveport, and finally down into the Houston terminal area. We might experience some turbulence enroute. I've asked our stewardesses to hold up the food service until we see how conditions are. We'll try to find an altitude where the air is as smooth as possible. In the meantime, sit back and relax, and it's a pleasure to have you aboard this morning."

Mike's PA's were about the best in the airline, some said; he had a friendly, convincing voice and often made scenic announcements, which few captains bothered about. The carrier had requested their captains to make more PA's and this annoyed some of them to such an extent that they made none during an entire flight. The federal air regulations do not require a pilot to make any announcements unless a safety measure must be initiated, and the PA's are entirely up to the pilots. Mike felt that it was good airline public relations to communicate with his passengers to ease concern during delays or turbulent air conditions. Mike realized it would be a rough flight, and in those seconds, as the plane slowly taxied towards 31-Left, he silently cursed himself for letting the spookers take hold, making him a prisoner, knocking his life into a series of small deceits. He often had periods of deep regret.

When the plane was near the threshold of 31, Jim contacted the tower informing them that they were ready in sequence. The tower acknowledged and as their turn came, the lumbering DC-8-61 turned onto runway 31-Left and pointed its nose into the wind.

"IA 467, you're cleared for takeoff."

"IA 467 is rolling."

Mike eased his feet off the brakes, made a slight directional correction, and the DC-8 picked up speed as the four turbines sucked in the damp morning air. At 138 knots they passed their V-1 decision speed and at 153 knots, Jim said, "V-R," and Mike eased back on the yoke, bringing the nose up into an attitude where the wings would attain their needed lift. Four-sixty-seven was clearing the ground, and a moment later the plane entered the low-flying scud and suddenly everything went black in the cockpit except for the red light illuminating the instruments.

"IA 467, contact departure control on 121.1. Good day, sir."

Jim switched the frequency identifying the flight. "Turn left and maintain heading of 240. Report reaching 3,000."

"Report reaching 3,000," Jim acknowledged.

The plane had lifted off routinely. The after-take-off checklist was completed by the flight engineer and the Stretch 8 followed the heading directed by departure control, which had the flight on its radar scope.

Mike rolled the plane into a left bank and they settled on the slow swing southwest of the airport. At two thousand they came out into a broken layer of fast-moving clouds and reentered another darker layer five hundred feet higher. The DME (distance measuring equipment) was tuned to the Robinsville, N.J., VOR and the distance to the station appeared as digits on the DC-8's instrument panel. The air was smoother than Mike had figured. They trimmed up the ship, reported reaching three thousand and after being cleared to the VOR they punched in the flight director, which would take the flight directly to the VOR, locking in on the ground transmitter signal.

Even before they reported in, a message came from departure control requesting the flight to switch frequency to New York Center; the center asked them to "squawk ident" and Mike pushed the button on the transponder. Two bright blips came up on the sweep scope in the long, loud, confusing Air Traffic Control room in Islip, Long Island.

Rain continued to pelt the plane as it struggled up through light to moderate turbulence over Pennsylvania. Just before they reached their cruising altitude, about twenty-two miles off the Harrisburg VOR, 467 picked up the severe turbulence. The plane bounced twice and then dropped rapidly. Mike felt his stomach jump into his throat. The autopilot took over and the plane returned to her course.

The air continued to be choppy for a time and the plane shook violently.

"We'd better take her off the altitude hold, Jim," Mike said.

One axis of the autopilot was snapped off and the copilot gently curled his hands around the wheel. Moisture appeared along Mike Hagen's brow; it was not fear but what he called his "M.S."—"Morning Sweats." He pressed the stewardess call button.

"Nancy, this choppiness might continue for a while. Keep everyone in their seats, I'll make a PA."

In the first-class cabin Peter Hanscom sat petrified by the turbulence. Flying through the inky clouds and the sight of the freezing rain hitting the DC-8 sent flashes of panic through the marketing executive and many others in the shuddering, racking aircraft.

Mike's voice came over the PA system again. "Ladies and gentlemen, this is Captain Hagen. We're at our cruising altitude now. The rough air we're having might give some of you concern. Please understand that these conditions are not unusual and our aircraft is stressed for anything the sky has to offer. It's uncomfortable, but the flight is proceeding routinely. We hope to begin our breakfast service as soon as possible; in the meantime, please remain in your seats with your seat belts securely fastened. Thank you."

Mike listened on the center frequency and chatter crackled back and forth as pilots reported rough air at all flight levels. There were constant requests for altitude changes, but it mattered little that December morning; one altitude was no better than another. There was rapid vertical air movement all over the Alleghenies and every route was experiencing the same acute flight conditions.

Pete Hanscom tried to concentrate on a publicity release as the plane was tossed about in the air and two seats behind him, someone vomited; the stewardess took the bags to the forward lavatory. That set off a psychological outbreak as two other first-class passengers started coughing, and the stewardesses knew what was coming. Some of the passengers felt no fear; they were comforted by Captain Hagen's deep, sure voice; others, especially women who were not frequent air travelers, began to associate the plane's violent motion with danger. The elderly invalid in seat 29-A was crying and two women, one in back and the other across the aisle, were trying to comfort the lady.

The flight was handed off to Cleveland Center and Mike asked for another altitude. Cleared to 35,000, where the turbulence was worse, he requested 31,000; finally, they went back to flight level 310. Mike took the wheel for a while and even though he felt his spooker wearing off and the hangover coming through again, his handling of the controls—the practiced dexterity—seemed to settle the plane down. He had an almost *perfect sense* of the ship's controls, knowing when to force them, when to nudge them, and when to let the plane take care of itself. He was more skilled at this than most IA pilots, some of whom let the autopilots run even in turbulence. Mike felt that since gyros could not feel the plane, they could only respond to motion and were slower than a good pilot's reaction. But this theory was controversial.

Half an hour later Mike felt the need for his spooker, gave the controls over to Jim, and stepped outside the cockpit. He took a paper cup from the drinking water dispenser beside the lavatory door, and then went inside. The two stewardesses were sitting in the jump seat opposite the lavatory. Usually when he went in for his spooker, they were serving. Today he forgot that they would be tucked in sitting by the lavatory.

Inside Mike reached under the disposal unit, felt the thermos, and pulled it through the door. He opened the top and poured the one hundred-proof bourbon into the paper cup, lifting it quickly to his lips. He drank hurriedly and poured a second drink. The plane took a hard bounce and part of the bourbon sloshed up into his face and down on the counter. He wiped it up, replaced the thermos, and stepped from the lavatory.

"How long do you think this will go on, Mike?" Nancy asked.

"I wish I knew. There's no sense in serving now."

"We have two passengers sick in first-class, five in second."

"I'm sorry. It's about the worst air I've seen in a helluva long time."

He smiled and winked at the girls. The younger one was visibly nervous; Nancy was calm. Engine-outs, rough air, mechanical delays—she had seen almost everything in eighteen years of flying.

At 9:55 A.M. they called Cleveland Center again and requested pilot reports on various levels; then were advised by Center that no levels were reporting smooth air but that the latest weather prog indicated improvement by 10:00 A.M. The time recorded from JFK departure was now one hour and ten minutes. They were coming up on Scotland VOR about fifty-three miles southwest of Indianapolis. Mike's spooker brought a calm to his head and his shoulder and neck pains seemed to ease as if a giant masseur had worked the kinks out. He looked over at Jim and smiled. It was a bold, confident smile that said to the younger man, "You're doing fine."

Mike punched the PA button once again. "Ladies and gentlemen, this is Captain Hagen. We have been informed that the latest weather advisory predicts more favorable upper conditions past central Illinois, which we'll reach in about forty-five minutes. The situation has been aggravated by several cold fronts. If the air settles down, we'll start our morning breakfast service and, again, we apologize for the bumpy conditions today. Thank you for your patience."

Peter Hanscom, who was fighting his own panic, was not very reassured by Mike Hagen's PA. He detected a highly abnormal message, even though the captain had spoken in low, reassuring tones.

The flight went into a gradual bank and started south at the Farmington VOR, the turbulence at 31,000 having subsided. At 10:55, Mike told Jim they could go back on the Fairchild autopilot, and then streaks of broken and fluffy clouds began to slide by the plane as it entered the back, or receded, side of the Tennessee low.

When the air was velvet smooth, soft morning light began to pour through the windows of N8907C. The passengers felt they had been rewarded for their bravery and Mike instructed Nancy to begin the meal service. Twenty minutes later the junior stewardess brought breakfast trays to the cockpit, but Mike said he wasn't hungry and told Jim and the flight engineer to go ahead. As they dug in, he slipped on his headset and called his dispatcher in Chicago on the company frequency.

"467. Do you have an update on Sigmet Charlie 4?"

"Roger, 467. Stand by." Pause. "Affirmative, 467. Sigmet Charlie 4 is cancelled. Sigmet Charlie 5 valid until 1300 CST indicates light turbulence over northeast Texas, area around Shreveport, Louisiana."

"Are you sure that says light?"

"Yes, sir. I'm reading it off the teletype."

"Bullshit!"

"Say again."

"Never mind."

Mike clicked off the button.

"Did you see that wind shear and the position of the jet stream on the board this morning?" he asked Jim.

"Yeah, I did."

"Would you say it indicated light, moderate, or severe turbulence?"

"More like severe, I guess," the copilot answered, knowing what the captain wanted to hear.

"You bet your ass!"

Mike was about to lash out at the company meteorological department, but he checked himself in time. Every airliner is equipped with a voice recorder in the cockpit and nothing can be said without the words being indelibly placed upon the slow-moving recording surface. For some reason, IA, an airline that prided itself on redundancy, had *two* voice recorders, *two* flight recorders, *two* autopilots, and two of many other things. "Those bastards are out there in the dark of night listening to the tapes, spying on me," he told his wife when he came home after his first trip in a "bugged" cockpit.

Actually, Mike knew it wasn't so. The tapes were installed because of federal air regulations to supply information in crash situations. And, of course, Mike learned how to "take care" of the tapes: that was lesson one.

Mike gazed at the crystal skies around them. The fear of hitting the turbulence haunted him; he remembered the statements of an airline crew that entered an area of extreme unforecasted turbulence. The captain of the 720-B, which was knocked around violently, told the investigators that immediately before the aircraft hit the shit, the outside air temperature dropped about ten degrees. Mike kept his eyes on the outside temperature gauge, and when it began to slide, he clicked his frequency button to 122.1 and called Little Rock Radio, asking them for pilot reports from the Shreveport area.

The transmission was picked up remotely by the Little Rock VOR receiver and transmitted over a ground line to the Flight Service Stations where the operator on duty placed the inquiry on the request reply circuit. The information Mike requested was spewed out of the Kansas City computer, which stored thousands of bits of weather data, plus pilot reports. In less than a minute the reply came up on the teletype.

"IA 467, I have three pilot reports."

"Read 'em off," Mike said.

"First one in sequence of time filed, 1120 central . . . a Gulfstream II at flight level 270 over Clarksdale, Arkansas, reported light turbulence. An American 727 at flight level 350 near Hot Springs reported light to moderate, and the third one says that a corporate pilot, flight level 280 over Fort Smith, Arkansas, flying a Turbo Commander, reported light turbulence."

"That's it?"

"Roger."

"Any updates on Sigmet Charlie 5?"

"No, sir, light to moderate turbulence forecasted."

"Okay. Thanks."

Mike looked at Jim. "Don't understand it."

The copilot shrugged his shoulders. Mike watched the temperature drop. Goddamnit, something was out there! Pilots are painfully aware of an empirical fact of jet flying: at times there isn't much difference between too slow and too fast, and all it takes is a good knocking in extreme turbulence to upset the plane.

Mike had a feeling it was coming. He slowed the plane down to its rough air speed; this day it was 245 knots or, as in pilots say, Mach. 8. Then he retrimmed the plane and pressed the stewardess call button. Seconds later, Nancy Halloway entered the cockpit, closing the door behind her.

"I believe we're entering an area of severe clear air turbulence, Nancy. Suspend the meal service immediately."

"We just start—"

"I realize that but I want the galley secured, all trays off the table, and everyone belted in, including you girls. No smoking."

She looked at him for a second, then turned and left the cockpit.

Mike started his PA. "Ladies and gentlemen, this is Captain Hagen again. We might be penetrating an area of clear air turbulence and, as a safety measure, I am suspending the meal service. The trays already out are to be returned and secured in the galley. I'm also putting on the No Smoking and Seat Belt signs. No one is to leave his seat under any circumstances until further notice. We apologize to those who did not receive our usual good breakfast, but this procedure is precautionary and we are initiating it for your safety. Thank you."

Peter Hanscom was just cutting into his scrambled egg patty when the junior stewardess removed his tray. His sense of fright returned, more intense than before. Even the blasé old-time businessmen were looking about nervously; the captain's voice seemed to carry a bit of apprehension.

Besides the apparent indicators he had noticed on the IA weather map and the temperature drop, there was something else that told Mike Hagen they were heading for an upset: his intuition. Some pilots get premonitions about the skies, just as sea captains possess a strange, unexplained sense of their universe. There have been many cases when a skipper said to his mate, "We're entering shallow water," only to be told, "No sir, the charts don't tell us that." Some skippers have odd perceptions about the water under them and know that the sea is shoaling, even though the charts say something else, just like Sigmet Charlie 5. Mike Hagen carried around certain cognitions of the upper air, a feel for the skies, evoked, perhaps, from having spent so much of his life above the earth. As he sat there looking out into the pinkish morning light, the pilot was certain they would hit CAT. It was just a matter of when. They were prepared. The jet was down to her rough air speed; everyone was securely fastened in; he even sent the flight engineer back to make sure. (One of Mike's dictums was *secure* seat belts because he knew the dangers of loose ones.)

The flight deck became very still as they waited for it to happen.

But nothing did happen.

They passed Shreveport, leaving that brown smudge of a city far to their left. Interstate 20 cut across the rich green-brown earth like an endless white ribbon tacked into the ground as far as the eye could see. Forty miles southwest of Shreveport, the flight came up on the long Toledo Bend Reservoir; Mike was working Ft. Worth center and he began his descent into the Houston terminal area. He debated whether to turn off the seat belt sign or not, give the passengers a chance to go to the lavs; they must be past the area of turbulence, or maybe it was never there and Sigmet Charlie 5 was substantially right.

The emotions of airline passengers are, obviously, in different places at different levels and some, like the business machine salesman in coach seat 25-C, had traveled so many times on recips and jets that he was almost totally immune to experiences in the air. He wasn't always aware of takeoffs and landings, and he had experienced so many bumps, hail pinging off the skins of aircraft, seemingly endless holding patterns and rough landings, that he simply sat back and slept or, at times, reviewed his sales reports. Nor was he scared when Mike made his PA about the possible turbulence, but others in the cabin became alarmed in varying degrees.

A couple of middle-aged women traveling together in first-class were clearly nervous, for this was only their second flight and they had not fully recovered from the previous rough air; they moved about in their seats and whispered to each other. The cabin had become very quiet as the low whine of the four turbines eased off.

The first jolt snapped everyone's head.

The business machine salesman woke up abruptly. There was an upward acceleration, a buffeting, and then the jet began to shake. Peter Hanscom dug his fingers into the arms of his seat. In an extremely turbulent situation passengers will suffer complete spatial disorientation, believing they are upside down when they are not, that the plane is diving when, in fact, it is going up. Peter Hanscom believed they were in a steep bank; as he looked out of the window, he saw the wings shaking and he knew that the turbines were about to come off their pods.

Then there was a crash. It came from the aft galley, but he thought it was the wings being ripped off. He closed his eyes and started praying, thinking of his wife and children. The plane was undergoing severe negative "G" accelerations and the passengers were assaulted by whirling blankets, pocketbooks, coats, and incredibly loud noise as they were shoved sickeningly down, up, and back against their seats.

Instead of diving, the jet was actually pitching on the flanks of a violent updraft. A whole sequence of critical events took place in spastic seconds, fragments of seconds. As the shock wave darted through the aircraft, the center of gravity changed leading to a shuttering high-speed stall. The plane began to climb with airspeed winding up dangerously.

For a few seconds in the cockpit they had no idea of their attitude, heading, or airspeed. Pencils, papers, charts, and jackets spun crazily in the air and the instruments vibrated so violently they began to blur and the small numbers and needles became fuzzy white streaks, impossible to read. The trembling young flight engineer sat with his eyes glued to the board in front of him as the racking and the noise intensified.

Mike gently, cautiously removed a little thrust; the climb was arrested and he nudged the wheel forward just a bit. It took eleven seconds to bring the plane under control, but it seemed like minutes to most people because their sense of time had been kicked off balance.

They had ascended fifteen-hundred feet in the climb and were far out of their assigned altitude. Once he had adjusted the speed, Mike regained his proper flight level which returned them to smooth, velvety air. The cockpit was silent; everyone's heart was thumping wildly.

"Nice handling, Mike," Jim finally said with a quaver in his voice.

"It'll be okay now," Mike said. "You all right?" he asked, turning around to the third officer.

"I've been better."

"Remember, fellows, if you ever suspect CAT, go to your rough air entry speed right away, and for godsake be sure everybody's tied down."

Jim peered over at Mike; he could not understand

how a man who was drinking could have forecasted the clear air turbulence and handled the plane in the way he did. The copilot chalked it up to Mike Hagen's experience. He was a high-timer. Jim's flight time was under 5,000 hours and he had never experienced anything like that even in military flying. He knew what the consequences would have been if a meal service had been going on when they hit the CAT; hot drinks would have been tossed around; there would have been injuries and possibly deaths. Jim's feelings for the captain were mingled; in one sense, he felt sorry for the man—his desperately unhappy marriage, his drinking problem—and yet, Mike Hagen had an air sense that was almost uncanny. Or was he just lucky? The copilot didn't know.

It took several minutes for the passengers to get their balance and psyches back. The screams that filled the cabin turned to cries of joy at being alive, but there was apprehension on many faces because they thought the airplane might still come apart, and why hadn't the captain made a PA? Was he injured?

But Mike was busy. He radioed Center immediately.

"What's happening up there?" the excited sector controller asked. "We've just gotten a bunch of pilot reports, on extreme turbulence."

"Copy this, get it straight. IA 467, a DC-8-61, hit extreme clear air turbulence at flight level 290,1105 central, sixty miles north of the Lufkin, Texas VOR. Get it on the machine right away. This shit almost broke us up."

"Roger. You ought to read some of the others."

"Can't wait."

As Mike clicked off the transmit button, the cockpit phone rang.

"Wow!" Nancy said.

"You bet it was a wow, baby. How's everything back there?"

"Absolute shambles."

"Anybody hurt?"

"Don't think so, but someone better check the aft galley. It came apart, and please say something to these poor souls—they're out of their minds."

"Okay, I'm coming back."

Mike was about to do something strictly against company regulations, but "screw it," he thought, as he lifted himself from the seat. Under the circumstances, he thought it advisable personally to talk with the frightened passengers and reassure them.

"Jim, keep her off altitude hold. I don't think we'll hit that shit again, but if we do, be gentle with thrust, very easy."

Jim nodded without turning around; he was pale, still a bit shook-up.

Mike passed the first lavatory and he wanted to duck in for a big, cold spooker. He deserved it, but as he looked at the chaos of magazines, books, attaché cases, and pillows strewn about the cabin, he decided to talk to his passengers immediately. They were looking up at him wide-eyed and nervous.

He spoke to the few in first-class. "Everything's all right now, folks. We've just experienced what is called clear air turbulence, but our entry speed was low enough to permit a shallow dive without an accompanying build-up of air speed. While this has been extremely uncomfortable for all of us, we never exceeded the limitations of the aircraft. As I said, everything's fine now and we should be landing in Houston in about twenty-five minutes."

They shook their heads and mumbled their thanks, and the pilot continued on to the coach section where he made the same speech, and then he walked up and down the aisle answering questions. Finally, he looked at the aft galley and seeing that nothing was structurally wrong, he returned to the cockpit as Jim Cochran was letting down into the Houston terminal area.

Nancy Halloway had been sitting in the forward jump seat when the plane was hit by the shock wave and she had heard a crash from inside the nearest lavatory. After the flight had settled down and she had walked through her compartment to see if any passengers needed assistance, she returned to the forward lavatory and opened the door. Inside she saw that an overhead compartment had come down and towels were piled up on the floor. She bent over to pick them up and was struck by a pungent odor, the unmistakable smell of bourbon. Odd, she hadn't noticed anyone going into the lavatory; they had been under seat belts most of the morning. The suitcase with its rack of little bottles was still locked; that was for the snacks on the next leg. She glanced once more around the lavatory, then shrugged; maybe someone had brought his own. Sometimes a very nervous passenger wanted a nip early in the morning but was too embarrassed to ask for it. Then she realized they would be on the ground in a few minutes and left the lavatory hurriedly to complete her prelanding duties.

Mike's pilot report, among others, set into motion a string of events. The terminal and area forecasts for Houston were immediately amended. The turbulence messages went on the line to the Kansas City high-speed computer and were relayed out on the circuits. A new sigmet was being prepared.

At the same time, the control positions working traffic in the affected area began to divert aircraft; twenty-nine planes—some commercial, others piston and corporate jets—slowed up to their rough air entry speeds. A few let down to the lower skies; others went into gradual banks away from the murderous CAT. Eight minutes later, Sigmet Charlie 6 came up on teletypes all over the United States:

SIGMET CHARLIE 6-DEC. 10-1128 CST.
CANCEL SIGMET CHARLIE 5. SIGMET
CHARLIE 6 VALID UNTIL 1430 CST. PILOT
REPORTS INDICATE SEVERE TO
EXTREME CLEAR AIR TURBULENCE

AIRWAYS BOUNDED BY TYLER, TEXAS-SHREVEPORT, LA., NORTH, SHREVEPORT-LAKE CHARLES, EAST, LAKE CHARLES-BEAUMONT, SOUTH, BEAUMONT-TYLER, WEST. DUE TO WIND SHEAR AND PROXIMITY OF JET STREAM EXPECT TO ENCOUNTER SEVERE, POSSIBLE EXTREME, CLEAR AIR TURBULENCE IN FORECAST AREA.

But it was too late for one flight that day.

After the flight touched down in Houston, many of the deplaning passengers paused on their way out to express their appreciation again to Mike and shake his hand. As a precaution, the invalid lady was taken off in an ambulance, and then Peter Hanscom came into the cockpit and showed Mike his company I.D.

"Sit down," Mike said.

Pete slid into the flight engineer's seat. "That was some ride, Captain."

"It was," Mike said with a victorious smile.

"Ever happen like that before?"

"Not exactly."

"I was wondering," Pete said. "How did you know we were going to hit that stuff?"

"I didn't. A hunch, that's all."

"Based upon what?"

"The weather map back at JFK didn't quite agree with the turbulence advisory."

"We could have had structural failure, I suppose?"

"Yes, there was a chance."

"And if people had been walking around, there would have been serious injuries? I think there's a lesson here. If this kind of thing can happen, perhaps we should make it a company rule to keep everyone in his seat as much as possible."

"CAT's difficult to forecast precisely, only one chance in a hundred that we hit the center of it this morning."

"Well, I don't mind telling you I was damned scared."

"I've had more comfortable flights myself."

"I'm going to report this to Fitz, tell him what a fine job you did."

"Thank you."

When Peter Hanscom left the cockpit, Mike pulled on his coat and went into the lavatory to retrieve his spooker.

Luckily, the thermos was still there. It had not been unleashed by the negative "G" forces exerted during the plane's struggle with the turbulence. He pulled it out and looked at it. He needed another drink, but he had his pace and timing down, so he simply shoved the thermos into his pocket. He often wondered what would happen if the thermos came loose and fell to the bottom of the disposal bin. How would he get it when he needed the spooker? He sometimes saw himself clawing away at the lavatory, ripping it open like a starved animal going after a trapped piece of meat.

When he came out of the lavatory, Nancy was waiting impatiently in the galley for the catering fellows to "sign her off," and she looked up and shook her head resignedly as he straightened his jacket and went back to the cockpit.

Mike had a Houston layover routine. Most of the pilots hung around Operations or went to the pilot's lounge, a gloomy place where a TV set was always blaring away, until time for the San Diego leg of the trip at 2:15 P.M. The captain had picked this flight sequence carefully because it would allow him enough time to check into the new airport hotel—a great circular building close by—where he would go upstairs to his room, order a melted cheese on rye, have a cold drink from his thermos, maybe take a bath, and nap for an hour or so. The rest helped him to feel relaxed and lifted enough when he reported in for the continuing segment to guide the DC-8 over the south end of the Rockies, across the desert to San Diego. A three-hour-and-five-minute flight, it usually put them on the apron at Lindbergh Field, San Diego, around 3:30 P.M. Pacific time.

Today, however, flight 467 arrived in Houston almost an hour late, and Mike knew his rest time in the hotel would be limited. The pilot was exhausted. At first he thought simply of calling Operations and telling them he'd had enough—logical, acceptable—but that would be a tacit admission that he had gone too far, and he earnestly believed that the spookers didn't affect his job performance. Mike realized he had crossed one line—daytime drinking—and he knew there was another line out there someplace. How far he didn't know; yet, he was certain he would not come near it. He had his own guidelines: the first day he called in sick after a night of drinking, if his hand began to shake, if his flying was in any way impaired, he would stop. Up to this time, none of these things had happened.

There was another reason why Mike didn't want to "deadhead"; the pilot had a date with Pat Simpson that evening in San Diego and he really wanted to see her. He suddenly realized he could delay the flight. Yes, that would be wise, conservative, and pilot-like.

"How are the control surfaces?" Mike asked the young flight engineer as he reentered the cockpit.

"No damage, sir."

Mike then felt the trim tab wheel. He nursed it back and forth, back and forth.

"Don't like the feel."

Jim felt it and shrugged his shoulders.

"I want this checked," Mike said. "Call dispatch."

The Captain's authority was supreme. All he had to say was, "I don't like it," and the flight would be delayed while the mechanics crawled over the equipment. And if the Captain said, "I *still* don't like it," new equipment would be pulled in. Mike knew it would take about an hour to an hour and a half to remove the cable inspection plates—enough time for him to enjoy the cool, dark room with his spooker.

When they reached Operations, Mike told the station manager, dispatcher, and the chief airframe mechanic about the severe clear air turbulence. They already knew. The dispatcher had seen it come up on the "A" wire and the station manager knew because he called the ambulance for the elderly woman in 29-A.

"You want all the bell cranks looked at, Captain?" the airframe mechanic asked.

"Yes, and the cable tension, especially the trim tabs." Mike turned around to the dispatcher. "It might take an hour or two. How about rescheduling equipment?"

"We have nothing due within five hours. I'll put it on the wire saying that we're holding the DC-8 for a mechanical. Tell 'em to stand by for a back-up. The best I can do is 89, inbound equipment from New Orleans, but that's five hours from now."

"See how the cables look," Mike told the mechanic. "Jim and Lou, stay with the bird and make sure everything is checked. We've had enough action for one day."

Mike picked up his flight bag and moved toward the door. Jim followed the pilot out and they stood in the bright, warm Texas sun. Jim touched Mike's arm.

"There's nothing wrong with those cables, is there?"

"You never know," Mike said, looking at the black macadam under his feet.

"Take it easy, Mike, we still have the West Coast leg to go."

"I'll be in the room. I need a little sleep, that's all. Bad experience—that fucking CAT!"

Mike walked along the concourse and through the main terminal to the International Hotel, where he checked into a small single room. N8907C was hauled away from the loading gate with the group mechanic in the right seat and Jim in the left. They started their

engines and the DC-8 taxied to a hangar on the far
end of the field where six airframe mechanics were
waiting to pull the inspection plates.

When he reached his room, Mike took off the uniform coat and flung it on the bed, reaching into his
flight bag for the icy thermos. He went to the bathroom
and poured himself a drink. He gulped the bourbon;
his nerves immediately calmed as he picked up the
phone and dialed room service for his usual sandwich
and a bowl of thick onion soup.

"Oh yeah, a lot of cream with the coffee."

He watched television for about ten minutes and
when the knock came on the door, Mike pushed his
drink under the bed and jammed the thermos back in
the flight bag. He signed for the food, ate the sandwich,
took a hot bath, and crawled into bed. About one hour
later, the phone rang waking him up.

"Mike, you okay?" Jim asked.

"Sure, just sleeping."

"Funny thing."

"What?"

"Well, we pulled all the inspection plates. There
was some sloppiness on one of the trim tab cables. I
don't know if it was the dive this morning or not."

"I doubt it. Anything else?"

"No, we looked over the whole undercarriage, all
the control surfaces, spoilers, flaps. Hydraulics tested
out. We replaced one fuse, but I think the ship came
through okay."

"Where are you now?"

"At the hangar. I called Operations. The flight's
scheduled to go out at 3:30 local."

"I'll be over."

Mike put in a call to San Diego. Just the sound of
Pat's voice made him feel happier. He told her the
flight was delayed because of mechanical problems.

"I'll work late at the office. We're behind anyhow," Pat said.

"I can't wait to see you," Mike answered.

He was feeling better, refreshed from the sleep and the thought of Pat. He dressed, studied his face carefully, and applied just a bit of the cover stick to the troublesome left cheek, and with his hair neatly combed, he went downstairs, paid his bill, and left. Jim was the only member of the flight crew who knew that Mike was checking into the hotel on the Houston stopover. No one ever saw Mike around Operations before it was time to check in again or in any of the three restaurants at the new Houston Airport. No one ever asked where the pilot went between flights, not even Nancy Halloway, who had flown the Houston-San Diego layover with Mike more than anyone else. Even though IA had stopped pairing the cockpit crews and the stewardesses' trips sometime previously to quash romances that were taking root on the layovers, the same crew members often flew together because of their seniority. Nancy Halloway had friends in San Diego and she liked the mild weather, so she frequently turned up on Mike's schedule.

The flight was boarded at 3:15, and after a quick look at the weather in Operations, which showed nothing very much over the western airways except a developing low pressure south of Portland, Mike felt relieved. As the plane was re-catered, Mike sat in the cockpit and felt the trim tab cable and tension of the other controls as the airframe mechanic looked on. Next to turbulence, Mike thought control failure was one of the worst hazards facing heavy aircraft operation; many times he thought of a cable coming off a pulley, the failure of the cargo door on the Turkish Airlines DC-10 near Paris, the feeling the pilots must have had with a wheel in their hands connected to nothing and the horizontal stabilizers of the big aircraft flapping like shutters in the wind sending the plane into a graveyard spiral. He knew from crop-dusting days that an airplane wants to spin if left alone; the only thing that prevents it is the wheel or stick you have in your hand, plus the stored up energy of altitude.

Mike cranked over the trim tab and he asked the flight engineer to go out and visually check the position of the trim tab on the tail assembly in the far wrung out position. He had never been asked to do that before, but on the other hand, he had never been in an incident like the one that morning, so he snapped to his feet and left the cockpit. As he did, Mike slid the thermos into his coat and made his way to the head. Inside he opened the disposal door and shoved in his spooker, the icy umbilical cord. He looked at himself and smiled to see if the bags under his eyes were puffier than usual; everything looked okay and he returned to the cockpit. He asked Nancy to bring him some coffee if she had time before they were airborne, and she brought a cup to the cockpit shortly after the manifest sheet was handed in by the gate attendant. The flight was signed off and they pushed the nearly full DC-8 from the jetway. The turbines were spun up, ignited, and the plane proceeded to the active.

"Mike, I almost forgot," Jim said, "you have a wire from New York Operations."

He handed it to Mike.

ADVISED BY HOUSTON OPERATIONS THAT FLIGHT #467, JFK-HOU, EXPERIENCED SEVERE TURBULENCE AND EXTREME CLEAR AIR TURBULENCE AROUND 1030 EASTERN TIME VICINITY OF SHREVEPORT. FAA REQUESTS COMPLETE PILOT REPORT. PLEASE COPY OPERATIONS NEW YORK. DO NOT SPEAK TO PRESS ABOUT INCIDENT. FITZSIMMONS RECEIVED WIRE FROM HANSCOM, V.P. MARKETING, ABOARD 467. SAID YOU HANDLED SITUATION EXTREMELY WELL. GOOD WORK, MIKE.

JOE BARNES, CHIEF PILOT

As they taxied, their ATC clearance came in. Mike took over and Jim copied.

The clearance was read back and Mike turned onto the active and they were cleared for immediate takeoff; he fed in the power and felt the jet surge ahead as Jim read off the knots. The DC-8-61 rotated and climbed smoothly into the bright, warm Texas afternoon, and at 2,000, they were under the control of center. They had three communications with the aircraft. The crew snapped on the autopilot, notched her into the Midland, Texas VOR, their first reporting station, and Mike sat back and took out a cigarette.

During the first hour he made a routine PA and around 4:30 the hollow, empty feeling returned to his stomach. Mike excused himself and walked out of the cockpit; he spoke to a woman passenger leaving the lavatory. Nancy was preparing her serving cart and happened to notice the conversation. She saw the captain take a paper cup and enter the lavatory. Ordinarily this would have passed her mind but she remembered that the pilot did exactly the same thing on the morning flight, and she couldn't understand why he didn't simply take a drink of water from the spigot that was located outside the lavatory door just under the paper cup dispenser.

Mike entered the lavatory, reached into the flapped door for his thermos, removed it, unscrewed the top, and poured the bourbon into the paper cup. He wanted to bring a slight dignity to his closet nipping and he thought the tiny paper cup was less degrading than drinking out of the thermos. He leaned against the bulkhead and felt the liquor running into his stomach, bringing the nice warm feeling with it. He placed the thermos back into its hiding place.

He looked in the mirror again to see if there were any small noticeable changes. By this time the pilot was sensitive to details, small changes in his appearance—his bloodshot eyes, their glassiness, the position of pupils, the bags under his eyes, the slight sweat lines on his brow, the rivers in his cheeks—and while the pilot placed his attention on the small parts of his face, he often refocused his eyes trying to visualize the entire effect. Yes, he thought. He still looked pretty good. He felt reassured and came from the lavatory and smiled at an elderly passenger who was waiting to use the facility, and then he used his key to unlock the cockpit door and went back in.

Mike took his seat and leaned back relaxed. This was the time of the flight day he waited for; the spooker refreshed him; the high-altitude airway heading west of Tucson was usually flown in tame air, and he could look into a lowering sun hovering over the southern end of the High Sierras; to the south, Mexico, and its lemony light, and the outlines of the Sierra Madre Mountains as they rose again out of the burnt sienna plains—the beauty of flying. Mike also liked the last part of the leg because he would be seeing Pat Simpson within a couple of hours.

Mike's eyes became heavy and he closed them, wanting to doze as the soft, warm rays sifting through the tinted Plexiglas window bathed his face. He shook his head and laughed silently to himself. Same cockpit. Same plane six hours later and he was going to sleep. His copilot was leaning on his elbow routinely looking at a chart resting on his lap, then down at the small numbers clicking away in the window of the DME. Over his shoulder, Mike saw the back of the flight engineer; he, too, was yawning as he made a log entry. It was a drowsy afternoon and Mike smiled to himself and thought that perhaps it was just such a time when the entire flight deck crew of a South American 737 went to sleep—a famous airline story.

There were one hundred and eighty contented, boozy, well-fed passengers sitting in the back and probably not one of them knew that only a few hours earlier this same plane had been nearly shaken apart.

What a fucking job, the pilot thought. Sometimes he was grossly overpaid for doing nothing—like that warm afternoon flying high above the southwestern desert—but that same morning, no amount of money could pay for his expertise. It was worth much more than the $55,000 he received annually. He had saved lives that morning, of that he was sure.

But this did not make Mike any more satisfied with his job and he remembered vividly, as if it were yesterday, the morning he started with Northeast, flying their junior routes in and out of Boston in a DC-3. The VOR stations were just coming in; the autopilots were cranky, and one had to fly to a great extent by visual landmarks. He had touch with the earth he loved; he saw the seasons change and he knew his way around the clouds because the old bird could not fly much above 10,000 feet. And in those days, you never went to sleep; there was too much going on to keep you awake. The pilot loved contact flying.

Over Gila Bend they received their inbound San Diego clearance, and less than an hour later they were on final for Lindbergh Field—coming down low over the hills of the city, sweeping almost level with hotels and apartment houses. Mike greased her on and taxied to the gate. He looked over at Jim.

"Hell of a day, huh?"

Jim saw Mike's face in the last light of day. He thought the pilot looked drawn and old. He wondered how far this man could go or where he would go, how it would end. One thing was certain, he didn't want to be aboard. How many times could a man go to the head before everyone knew, or before he misjudged or misread something and caused hundreds of deaths. Jim thought about his family. He would do what he had wanted to do for a long time. They wrote up the inbound log and said good-bye to each other. Mike went to the lavatory and removed his spooker. He thanked the stewardesses. December 10,1974, was almost over.

Two

Pat Simpson sat waiting for Mike's call at her drawing board in the office of a San Diego advertising agency. At thirty-two, tall and slender, more striking than beautiful, she had been recovering, slowly, from a broken marriage when she first met Mike Hagen. Now she thought she had never been happier. The pilot had done much to restore her wounded psyche.

On days when Mike was due in, she waited at the office until he called her from the airport; then they would drive together to a Mexican restaurant they both liked, then to her beach house at Coronado, just south of San Diego. She would leave early the next morning for the office, and Mike would take a cab to the airport for 602, the 11:30 departure back to New York.

The phone rang, and she smiled in anticipation of the thought of Mike's warm voice.

"Darling."

"Uh, this is Jim Cochran."

She hesitated a moment, trying to place the name. "Who?"

"Mike's copilot. We've met a couple of times."

"Oh yes, of course." She remembered the amiable, sunburned young man. Her heart sank.

"Is anything wrong?"

"Everything's all right. We're on the ground here. But I just have to talk to you about Mike."

"What is it?" she asked, her voice rising with apprehension.

"Well, I don't know quite how to say this, but Mike, you know, drinks a lot."

There was a pause, and then her curt response. "Is that what you called to tell me?"

Jim got the message, but once he'd decided to say something he wasn't going to be put off by a tone of voice.

"Look, I'm awfully sorry to spring this on you, but I was hoping you might say something to him. Mike's a damned fine pilot and this morning he pulled us out of a bad situation, but he's drinking during the flight and that makes it my business, too."

"Drinking while he's flying? You're crazy." She knew Mike drank, illegally, on layovers, she drank with him. But on the job?

"No, he's been sneaking them."

"How?" she said. The hand holding the receiver was beginning to tremble. It couldn't be true, not Mike, he couldn't do such a thing.

"He has this thermos filled with bourbon and ice. He hides it in the head. I used to see him going to the lavatory all the time and I asked him about it because I thought he was sick or something."

"How long has this been going on?"

"About a year, I guess. It used to be just once or twice, but you know, they say one drink in the air is worth two on the ground. You can't hide something like this forever; somebody's going to find out. If he gets caught, they'll bust him and he'll never fly for anybody again, not even freight."

"Jim, I've seen *you* take a drink on these layovers."

"I know. A lot of guys do, and it's against regulations, but that's a long way from nipping on the job."

She refused to accept what Jim was saying, yet something deep down told her it was true. "Does anyone else know?"

"I don't think so. Mike's careful as hell but he's risking too much, and it's only going to get worse. Don't tell him I called you, but I didn't know what to do." He paused for a second and then with difficulty said, "Frankly, I don't want to fly with him anymore. I've got a family to think about."

"When this started, why didn't you say something? You're as guilty as he is."

"I did. We talked, but Mike doesn't really believe he's got a problem. Look, Miss Simpson, I'm concerned about Mike. He says he can stop anytime, but I think he's lost control and, frankly, it scares the hell out of me. I'm in that cockpit, too."

"Oh God, this is awful." It was true, Pat felt it.

"I know. He's got a career at stake here and a lot of lives in his hands. There's going to come a time when the booze affects his flying and I don't want to be there."

"I don't blame you, Jim. I'm glad you called me. I'll speak to him right away, do what I can."

She took Jim's home number in New Jersey and put the phone down and crossed to the window; long layers of stratus clouds dimly lit by the afterglow hung over the Pacific and from her office on the brow of a high hill, she could look down upon the runway at Lindbergh Field. Blue taxiway lights were mingled with the white runway markers; a 707 passed her view and settled down toward the threshold. Her eyes followed the silhouette of the plane and she saw the tail strobe as it turned off the runway. A second plane came by, losing altitude exactly the same way, then a third, a fourth, a fifth. Each one was at a precise position when it passed by her window; she lined them up with a radio antenna on an adjacent hill. It was as if they were all sliding down a long cable attached to the sky someplace, and she thought about the men inside looking out the front windshield. Were they mechanical, plastic pilots who brought the planes down the alley exactly the same way, or was it just a learned reflex, as simple as a man folding dough for pretzels?

Did they drink like Mike Hagen? As she watched more planes land at Lindbergh, the significance of what Jim Cochran had said tore through her. She felt helplessness, and then a rising panic.

As Pat stared south toward darkened Coronado, she thought of the first time she ever saw Mike Hagen. She never forgot what she noticed first about him; even now, it made her smile a little. He had freckles on his slightly rounded belly, little freckles that formed a cluster about his navel.

She had set up an easel at the end of a pier in Coronado and was struggling with a wet watercolor wash. She stopped to light a cigarette and happened to look aside. Her gaze fell upon a roundish belly full of freckles. Her eyes slid upward and she saw another mass of sunbleached freckles all over a big face with a pleasant smile. He wore a baseball cap and carried a fishing pole. Mike Hagen.

"Am I making you nervous?"

"No more than the painting," she answered.

"I used to sketch a little bit myself. Teacher said I was pretty good."

"What did you like to draw?" she asked, putting down the brush and giving up the watercolor attempt.

"Airplanes. Crop dusters—two-wing jobs."

"Do you fly?"

"I'm a captain with Intercontinental."

This surprised Pat because the man standing in the hot sun at the end of the pier looked more like a farmer, a Texas cattle raiser.

"Are you from Texas?"

"Do I sound like a Texan?" Mike said.

"Sort of."

"I'm from Florida, but they say Florida people don't have accents because they're all foreigners. My father came from Maine—had a twang. We lived near an Ag strip south of Homestead. The pilots were Oakies, Midwest crop sprayers. The others were crackers, so I grew up sounding like a western cracker, whatever the hell that is."

She laughed, liking Mike Hagen from the start, the out-going, matter-of-fact way he spoke, his earthiness and openness.

She and Mike sat on the end of the pier and talked and she ended up letting him start another watercolor by laying the broad areas of the sky with a big brush loaded with Cerulean Blue. It was rather funny and the blue dripped off the paper onto the dock. They continued laughing and talking at a small seaside restaurant where she often went. Now she recalled that he had some drinks at lunch; but she hadn't thought anything of it.

Later she was too much in love with the big, grinning Mike Hagen to ever think about his drinking. He never seemed to be drunk; when he drove her Jaguar, it was with care and precision; he never stumbled, slurred his words, or forgot things. She thought alcoholics were disturbed, brooding people who sat alone in dark bars. But there was nothing outwardly wrong with Mike Hagen except his marriage, and he told her that it was downhill almost from the beginning. Mike didn't appear to be an unhappy man any more than he appeared to be an alcoholic.

The only time she recalled ever seeing him drink during the day was on their vacation in Hawaii when they'd sit under the thatched-roof bar by the pool and order large, fancy concoctions. She hadn't thought there was anything wrong; the pool bar was always about six deep with carefree vacationers. Some of them even started at ten in the morning. Mike, she remembered, never went to the bar until noon, and in the evening he would have four or five drinks.

To her, he just drank a lot; she didn't know how much was too much. Their love affair had been going on for almost three years and they had never had a serious argument; she thought Mike Hagen was one of the most dependable, straightforward men she had ever met. The call from Jim made her angry, then fearful. Who the hell was he to be calling her up, telling on Mike? Cocky bastard. But underneath she knew it was probably very much on his mind, something he had been wanting to say for a long time.

What was she to do? She couldn't tell Mike about the copilot's call and when Mike's phone call came a short time later, Pat was still at a loss.

He looked the same to her, a bit tired perhaps. He told her about the day's problem with the clear air turbulence as they drove from the office up to La Jolla. All through dinner she listened and watched him carefully; the pattern was no different—four bourbons, no trace of intoxication. She decided not to wait until they got home.

"Mike, I've got something on my mind."

"Yeah, I thought you were kind of quiet tonight. Something the matter?"

Pat reached across the table and took his hand. "In a way, something *is* the matter. I'm worried about you. I think you drink an awful lot for someone who has to fly a plane."

He smiled, sipping his coffee. "You're right. I know I drink too much."

"Why do you do it, Mike? Aren't you jeopardizing your job?"

"Yes," he said mechanically.

"Doesn't that bother you?"

"You know what I think about this kind of flying —we've talked about that."

"But what about the passengers?"

"I'm not endangering them. Today I'm sure I saved some lives." He took both of her hands in his, grasping them with warmth. "Pat, I really don't think my drinking is going to harm anybody. It doesn't affect my flying."

"Isn't there an airline rule that you're not supposed to drink twenty-four hours before a flight? You've had several big drinks tonight and you have to fly in the morning."

"But I've been drinking like this for years. I can hold it. In all the time we've spent together, have you ever seen me soused? There are plenty of people around here who drink a hell of a lot more than I do, shuffling, slobbering drunks. Have you ever seen me like that?"

"No," she said, "you know I haven't."

"Well, stop worrying then."

"Darling, no one can drink as much as you do and not have liver problems or something. The body breaks down. I don't want that to happen to you."

"I'll let up a little if it'll make you feel better."

"Mike, there must be a lot of pilots sitting in restaurants tonight who have to fly in the morning. How many do you think are drinking?"

"I'd say ninety-six out of one hundred aren't. Those who are drinking, probably are having a beer, a glass of wine, perhaps a Scotch or two—no, just one. The fellows are very careful for the most part and they should be. Very few places a guy can earn close to sixty thousand without a family business or college."

"And you've just had four drinks! How can you have one set of standards for yourself and another for everybody else?"

"I can handle it."

Finally Pat came to the question she'd been dreading to ask.

"Mike, I want you to give me an absolutely truthful answer. Do you drink during the day?"

Mike Hagen didn't say anything for a minute. "Yes, goddamnit, I drink during the day! Why do you ask that? What difference does it make?"

They didn't discuss it further until they reached Pat's small, well-furnished house in Coronado. She made coffee and he took a straight-up brandy with it the way he always did.

"Mike, I wasn't kidding about the drinking.

Promise you'll see somebody back east. Please, darling, for your own sake. This thing has got to be cleared up now. If you won't do this for me then I don't want to see you anymore." She was surprised at the sharpness of her words.

At that moment the phone rang. It was the worst possible timing for Pat. Mike listened to the ring with relief.

"Yes?" Pat answered.

"Jim again. Mike there?"

"Just a minute," she turned to Mike. "It's for you, it's Jim. But I really meant what I said, Mike."

"What's up, Jim?" Mike's voice was hearty.

"Joe Barnes called from New York. He wants you to call him."

"Okay, thanks."

It was almost 2:00 A.M. New York time and Mike wondered if he should be calling the chief pilot at that hour, but they were close friends, so he went ahead.

"Hello, Joe, sorry to call so late. Cochran left a message."

"That's all right. Did you get my wire?"

"Yeah. Picked it up in Houston."

"You certainly did one hell of a job yesterday morning. Did you hear about the Inter-Texas flight?"

"No."

"They were around Shreveport same time you were. Goddamned CAT caught 'em in the ass. They dropped 4,000. Christ, half the plane came apart inside. One killed, twenty-two injured, five critical—broken backs. They made an emergency landing in Shreveport."

"Jeez, what kind of equipment?"

"Seven-twenty-seven. Their galley came loose and crushed a stewardess. The F.A.A. called, Lewiston himself, they got the report on your turbulence and how you handled it. Not one injury, even that old lady. They want to know how you got through and Inter-Texas fucked up. How did you know?"

"Over 26,000 good hours in my book. That's how I knew."

"I told Lewiston that our Captain Mike Hagen had forgotten more about flying than half these clowns in the air today. I told him we don't drive planes, we fly 'em, Anyhow, here's the point. You know they've been doing research on clear air turbulence for years. They want to send a team of safety experts out on an Air Force jet early tomorrow morning. They're going to interview all the flight personnel—you, Cochran, the girls, everyone—and they want to go over the plane. I called Fitz right away and he says it's a hell of a compliment. He wired dispatch and San Diego operations. We're going to hold your equipment in the hangar for inspection and the entire flight is being replaced with inbound Portland equipment. I'm coming out, too, on 305. The first meeting is scheduled for 1:00 Pacific. And by the way, Mike, we've got you up for a safety award. Maybe a thousand dollars. Oh, almost forgot, there was a report from Houston that you ordered the equipment completely checked, the inspection plates off. Damned good thinking. They found some problems in the trim tab cables. F.A.A. wants to know how you figured that one out?"

"A feeling."

"A what?" the old chief pilot said in his crusty manner.

"A certain feeling. The wheel was slightly different," Mike said, telling a convincing lie.

"Well, it was a damned smart precaution. In fact, they've grounded the Inter-Texas 727, going over every inch of the equipment. Mike, nice going. I wish we had a hundred guys like you."

"Thanks, Joe. Thanks very much. I needed a boost tonight."

"Well, you got one. See you tomorrow, F.A.A. Building, room 297, at one. Good night, Mike."

A broad smile bloomed on Mike's face. He walked over and kissed Pat.

"The company's chief pilot is coming out here tomorrow with the F.A.A. investigating team. An Inter-Texas flight hit the same air—one killed, over twenty injured—and you talk about me not being able to fly. Ask Joe Barnes if I can handle the equipment. Ask him."

She was about to say something, but she remained still and shared with the pilot the blurred happiness of the moment. He filled his glass; she did, too, and they took a blanket out to the beach and watched the bright moon and small clouds sailing in from the sea.

Nancy Halloway checked into the El Cortez Hotel with the other stewardesses. A short time later her date, an electronics salesman, picked her up and they went over to Mission Bay for Polynesian food. When she returned to her room around midnight, Nancy found the message from Crew Schedule that the crew had been taken off 602 and were to report instead to the F.A.A. Building for a preliminary hearing on the turbulence experienced that day. She felt a twinge of irritation because she had theater tickets for the following night; now they wouldn't get into New York until very late or possibly the following morning. Another evening screwed up.

The glamorous job had become a strain: one endless meal service after another, smiling at people who asked the same, stupid questions, crazy hours. It was not the life she thought it would be when she boarded her first IA plane, a Convair 140, for a sixty-five-minute flight from Harrisburg to Baltimore on a spring day in 1957. That was many years ago. But then, Nancy hadn't thought she'd be around this long. According to the airline's P.R., the average stewardess left within two years to get married, supposedly the ideal mate after IA's training.

Three

The jurisdiction for the incidents of clear air turbulence over Louisiana on that December 10 fell within the bounds of several government agencies, among them the National Transportation Safety Board, an independent fact-finding group that works closely with the Civil Aeronautics Board, the Federal Aviation Administration, and the aircraft manufacturers. There are many views on N.T.S.B.; no one disagrees with the fact that they are the best in the world when it comes to finding out what happened and why when there are accidents. But some critics feel their procedures for preventing accidents, their sending out directives with enough punch and enforcement, accompanied by punitive measures, leave much to be desired. The Board itself says that's the F.A.A.'s job. Others claim there are too many agencies, bureaus, and various establishments controlling pilots and planes, that some sort of super-agency should take command.

After pilots' reports came in relating to the various December 10 CAT incidents, the N.T.S.B. moved with utmost speed. There had been five other incidents of planes encountering turbulence that day: Southeastern's Houston-New Orleans flight; a Louisiana Commuter airline over Fort Smith; the American 727 incident near Hot Springs; and a private flight on oxygen in the vicinity of Clarksdale, Arkansas. But the flight that sparked the investigation, of course, was the Inter-Texas tragedy because there was a fatality and many serious injuries. The N.T.S.B. declared that the December 10 situation was a major meteorological condition and worthy of a priority investigation.

Six planes had reported the situation; four of them were equipped with flight and voice recorders, two of them were not. But the air safety experts working on the problem were looking for some correlation among the six. Most of all, they were interested in one preliminary fact that presented itself that day.

Of the five ATR-rated pilots in command on that day in the vicinity of Louisiana cruising between 28,000 and 41,000 in clear skies, one pilot, Mike Hagen, apparently knew that his aircraft would enter the core of extreme air movement when the others with just as much regulatory licensing and available weather information flew into the situation with no sense or indication of what was about to happen. Why? What did one pilot know that the others didn't?

Further, the same plane was grounded in Houston by the Captain. The other aircraft were sent on their way *without* control surface or cable inspection. Why? What did the IA pilot suspect? Why did he order the removal of his inspection plates? Was there apparently an off-tolerance condition in the horizontal trim tab control lines? The safety board, among others, wanted facts. They began by grounding every plane that had experienced the identical air disturbance.

Two investigating teams left Washington that afternoon aboard F.A.A. planes and Air Force jets; they would be predominantly concerned with the Inter-Texas and IA incidents—and mostly with Mike Hagen's story. N.T.S.B. directives of December 10 continued into the night on the F.A.A. wire to local branch chiefs:

REMOVE IMMEDIATELY FLIGHT AND
VOICE RECORDERS FROM N8907C, DC-8-

61, LOCATED SAN DIEGO. HOLD CREWS
FOR INTERROGATION. EXPECT FURTHER
INVESTIGATION ALL GROUND CONTROL
PERSONNEL, WEATHER PERSONNEL
AND FORECASTERS IN REGARD TO
CLEAR AIR TURBULENCE CONDITIONS
EXPERIENCED IN AREA
APPROXIMATELY BORDERED BY TYLER,
TEXAS-SHREVEPORT, LOUISIANA,
NORTH; SHREVEPORT-LAKE CHARLES,
EAST; LAKE CHARLES-BEAUMONT,
SOUTH; BEAUMONT-TYLER, WEST.
FLIGHT LEVELS 28–41. INTENSIVE IN-
VESTIGATION ALL PILOT REPORTS
THIS AREA BETWEEN 0800–1130 C.S.T.,
DECEMBER 10, 1974.

The flight recorder installed on N8907C was a
Fairchild unit, model number F2424, and it kept a record of the five main indications of a plane's direction
and inertial forces. The first readout, and perhaps the
most important in the case of the IA flight, was the
"G" force gravitater, which would tell what negative or
positive "G" forces had been exerted against the aircraft at any one time. The recorder also read out the
aircraft's magnetic heading, indicated airspeed, altitude, and recorded time. By feeding these five data
sources into a control program, the investigators might
be able to piece together the answer to what happened.

Four investigators showed up in San Diego the
next day.

Everyone wanted to meet Mike Hagen.

By 5:00 that morning the flight recorder had
been removed from N8907C and taken to the F.A.A.
regional office for readout plotting. The pilot in the
meantime was sleeping off seven outsized inputs of
Old Grand-Dad. By 9:00 A.M., the plot was nearly
completed and it showed a very interesting pattern: the
plane entered the climactic CAT at a reduced airspeed, 245 knots; during turbulence the maximum in-
cremental "G" forces were about 4.8, going from plus

3 "G's" to 1.8 "G's" negative. When the investigators compared notes with the Inter-Texas 727, her flight recorder, a Bendix, showed a lower exertive "G" force pattern, and the accelerative sweep was far more moderate; yet, there had been one fatality on that plane and three of the fifteen people still in the hospital were on the critical list.

The N.T.S.B. was searching for one deposition: was there an operational lesson to be learned from the CAT incident? Their questions, the voices on their sophisticated recording and monitoring equipment, would never reveal the most imperative link in air safety, the human factor—the strengths, wisdom and weaknesses of that band of men who sit in the left cockpit seats of the giant flying machines. They could not get inside the head of a man like Mike Hagen, and if they could, if they had been able to see this pilot at Ellen's Place, the bitter paradox might have changed the course of all the procedures and operatives.

Joe Barnes was a big, lusty man born into a midwestern pioneering tradition. He was the last of his generation, a dying breed. The men who grew up with flying were disappearing back into time, absorbed by the airline corporate structure and the sophisticated milieu of modern flying. Joe was a colorful man. You could tell by looking at him that he was a pilot; he had the rough-edged face, warm, crinkly eyes, and a strong jaw. He had been a senior ranking captain at IA when he decided to become a check pilot working under IA's Chief Pilot for the base, Fred Darrows. When Fred reached sixty and retired, Joe stepped into his job.

Joe was well-liked and a legend around the airline industry because he was the only man left on the operational side of the airlines who had actually flown a Ford Tri-Motor on regular service. He was fifty-nine—six months away from giving up his desk at IA—and he planned to return to the Midwest somewhere and perhaps buy into a small, fixed-base opera-

tion. He would never leave flying because he grew up
in the infant days of barnstorming, and he wanted to
die not too far from a flying field.

Joe's mother died when he was born, after which
his father, a third-rate vaudevillian, bought an ancient
projector manufactured by the Edison Company along
with a library of old newsreels and some Biograph
pictures starring, among others, Lillian and Dorothy
Gish, Mae Marsh, Blanche Sweet, and, of course,
"Little Mary." He became an itinerate motion picture
exhibitor, touring the Midwest, especially around
southern Ohio and western Illinois, with weekly attrac-
tions of movies that he showed in tents. The admission
was a dime, and for those rural communities without
nickelodeons, the tent show represented cheap, popular entertainment.

From the age of about thirteen Joe was the ad-
vance man for his father and he moved ahead of the
tent show putting up posters and slipping handbills under doors announcing the arrival of the spectacular entertainment thrill—the new marvel—moving pictures.
For a while, as Joe told the story, they had a few live
dancing girls, but this was halted when complaints began to pour in from local church leaders. (The
Barnes tent shows were concentrated in the deepest
areas of the midwestern Bible Belt.)

The inevitable happened. The Barnes Tent Show
came across Willie Hinds and his Flying Circus, and
the two traveling acts merged into an air and tent spectacular with some success. Willie Hinds, who had been
a pilot in World War I, taught Joe how to fly a Curtis
biplane. The year was 1930. Joe Barnes was fourteen
and he flew with the flying circus, even wing-walking,
without an official license, until he was seventeen, the
minimum age in those days. In 1933, Joe Barnes received his certificate to fly. He was proud of this and
the small piece of paper, framed and yellowed, was
mounted on the wall of his La Guardia office.

Two years later his father retired from roadshow-
ing and Willie Hinds was killed on takeoff from an Il-

linois cornfield, so Joe went to Detroit joining Western
Air Express as a copilot. He quit the airline in 1938
and spent two years crop-dusting in Kansas before he
was hired by Trans-Continental Airlines as copilot to
fly their new DC-3. In 1941, at the age of twenty-five,
with over 12,000 hours, Joe Barnes left for the Army
Air Force where he flew seventy-eight missions over
Germany with the Eighth. He received the Air Medal,
was shot down twice, but managed to reach England
each time, and then in 1945, he returned to Trans-
Continental. The company received its first overseas
route in 1949, changing the name to Intercontinental
Airways.

Joe grew up with all the equipment; he saw the
DC-3 retired, the coming of the short-range Convairs,
the Connies, the DC-8's, and the 747's. He started in
open cockpits and ended in the three-story office of the
747. No one, including Joe, knew how many hours he
had put in his nine logbooks. There were 34,000
logged for military and commercial cockpit time, but
Joe estimated he accumulated another 4,500 while
crop-dusting or flying with the Willie Hinds Circus in
the days before flying became a logjam of numbers,
procedures, and record books.

Joe Barnes met Mike on IA's transcontinental
service, JFK/LAX, in 1968 when Mike was flying copilot on the senior flights. They had flown together
several times when Joe asked the younger pilot how he
got into flying.

"Crop-dusting in Florida," said Mike. "Citrus
spraying while I was going to the university."

"No shit. I used to be a honky-tonky spray devil
myself," Joe said.

It was the first time he had ever sat in an IA
cockpit with a man who learned his flying by letting
down foul-smelling, eye-blinding fertilizer or pest kil-
lers while trying not to hit trees, electric lines, poles,
water towers, windmill pumps, all the enemies of low-
level precision "row" spraying. Joe asked his copilot a
few probing inside questions about dusting and in a

couple of seconds, the captain was sure that Mike Hagen had edged double wingers in and out of the fields, following the "crop year" laying down that beautiful, high-paying shit. In the eyes of the older pilot Mike Hagen immediately gained enormous stature, a fellow crop duster. An "Ag" pilot knew what it was all about: the small, private, closed world of those great half-crazy pilots who sprayed crops, followed the seasons, and saw some poetry and beauty in rural America— the taste of the earth, Joe called it.

"Yeah, goddamnit," Joe told Mike, "these fucking big things just go too high. I like the low world."

From that moment in the cockpit of the DC-8-61, somewhere west of the Gila Bend VOR at flight level 39 on a March day in 1968, the two former contact flyers shared a fellowship and a respect for each other that rarely exists between modern airline pilots. When Joe became chief pilot he never allowed Mike any special breaks, never singled him out for preferential treatment, but Joe gave to the younger pilot something very special—his knowledge of flying and of the temperament of the air. Joe Barnes didn't have a son, and soon after that 1968 flight, he began telling Mike everything he ever knew, and, in a way, Joe thought of Mike as the son he never had.

When the reports of the December 10 incident began to reach the Chief Pilot's office, Joe felt a very warm, special pride. His student had done well. He had saved lives and placed the carrier in a favorable light. This meant quite a bit to Barnes because unlike Mike Hagen, he was a company man all the way, blending, sifting, sorting, delineating between the needs and problems of his 270 New York-based pilots and the imperatives of the carrier. That was Joe Barnes's extraordinary contribution besides all the legends that surrounded the man.

Before the hearing Mike and Joe met at the underground bar of the Del Coronado. Joe ordered

Scotch, Mike his usual Old Grand-Dad with three rocks.

"Isn't it strange how things come 'round," Joe began. "Here we're sitting on the edge of Lindbergh Field where Ryan built the *Spirit of St. Louis*. We're back at the same field, forty-seven years later, talking about something that happened to a giant airplane, how it almost got the shit knocked out of it by the crazy upper air."

"That's right, forty-seven years, and we're still experimenting. Probably we'll keep right on."

"I hope so," Joe said. "Flying is getting so mechanical. You brought the human factor in yesterday. Level with me, how the hell did you know you'd hit that stuff?"

Mike hesitated and a smile crept across his red face. "I didn't."

"That's what I thought."

"But I did see that position of the jet stream, near the low, I mean. Also, advisory 39, the light to moderate turbulence warning, didn't seem to reflect the situation if the weather map was right. I remembered something else. Once when I was on a leg over Arkansas—or was it Missouri?—doesn't matter. I was sitting in Convair equipment—yeah, it was my first right-seater. Anyhow, all of a sudden, we hit this CAT shit, dropped a good 2,000, quick accelerations, all that. The steaming coffee flew up and rained back down on my cock. Jesus Christ, ever have that happen? I'll never forget it. I was about ready to leap out of the plane."

"So, that's what did it, a frizzled cock!" Joe Barnes laughed, a deep, rumbling belly laugh.

"Yeah, and I could see all those passengers sitting back there with their little burned cocks," Mike said. "So, I was monitoring the pilot reports; they weren't too serious, no severe stuff. I never knew, Joe, I just took precautions."

"I figured that," the chief pilot laughed. "But this

afternoon Fitz wants me to come on strong, like we always tell our pilots to do more than necessary."

"Am I supposed to say that?"

"No, I'm going to give the hearing an opening statement on behalf of the company, some bullshit. Then you agree and tell them how you sensed the CAT and you thought safety was more important than a lukewarm breakfast. That's all. Don't lay it on too much, just enough for believability."

"Joe, you know if we tried to keep passengers under seat belts all the time they'd get pretty annoyed."

"That marketing V.P. you had aboard was certainly impressed. Called Fitz and told him you were a remarkable pilot."

"I tried to figure it all out years ago—how I would handle the machine if we ever hit the shit."

"No fears, Mike?"

"Some."

"What about that trim tab cable?"

"I don't think it had a damned thing to do with the CAT."

"N.T.S.B. says otherwise."

Mike shrugged. "So, they earn their medals."

"Don't play it down too much, Mike. Remember, someone was killed on the other flight; you got everyone through. That's what counts."

"I'll say my lines. Don't worry."

" 'The line's policy is always to have its captains take every meteorological condition into consideration,' something to that effect."

"Sure, but you and I know it's bullshit. Every carrier is the same."

"Do it anyway. You could be chief pilot at IA someday."

Mike did not answer. He looked across at Joe Barnes, seeing the dim outline of another era sitting in the darkness of the bar. It was ironic, Mike thought, talking about all the flying experiences over stiff drinks.

* * *

The hearing was held in the bare conference room on the second floor of the Federal Aviation Agency building adjacent to Lindbergh Field. What had happened in the cockpit of the IA flight on December 10 was fairly well established by the investigating team before the oral testimony began. Flight and voice recorders told the story. The government safety officials sat around the long, partly chipped conference table with its pitchers of water and yellow pads, waiting to hear what the flight instruments had not told them. To one side, a reporter tapped away and at the end of the room there was a cheaply framed picture of Lindbergh and an American flag.

Jim Cochran's testimony in general praised the work of the captain and this was echoed by the twenty-five-year-old flight engineer, one of seven blacks in IA's flight department.

Each stewardess told her story, how the plane seemed to be at the mercy of the violent air currents. When asked if they thought the passengers would have been flung about if they had not been strapped in, the women told the hearing that the jolting and shock wave were so severe they were sure injuries or death would have occurred. After describing the early stages of the flight, the turbulence over Pennsylvania and Ohio, Nancy Halloway told the investigators they began their meal service.

"And then what happened?" the investigator asked.

"Captain Hagen rang and I went to the cockpit. He told me to pick up the trays at once."

"Was the plane in any turbulence at that point?"

"No, it was very smooth."

"Did you consider Captain Hagen's instruction unusual under the circumstances?"

"Yes, sir."

"How long did it take you to collect the trays?"

"Well, I called the coach stewardesses first, then we started picking up in front. It took about five minutes to get the trays stowed as we didn't have too many in first-class that morning. Then the second stewardess and I went back to help out in tourist section. They had a lot more people, of course."

"How long was it between the time Captain Hagen told you about the possibility of clear air turbulence and the time you were buckled in?"

"Maybe ten minutes."

"That's about right, because it was fourteen minutes between the time Captain Hagen gave the command and the first indication of turbulence, according to the flight and voice recorders. Now, Miss Halloway, this is important. Could you have had the entire breakfast service put away if the plane had been full?"

"No, because we had problems. The passengers had been pinned in their seats during the early part of the flight. When we got out of the first turbulence, everyone started getting up, going for magazines, standing around talking. A lot of them were nervous during the rough air. Some had been sick, and they were glad it was over. We had trouble rounding everybody up for the meal service."

"Were all the first-class passengers in their seats when you got the message about the suspected clear air turbulence?"

"A few were still roaming around, and when the captain came on and said we were heading for turbulence again, no one believed it. Anyway, they didn't pay much attention. We practically had to force some of them into their seats."

"Have you ever experienced clear air turbulence before on any flight?"

"Yes, but not this severe."

"Has anyone ever issued you emergency instructions before when the air seemed to be perfectly safe?"

"Yes, when I began flying, they didn't have jets —" Nancy smiled and they all chuckled.

Joe Barnes who was sitting in on the hearings said, "Darling, when I started, planes had two wings and we sat outside." They all laughed again.

"Miss Halloway," the government official said with a wink, "you were talking about the pre-jet age?"

"Yes, we were in a DC-6 to St. Louis and the inboard engine broke an oil line. The captain turned on the No Smoking and Seat Belt signs. We made an emergency landing in Cincinnati, but no one was hurt. We used to have mechanicals all the time with prop planes."

"Now, tell us about the clear air turbulence you experienced on flight 467 yesterday."

"I was in the jump seat. It seemed crazy in the beginning because the last glimpse I had of the sky before I buckled myself in was bright blue, no clouds or anything. There was a slight bump at first, then things settled down. All of a sudden, the plane went up in the air very quickly; then it began to vibrate. It went on for a long time. People began to scream."

"What did you think?"

"I thought we were going to crash. It seemed forever before anything happened; finally, I heard the engine sounds change. There was a lot of noise, a thump from inside one of the lavs, I remember."

"What were the reactions of the passengers after the plane settled down?"

"Most of them were zombies. Several were crying. A couple of old people in front had their arms around each other as if they intended to die together. When I walked by, the old woman grabbed my arm and said I was wonderful. Actually, I hadn't done anything."

"And what would be your duties in a situation like this?"

"After seeing that everything was okay in my end of the cabin, I went aft to check with the girls, see if I could help. There was a very loud noise from back there during the turbulence and I thought maybe the side of the plane had blown off."

"When you reached the coach section, what did you find?"

"One of the girls rushed up and said the galley

bulkhead had come apart and there was hot coffee all over the place. It was a mess. I called the captain, made a report, and he talked to the passengers and calmed everyone down."

"Did the coach passengers have the same reactions you had observed up front?"

"Yes, some were crying. One lady was hysterical, but most seemed to be in sort of a shock. Then they began talking, telling each other how they felt. It was a terrifying experience. I think it was the worst thing that ever happened to me flying."

"Do you have any recommendations, Miss Halloway, with regard to what you observed?"

"Well, it's a good thing the seat belts were on. I'm sure anybody walking around would have been killed. From where I was sitting, I could see stuff flying everywhere—blankets, pillows, magazines. When turbulence is expected, of course, we don't serve meals or let passengers out of their seats, but if you don't know it's coming, I guess all you can do is suggest that everyone keep his seat belt on all the time. We do that now, of course, but it doesn't do much good. You can hardly blame a passenger for not wanting to be caged the whole time he's aboard."

They thanked the tall, blond woman and called Mike Hagen. The bald truth of the matter, of course, was that the pilot didn't know for sure that the CAT was coming. Mike had played a hunch; it was the rare joining of luck and experience that sometimes pays off.

"What was your clue, Captain Hagen?"

"I saw the position of the jet stream yesterday morning. I figured the relationship to the wind shear and it seemed to me that Sigmet Charlie 4 didn't quite agree with the map. Frankly, I didn't know which was right, but then the temperature began dropping as it does sometimes near turbulence."

"I see, you just sensed that serious clear air turbulence could be in the region. How did you know that the cable on the trim tab was loose?"

"It felt different."

"You could actually feel it in the trim wheel?" the man asked skeptically.

"Sort of."

"What recommendations do you feel we could introduce, based upon your experience?"

Mike could hardly suggest that every aircraft flying in a zone of suspected turbulence suspend meal service and slow the equipment down; it would disrupt the entire airline business.

"I think the downgrading of turbulence sigmets should be handled very carefully," he said. "That appeared to be the problem yesterday. If I were the forecaster, Sigmet Charlie 5 would have been worded differently."

The discussion brought up several interesting points. The Airmet, designed as a warning for light aircraft under 12,500 pounds, and the Sigmet, intended as an interim warning for all aircraft, did not really meet the requirements of a "significant" meteorological phenomenon; the wording of Sigmet Charlie 4 simply said light to moderate turbulence. It became apparent during the discussions in San Diego that weather forecasting, even in this day of advanced monitoring and reporting, is still an infant science, if, indeed, it can be indexed as a science.

Sigmet Charlie 5 originated from the Houston forecast center and it was based upon pilot reports and information that Mike received from Little Rock radio drawn from the Kansas City computer via the reply circuit.

It was obvious what happened.

The forecaster, seeing the reports and then looking at Charlie 4, noticed a discrepancy in language. No severe or extreme turbulence was reported in the Texas-Louisiana rectangle, which didn't mean, of course, that the CAT wasn't there, only that no planes had encountered it, or perhaps, the vertical gusts were not fully developed at the time the Sigmet was downgraded. In the vernacular of the weather bureau, light turbulence means small bumps causing slight discomfort; seat belts are not normally required. Moderate turbulence is considered to be a flight condition that calls for fastened seat belts. There is some latitude between light and moderate turbulence and while one pilot might snap on his seat belt sign in a situation, another may feel it's unnecessary.

But there is *no* doubt when a plane hits severe turbulence. It is defined as follows: "Aircraft may be out of control momentarily. Occupants are thrown violently against belt and back into seat."

The exact definition for extreme turbulence is even more acute: "Rarely encountered, aircraft violently tossed about, practically impossible to control. May cause damage."

The hearing ended at 5:10 and Mike went immediately to his hotel room and took a long drink from the thermos. It was just about time; he could feel that gnawing, familiar urgency coming on. He called Pat then and told her about the hearing and the congratulations from the Administrator. She bit hard on her tongue, wishing the incident had never occurred. What irony she thought.

That night before dinner at her beach house, and after, the pilot drank heavily.

Angry, Pat said, "You've got to straighten yourself out. I'm not going to sit around worrying about you all the time. If you can't figure out what's happening, you're a complete idiot!"

"All right. I'm not flying tomorrow and I promise you I'll go to A.A. when I get back. Don't worry about it, I'm no Ray Milland. I haven't dropped a weekend yet, baby, and I'm not going to start."

Four

IA's eastbound SAN-JFK nonstop took off from Lindbergh Field twenty minutes late. The equipment was the same DC-8, N8907C, which had been carefully inspected by the F.A.A. and put back together, and signed off. Mike decided to deadhead back and he was replaced by a captain from the carrier's Los Angeles-base reserve list who flew down on Western Airlines since IA had no crew base in San Diego. Mike told Joe Barnes jokingly that he was going to relax and ride in first-class on the way back, just as Fitz had promised them.

Joe was pleased because he wanted to talk company policy; he saw the possibility of a bonus coming up for this and wanted to go over the story with Mike again. Joe wished to make sure that everyone—Cliff McCullen, flight vice-president, and his boss, Fitz—knew what a splendid job the IA New York-based flight department had done.

Actually, the record spoke for itself: IA had the best service story of all the first level U.S. flag carriers. In the history of the airline there had only been three major crashes: a midair with a military plane over Utah in 1956, a DC-7 flight in which fifty-two passengers and crew were killed; an inbound DC-3 crash at Cincinnati in bad weather in 1948 that killed all passengers and crew; and the carrier's worst crash, the 1967 collision with a Swiss mountain when all aboard the 707 were lost. There were other accidents involving IA, but they were hardly remembered since there were few fatalities although there were some injuries. The carrier also had its share of embarrassing mishaps.

One had happened only two months after Joe Barnes sat down at his new La Guardia desk. It took place almost under his nose. He received a call from the IA dispatcher:

"Shit. One of our inbounds just crashed on 22."

It was raining and bitterly cold. Joe sprang from his seat, ran from his office and jumped aboard one of the yellow airport security cars, which raced to the location. About halfway down runway 22, one of IA's 727's was leaning in the snow, the nose wheel and left carriage collapsed. The passengers were sliding down the emergency chute.

"Hold it there! For godsakes!" Joe yelled up at the door.

There was no fuel leakage and he ordered the crash equipment to evacuate the passengers via ladders. As soon as a ladder was placed against the plane, Joe hopped up the rungs two at a time. It was bad form to enter the plane before the passengers were out, but from his years with the carrier, he knew the most closely guarded secret of all: get to the pilots first, if they're still alive. (Lesson number *one*.) When Joe reached the cockpit, he slammed the door and made sure the master switch and voice recorder were off. Only the copilot was there.

"Get the captain in here and the second officer."

"They're helping with the evacuation."

"I don't give a fuck. Get 'em! If you don't know who I am, I'm the Chief Pilot."

"I know who you are," the shaking young copilot said.

He bolted from the cockpit and returned with the rest of the crew. Joe slammed the door behind them.

"What the fuck happened? They'll be here in a minute—quick!"

"It was my fault," the young copilot said. "I clipped the end of the pier with our left undercarriage."

"Why were you so low on the threshold?"

"We got a little behind the power curve. I had to lift the wing to make a correction and the gear snagged it."

"Did you hear something?"

"No," the Captain said. "But we saw the green light on the panel go out. I took over and as we rolled out, the nose wheel went."

"Okay," Joe said. "Here's what happened. Listen closely. The plane was making a normal landing, and all of a sudden, the gear collapsed. Do you have that?"

"Yes," they said.

There was a knock on the door. The F.A.A. was there.

Joe opened it. "Lucky thing," Joe said, "these guys did a beautiful job. Beautiful. Congratulations again, men."

"What happened?" the F.A.A. representative asked.

"That goddamned gear collapsed, just collapsed. It's under the plane."

"Just collapsed?"

More F.A.A. men arrived, then more IA officials from the New York office. The plane could not be removed from the runway, which was closed until the accident team arrived two hours later. By then the news people were there. IA managed to hold off photographs saying that there was gas on the runway and they were not allowed out until the F.A.A. okayed it. (A deal IA made with the airport.) So the photographers never got close enough to photograph the plane, but there was little sense anyhow since there were no injuries. The story appeared in one New York paper:

LANDING GEAR COLLAPSES AS PLANE
LANDS AT LA GUARDIA.
An Intercontinental Airways 727, Flight 62 from
Detroit to La Guardia, experienced a landing
gear failure yesterday after it was on the runway,
but no passengers or crew members were injured,
nor was there a fire. Airline officials said an
investigation would be launched to establish the
cause of the landing gear failure.

When the crane lifted the plane up, there was no landing gear underneath, naturally: it was in the water at
the end of runway 22's threshold, a pier extending out
into Flushing Bay. The divers found it the following
morning, but this part of the accident never made the
papers. Joe Barnes was secretly congratulated by Cliff
McCullen and Pete Hanscom for his quick work.

While having the best safety record of any first-
level carrier in the category of fatalities, IA had, by
far, the greatest occurrence of planes landing at wrong
airports: five in 1936 alone, and twenty-nine throughout the carrier's forty-four year history.

Mike had slipped his spooker into a coat pocket
and after boarding 602, he entered the second forward
head, opened the trap door, and attached his lifeline.
Thirty-five minutes after takeoff at 1:30 MST, the
stewardesses began their luncheon service. When the
drink cart came by, Joe nudged Mike.

"Come on, we'll gas up."

"No thanks. Never drink during the day. I'll have
ginger ale," Mike said.

"Give me a double Scotch and soda," Joe said.

The drinks were served and Mike excused himself
and went forward to the head, took a paper cup, and
had his third spooker of the day, the first two having
gone down in his hotel room.

The old Chief Pilot talked over the early days
with Mike Hagen. To have entered flying when it was
new was a joy to Joe Barnes, a special privilege. He
had experienced little pain or loss in his life. Joe was a

vibrant, sturdy man who was born perfectly into his time, and in some ways, he and Mike Hagen were alike. They both were basically rural people; they liked crops, dust, fertilizer, and the smell of hot oil in an open cockpit—the richness and pleasure of flying the way it was. Joe rambled all the way back east—drinking three doubles—as he spread his joyous life out before Mike Hagen.

When the flight landed at JFK, Mike said goodbye to Joe Barnes, and the pilot agreed to write a memorandum for his chief on clear air turbulence and the measures they could suggest as a precautionary company policy, if any. Mike saw Jim moving toward his car in the parking lot; they waved at each other and then Jim came over.

"I want to say it was some job you did the other day. I'll never forget it. But just as a friend, Mike, I think you ought to cool the booze. I'm sorry to have to say this, but it's getting worse. I'm flying up there, too, and there'll be a day when I'm not too sharp and I'll need everything *you* have."

"I realize," Mike said solemnly. "I'm going to do something about it. Jim, stick by me for a while, will you?"

"You know I will. Anything I can do, I'll do. But I want you to know that I have a responsibility here—to the passengers and my family. I want to make sure you know my position. You're not in one cockpit, me in another. We're all on the same flight deck team, right?"

"Sure, Jim, sure. Thanks."

Mike waited a minute until he saw Jim's Chevrolet go by, and he waved at his copilot again. The pilot got into the front seat and put his head between his hands.

"What happened?" he said out loud. "How?"

He would begin by *not* stopping at Ellen's Place. That was the first step.

Mike drove out of the maze of JFK entry roads that twist from one terminal to another and feed into the main artery of the airport. It had started to rain lightly, but the weather was warm for December and the roads to Ridgefield would not be icy. Ahead he saw the line-up of cars. It was 8:30 P.M. and all the flights seemed to have terminated at once on that rainy evening. The roads leading out of JFK were inadequate, and sometimes on hot summer nights it would take forty minutes to get to the Van Wyck Expressway. This was another reason for Ellen's Place, an excuse; but a practical one, for as soon as the pilot cleared the airport, he would turn off, moving onto local, uncrowded streets toward the hidden dark bar nine blocks away.

He came to the turn-off almost thirty minutes later. He *needed* Ellen's Place: the traffic was worse than usual because of a minor car accident just north of the JFK entrance. But he went past the exit and felt a small victory. As the Nova moved through the Bronx on the highways jammed with homebound shoppers and commuters, he felt the empty, painful sensation in his stomach and head. He thought about stopping at a gas station and carrying his spooker into the men's room, but drinking in a fetid lavatory revolted him, so he continued, trying to think where he could stop: Pelham, he had taken one or two in a bar there, a small, pleasant, dark place—or was it New Rochelle? He couldn't remember. But he got off the New England Thruway at Pelham and proceeded up the Post Road, passing several truck bar and grills and finally, as the rain became harder, he pulled off the road into the parking lot of a place called the Candlelight Club. He changed into his mechanic's jacket, put on his dark raincoat, and ran in. He sat with two or three lost-looking men and sipped the bourbon that a taciturn man behind the bar poured for him and, refueled, set out again for Ridgefield.

He was *disgusted* with himself.

"I can't even get home," he said aloud. "I can't even get home."

* * *

Ridgefield, Connecticut, is one of a string of old pre-Revolutionary towns running up through Fairfield County in an area that is generally called the soft foot-hills of the Berkshires: pleasant, rolling terrain dotted with maples, elms, oaks, and hickories, and among the lush foliage, clusters of magnificent houses dating back to the late 1700s and early 1800s. It is an area for antique lovers, authentically quaint, and was newly discovered by publishers and advertising men who settled there after the local gentry sold out to the new rich and moved farther into more rural Connecticut.

Then, other affluent groups moved in: executives working for large corporations that had left New York City to base themselves in hidden glass buildings amid the greenery of southern Connecticut, and too, a new generation of pilots. They flew infrequently and earned around $60,000, more or less, depending upon the equipment and routes they flew. Many captains chose Ridgefield because it was just about an hour away from JFK (if one drove at three in the morning in good weather) and the rules of the airlines stated that a pilot had to reside within an hour's drive of the airport. (Ridgefield and the towns around it sat on the outer JFK limit.)

The Hagens moved to Ridgefield shortly before the heavy influx drove up real estate prices. They bought a large old place, said to have been built in 1781, which stood on the brow of a slight hill; it had a fine yard with four maple trees, two oaks, apple trees, remnants of an old orchard, and all this was placed on almost three acres of ground.

But age, Mike found, had its drawbacks, and from the beginning things began to go wrong: plumbing, shingles, wiring, stone steps, the stove, rain gutters, rotten beams, finally the oak that came down on the pitched roof one winter. Each year there was a project and on a copilot's salary, Mike fell behind although he did much of the work himself. His younger daughter had been born there in 1961 and he learned that raising two daughters in an area where other children had wealthier parents was expensive and often embarrassing. They could not join the country club until he was raised to the position of captain; even then it was difficult to tie all the financial ends together.

Jean. She was a thirty-nine-year-old dreamy woman who was aging unwillingly. She had a drink now and then, but she put it away poorly, and her disposition, Mike thought, was deteriorating a little year by year. They had met when he was crop-dusting, working the citrus groves around Indian River, Florida. He was refueling his Stearman one day and she landed at the small Ag field, claiming to be lost. At the time, Jean was taking flight lessons, along with water-skiing lessons and scuba lessons at a minor women's junior college in Fort Lauderdale. Her family lived in Jacksonville; her father was a fairly successful real estate dealer and her mother was a snobbish woman from an old Nashville family and quite a bit of this rubbed off on Jean, their only child. Mike was attending the University of Florida at Gainesville and in the summers he worked as an Ag flyer. Life at the Ag strip was pretty lonely and when Jean arrived there that day it was like a gift from heaven. She was blond and pretty and took an immediate and lively interest in Mike. Before long they were involved in a love affair and a few months later, were married—in a lavish wedding in Jacksonville. Jean's father was quite pleased because he liked the young pilot. Her mother, who had dreams of a society marriage, was not.

"What's the future for a crop sprayer?" she asked her daughter.

After Mike graduated from the university with a degree in agriculture, he continued crop-dusting and Jean worked part-time for an artificial flower factory in Fort Lauderdale.

She had shown quite a bit of talent for art and sculpture and she became a model maker for the plastics company designing fake exotic plants. But she was no happier than her mother had been with Mike's job and urged him to join a commercial airline, which would guarantee steady employment and some respectability. He resisted, but when he realized she'd never be happy as the wife of a crop duster he gained an air transport rating from a local school and flew junior routes as a DC-3 copilot with Northeast. He joined IA in 1957 and was transferred to the carrier's New York base; Jean stated emphatically she would *not* live in Jackson Heights, or any part of Queens, where most of the younger copilots settled and when they moved to Ridgefield, the pressure was on.

They had saved only enough to buy the house and Jean's tastes were well developed for a small town girl. They became more extravagant each year; the clothes came from Saks Fifth Avenue instead of the local dress shop; their daughters switched to private schools. She always wanted to look ten years younger than she was, and she frequently visited expensive health farms; twice her face was lifted by a prominent New York plastic surgeon. When her father died, he left her some money but she quickly went through that.

As the bills mounted, Jean said they needed supplementary income. Mike studied for a flight instructor's rating and began teaching at the Danbury, Connecticut, airport some seven miles to the north, but it was soon apparent that the money he earned from that job was inadequate.

"I guess I'll have to find something else," he said to her, hating what she was doing to him because he loved teaching people to fly, telling them the things he knew, engendering a love and respect for the air.

"I should think so. What do you get, a hundred and twenty dollars a week for that nonsense?"

"It's *not* nonsense."

"Poverty wages, that's all. We need a steady business that will grow. We have to put the girls through college and I don't mean some state teachers institution."

"You can always send them down to your alma mater to learn water-skiing." Mike noticed sarcasm had become a part of his daily speech. Jean ignored his acid comment.

"I'd like to start an artificial flower business, mail order. I know how to sculpt the original and have moulds made."

"And what would this great idea cost?"

"About fifteen thousand to get going. I was talking about it to Bill Cousins. He's a chemist and he said he'd invest in it. We can borrow the rest. He has a marvelous gimmick, a spray that'll make the flowers smell. Different jungle scents. You have a lot of time off so you can help me run it. I'll make the flowers, you run the business."

"Jean, for Christ's sake, I'm a pilot, not a florist."

"Well, all the pilots around here have second jobs. Nick Baldwin has made a fortune in real estate and Ralph Higgins has a mail-order furniture business."

"But artificial flowers? That's for pansies. Hah!"

"Funny, Captain. You'd better think of something because we can't send the girls to college plus everything else on a mere pilot's salary."

Jean prevailed, as usual.

They went into synthetically scented artificial flowers, operating out of a small office in Ridgefield. Jean worked hard at first and the moulds were very successful, being handled by a Boston plastic jobber, but as the competition grew Mike had to put in longer hours and, in the end, Jean worked less and less, caring more about her looks than her work.

When Mike reached home, Jean greeted him with a "Why the hell didn't you call?"

He ignored it, noticing that she had been drinking, and pushed past her to set his heavy bags down. Karen and Debbie had homework spread out on the dining room table, and they both jumped up when Mike came in.

"Hi, Dad, where you been? We were about to send out Mod Squad," Karen said.

Plump, serious little Debbie ran over and gave Mike a big hug. "We were worried. Did you have any trouble?"

Jean broke in. "You never think about us at all!"

"Jean, for Christ's sake. Give me a chance. I wired."

"I never got it."

"Well, I did. We had a turbulence problem and they held us over for a hearing in San Diego."

"What kind of problem, Dad?"

"I'll explain later, muffin," Mike patted Debbie on the head.

Jean told the girls to go upstairs. She turned toward Mike, "There's one hell of a lot of orders and things to do at the office. We're way behind."

He threw his coat on a chair and went directly to the bar, poured some bourbon and turned around and laughed at Jean.

"My lovely, concerned wife. You didn't even ask me what happened. All you're interested in are those goddamned stinking flowers!"

The two girls looked at each other resignedly and gathered up their books. They knew what was coming.

Jean started toward the den. "We're rattling your father, girls. The pilot of all time has come home in a mood, a goddamned mood. There's a turkey TV dinner in the icebox," she yelled, slamming the door behind her.

The following morning Mike went to the office over the local hardware store in Ridgefield. It was three rooms jammed with foul-smelling, exotic, outsized flowers, shipping boxes, orders and piles of other business junk that overwhelmed Mrs. MacGregor, the elderly, retired schoolteacher they employed. Mike spent the morning shuffling orders and by 11:00, he was ready for the spooker. He went into the small side bathroom and unlocked the icebox door. Mrs. Mac-

Gregor, who was a little hard of hearing, knew he nipped now and then, but she didn't particularly think anything of it. The pilot never changed his smile, raised his voice, stumbled downstairs—things she associated with those who drank heavily. On the other hand, Jean Hagen, drinking much less than her husband, was often caustic and smelled of booze when she thumped into the upstairs office. Mrs. MacGregor naturally associated Jean with a drinking problem, not Mike.

That was his problem.

He drank *too well*.

As he leaned against the icebox bringing the cold drink to his dry lips, the pilot looked down on Main Street, seeing familiar people walking about, in and out of the hardware store, the drugstore, same women with same children and station wagons. For a split second, he pictured a crop duster working a field somewhere south of the Indian River laying a grayish trail over the Valencias.

A flick of a strange lens.

Bearing down on him was the promised telephone call to A.A., an admission that he was in trouble. Was he? No, Mike thought; he didn't need a bunch of reformed drunks to hold his hand and swap horror stories, "holier-than-thou's" commiserating over coffee telling it like it was when. But he knew Pat would question him so he might as well get on with it. Where? He couldn't go across to the Presbyterian Church where a prominently displayed sign announced the A.A. meeting every Wednesday night; it would only be a matter of days before Joe Barnes and the IA flight department heard that one of their high-time captains was so deep into the sauce that he needed Alcoholics Anonymous. Anonymous? Ah yes, a mystery drinker, not Ridgefield, or even the towns nearby, for this part of Connecticut was small and everyone knew everyone else in what Vance Packard called the "exurban belt."

Then the idea came to him.

He had a biplane at the Danbury Airport and he

would put it to work; fly to A.A. The thought of a pilot showing up in his open plane for the weekly "drunk talk" amused him; he thought it was the ultimate flaunting.

Mike took the New York sectional chart and studied the airports ringing the area: Bridgeport and New Haven had landing lights, long hard-surfaced runways, and radio navigational aids. He would find a group that met near the airport. Perfect strategy. Which city would have his sort of drunk? (In the back of his mind he wanted something, anything, to come out of the meeting. He loved to drink and he'd *never* give the bourbon up, but he wanted to throw away the damned thermos, never see Ellen's Place again, and make it through the day without needing a fucking boost to get over the previous night. An obvious solution would be to knock off the nights before, but that he couldn't do, or at least, not yet.)

He dialed the Bridgeport A.A.

"Alcoholics Anonymous," a woman said.

"I'd like some information please. Where does your group meet?"

"At the Catholic Church on Marion Street, Tuesday nights at eight."

"Is that near the airport?"

"Not exactly. Are you from Bridgeport?"

"No, Danbury."

"There's a group that meets in your area. It would be closer."

"Ah, there's a problem."

"Well, you're certainly welcome here. If you need any help now, I could have someone call you back."

"I *don't* need any help!" Mike shot back. He slammed down the phone.

He wanted to fly. It was 11:30; he went back to the bathroom and took another half a spooker that cleaned out some of his anger.

"I'll be away for the afternoon, Mrs. MacGregor. I'm going up to Bridgeport on business."

"All right, Mr. Hagen."

Mike Hagen knew the limits and routine of constant, experienced drinking; how far he could go, what he could do and not do. If he were going to fly his biplane that afternoon, he could not take off with two spookers in his belly unless he took on a cargo of hot, greasy food to help counteract the morning bourbon and line his gut for the next spooker.

It was crisp and bright that December afternoon, low cumulus clouds moved over the Connecticut countryside from the northwest and the temperature was somewhere around forty-five, Mike figured. He got into the Nova and drove north toward the Danbury Airport. He turned into the large trucking diner just to the right of the airport entrance and piled into a large order of bacon and eggs. After two cups of coffee, his head was clear and he headed toward the field.

As he drove along with the windows down and the air hitting him in the face, his thoughts bounced back to Florida: he was walking home from church, watching the old working biplanes slip onto the dirt-strip sending up a cloud of nut-brown dust as the wheels hit, and there was always the whine and the crack of an old radial turning over. He had spent every minute he could at the field among the rough-edged flying cowboys, men who worked the crops down through Louisiana and Alabama for the various seasons, always ending up in south Florida for citrus dusting, the last stop before they would binge it, sober up, feel sorry, and fly north to repeat the crop cycle. Sometimes those cowboys would take him up, but he was so short as a teen-ager that he couldn't see over the front cockpit lip unless they strapped him onto a pile of old Miami telephone books.

"When yuh get up tall, kid, so's yuh can see over the cockpit, we'll teach yuh to drive one of these 'tail-draggers.'"

Mike did shoot up in his sixteenth year and he had saved enough money for lessons, but not in a Piper Club trainer. He talked a citrus sprayer into letting him learn in a weathered Waco UPF-7 that had been retired from spraying because she was a bit twisted. Still, the old bird flew and was certified airworthy as if she were determined never to give up the air. When Mike went up alone the first time, he was at the stick of this angry but beautiful, rugged two-winger, one of the wire and cloth jobs with a radial engine in front spitting out over two hundred horses; it was all there: the big bird, the whistling air, the loneliness, and that great hungry sky he loved.

Mike was licensed in just forty hours. He started laying insecticide on Valencia groves for seven dollars an hour when he was only sixteen and years later when Mike bought a plane, it was an antique Waco, the exact model in which he had soloed. He was forever trying to recapture the past as if to put a halt to the insidious transit of time. It took seven months to locate the plane; most of them had wasted away, rusting in cornfields; a generation of great planes was gone except for a few sitting it out in air museums or in the hands of antique plane collectors. Mike placed an ad in *Trade-A-Plane*, a national weekly newspaper:

Airline pilot wishes to buy unmodified Waco UPF-7. Does not have to have current airworthy certificate, but must have original unmodified airframe and powerplant. Top price paid.

A letter came in from a farmer in Kansas who said he thought he had such a plane in the barn—it had belonged to an uncle. Mike went out to a small town about thirty miles from Wichita and when they slid open the barn door, there was an old, faded UPF-7. The pilot didn't need to see the registration plate—he knew his Wacos, every model. He walked in around the dark barn, feeling the plane's loose struts, tearing off a small piece of fabric that came apart in his hands. She needed work, thousands of dollars, but it could be done and the pilot knew how because he loved the plane, was familiar with her temperament, heart and soul. As he gazed at the skeleton, he wondered how many good men had sat in the small cockpit.

"Ain't much to look at."

"It's not," Mike told the farmer. "How long since she's flown?"

"Fifty-six or seven. Luke used to fly her around a bit, then he took to his bed. Poor guy—arthritis—worst the doctor had ever seen."

"What do you think the plane's worth?"

"Don't know. Someone offered me two thousand, or was it three? She was almost flyable then. Now, she's junk. How about a thousand?"

The deal was made.

Mike took the family car and with his older daughter, Karen, who was twelve at the time, drove all the way out to Kansas in 1971. Together they disassembled the plane, marking each part. Then they set up a block and tackle over the barn and hoisted the old fuselage onto a flatbed trailer. The wings were fastened to each side and they headed east. The pilot never forgot that summer; they came home the slow way, making stops at the National Air Museum and the Edison Museum, and Mike and his daughter enjoyed their time together.

The pilot had rented a corner of a hangar on the far side of the Danbury Airport and the Waco was installed on blocks. Whenever he could Mike went to the hangar to work on it. He removed the old fabric, took out the rotted wing spars, and replaced them with well-seasoned spruce. The plane was a bare skeleton, but the pilot checked every weld in the tubular airframe—fixing some, smoothing others—and in his cellar he had made a new instrument panel out of rare burled walnut into which he set modern flight instruments ringed with highly polished, top-quality brass. It was a work of love, an odd kind of pilgrimage back into the Florida of the forties. Jean said nothing about the plane and never came to the damp, lonely hangar to see what was going on. "That goddamned nonsense is

depriving the girls of a college education," was her only
comment.

The plane was sprayed with lacquer five times—
blue and white, the exact colors of the Waco he soloed
in many years before. Mike rebored each of eight radial cylinders in the old Jacobs engine. He had learned
his engines from fixing his father's tractor, followed by
years of working in the hangar at the Homestead Ag
strip. When the freshly painted, dope-smelling plane
was finally rolled out one bright spring day, it was
doubtful that a more perfect Waco ever emerged from
a hangar. People around the airport—the hangar rats,
rubbernecks—held a party for Mike that afternoon:
beer and hot dogs cooked by the side of the hangar.
His children attended, but not Jean. The event was
capped off by Mike himself. He put on his old cracked
leather flying jacket and a helmet, climbed into the
newly licensed Waco, wound up the power plant, and
the old clunker kicked out puffs of blue-black smoke.

He fed in the power, the plane rolled down the
cement runway, the tail came up, he held the stick forward for a moment, and then his beloved Waco lifted
off. It went higher and higher over the green Connecticut hills. He had thought about pulling a few inside
loops or Cuban eights, but he wanted to refamiliarize
himself with the plane so he just flew by the crowd at
hangar level and waved. The ship was wheeled back
into the hangar. Everyone, including Mike, was satisfied. He got into the car and drove his daughters back
to their Ridgefield home. The whole project from barn
to roll-out had taken fifteen months and six thousand
dollars. It was worth every cent of it, he told his wife.

"Bullshit!" she cracked.

He parked the Nova by the side of the hangar,
waved to one of the regulars, a man struggling to re-
build a Cessna 195, and pushed against the hangar
door. It groaned on its rusty tracks as it slid back. A
shaft of bright afternoon light touched the blue Waco

perched like a bird, eager to rear its tail and spring for the outside air. Mike walked around the plane, feeling, tapping, and rubbing. He checked the oil and wiped some dust from the mirror-like prop, a chrome job that had cost him four hundred and thirty dollars. The propeller had to be balanced before it was refastened to the hub of the radial engine and he liked to see the sun flashes bouncing off the prop as it went around. "With a psychedelic fan, they know I'm coming," he told people.

But pilots and ground people would realize the Waco was coming without a splatter of sunlight off the chrome prop, for the old engine had a roar and a clatter all its own, the unmistakable throaty voice of an open radial, a sound seldom heard anymore. Mike put on his flying suit, not one of those you ordered from an advertisement in the flying magazine: this was a real one with a moth-eaten fur collar and cracked, oil-stained leather that squeaked as one walked. It was all held together, more or less, by heavy buttons and a rusted belt. He bought it for two dollars from an old Florida crop duster who was about to stuff it in the ashcan because it had collected too many smells over the years: oil, gas, sweat, fertilizer, caked mud, cow and hog shit, and everything else gathered over a lifetime of spraying. Jean was too embarrassed to give it to the cleaners, so Mike took it around himself and told the man to put the strongest stuff he had on it.

He climbed in, put on his helmet, adjusted the sectional on his lap, and with the throttle cracked and the big machine in front primed with a few shots, he hit the electric starter, one of his few concessions to progress. It whined, coughed, choked, sputtered, and finally caught, knocking out a puff of blue-black smoke. He smelled the hot oil and his ear okayed the sounds as the engine warmed up and the tone evened.

He taxied her down to the active, checked his magnetos, and fed in the power; the runway blurred under him and he brought the tail up, finally the wheels. The engine thundered and the chrome prop chewed the still air, taking the Waco higher and higher. The brown fingers of the bare trees reached up, but they would not get him and he spit down at the hills with joy; Mike was in his own fragment of the universe, a better one, a freer one. He climbed up through the puffy canyons, one more beautiful than the other, into the new, fresh world he loved. Sitting outside, the clouds seemed bigger and the rush of clean air past his face completely unclogged his head. Mike called it his air therapy; it dampened the flow of a new spooker and flattened out the ache for another.

Higher and higher.

They were eating up the sky. He leveled out at 7,000 on top of a round-edged cumulus drifting by. Mike chopped the power and put the plane into a dive as the altimeter unwound. With a close look at the airspeed, he pulled back the stick and the bird curved up into the deep blue of the higher sky; he fed in full power and the Waco set on her tail, going up and over. He cut it on top, hanging blissfully upside down, seeing the world, perhaps, as it was. Then to complete the inside loop he worked the stick again and the ship came around.

He was laughing.

Mike went again, pulling her up with full power until he hit the top and he curved off performing a difficult acrobatic maneuver, the "Split S." As he leveled once more, he searched for a hole in the cloud cover. When he found it, he put the plane into a spin. The earth whirled beneath him and he kicked in left rudder to straighten out his right spin, pushed the stick forward, then applied power.

"Don't think I can fly, Jim Cochran? Shit! Very few guys can do this, baby, so wherever you are, Jim Cochran, Pat Simpson, Joe Barnes, hope you're watching. This is dedicated to you, kiddies."

The pilot pulled a perfectly executed "Cuban Eight" for them, for himself, and satisfied, he put the Bridgeport omni frequency in the window of his "magic machine." The white bar centered, telling him the radial to the station; he banked around to the magnetic heading and flew off on his A.A. reconnaissance.

Twenty minutes later he called the Bridgeport tower on the portable transmitter and received landing instructions. Once over the airport, he decided not to take a long final like the Piper Cherokee in front of him; instead, he came in high, astride of the runway, and then slapped the heavy Waco right down on the numbers with an acute crop duster's slip.

"Biplane 54 Echo, please observe traffic pattern."

"This is biplane. Sorry," Mike said.

He taxied the plane up to the gate where a crowd gathered to see the antique and when he climbed out of the cockpit, the kids gasped. Not only were they seeing a beautiful old plane wrenched from the past, but the man who climbed out in his battered flying suit and goggles was a real aviator!

The twenty-minute cab ride to the Catholic church on Marion Street took him through a drab and grimy neighborhood, rows and rows of pre-World War I multi-dwellings jammed with Greek and Slavic families. Mike thought the young, first-generation Americans who left these houses during World War II for the battlefield must have welcomed the call. The church was as he imagined, a leftover from the nineteenth century, the moral spiral over a place which was poor, meaning Catholic.

"Want me to wait?" the cab driver asked.

"Yeah," Mike said as he opened the door and walked into the dark church, which smelled of incense, cheap candle wax, old cracked varnish and polish. There was a parochial smell in the place, a smell of decline.

"Can I help you?" came the soft voice from the shadows.

"Is this the place where the A.A. people meet?"

"Yes, that's tomorrow night, eight o'clock. Are you in trouble, my son?" the priest asked after studying Mike for a minute.

"I'm not in trouble," Mike said harshly.

"Are you from the parish?"

"No. Thanks, Father," Mike said, moving toward the door.

On the way back he thought about the alcoholics sitting in the damp, hoary basement recounting their drunken sprees to one another. It was a wonder the poor bastards ever stopped drinking; cheap bar Scotch was probably the only way to brighten their gray and brown lives.

"Oh shit," he said aloud, depression settling over him.

At the airport he got the number for Branford A.A. A man answered, and this time Mike was prepared, "I'm from out of town. Do you have a group that meets in Branford?"

"On Thursday nights, seven thirty, at the firehouse."

"What's the address?"

"On the square. You can't miss it. You new here, huh?"

"Yeah."

"Well, come on around. We have some speakers coming in from New London."

Mike wound up the Waco again, took off, and twenty minutes later, he was in the traffic pattern of New Haven's Tweed Airport following a Pilgrim Airlines De Havilland Otter down the alley on final. Again, the people around the airport twisted their necks to see the unusual old bird approach the terminal. He took a taxi the short distance to the firehouse and strolled about the Early American town that clung to its heritage without looking restored.

He thought he would like these ex-drinkers and the firehouse wasn't too far from the airport. At 5:30 that evening, as the lights blinked on at the airport, the pilot pointed the nose of his Waco down the active and took off into the chilly night. He was cold and the sharp, tingling air hitting his face took his mind off the desire for a drink. It was past spooker time and he bent the plane to the right and passed over New Haven.

Taking a bearing on the compass, Mike played that course until he recognized the pattern of familiar headlights moving up Route 7 and, finally, the runway lights of Danbury Airport popped into view. He called the Unicom for runway information, eased off his power, and dropped out of the black sky, laying his Waco right on the numbers. But the landing was hard, followed by a bounce. He didn't quite understand what happened. It was probably the restriction of night vision. Of course, that was it.

Thursday. He had ruled out the dreary Bridgeport group and called Pat to tell her he was going to join the Branford, Connecticut A.A. chapter. He *didn't* tell her how he was getting there; that was part of his delicious secret. He flew through the chilly darkness dressed in a thick wool sweater under his flying suit, and after he had the Waco parked by the New Haven Terminal, he called for a cab, instructing the driver to return to the firehouse in about two hours.

There was a small cardboard sign, "A.A. Meets Here, 7:30," attached to the bumper of the ladder truck that had been pulled outside for the meeting. Inside the bright bare firehouse were rows of fold-up chairs and a small speaker's platform. As soon as Mike ambled in, a balding man with a large smile raced toward him, his eager hand outstretched.

"Hello, are you one of the speakers?"

"No, just from out of town," Mike answered, looking at the self-satisfied ex-drinker.

"What group are you in?" the man asked.

"Homestead, Florida."

"Good to have you. Planning to attend the closed meeting?"

"Not tonight."

"Be with us long?"

"I don't know yet."

"Business trip?"

"Sort of."

Mike wanted this friendly sort to disappear and

he almost decided to fly back to Danbury at once, but he dismissed the thought and stayed.

"Want you to meet everyone at coffee later. Never had a guest from Florida before."

"Shove the coffee," Mike muttered under his breath. "I'll have an Old Grand-Dad."

The meeting was just as Mike imagined: the first speaker, an elderly retired schoolteacher who nipped out of desperation or loneliness, told a funny story of her intoxicated days, stepping on the dog, falling over the mailbox, clipping zigzagged hedges after a few in the kitchen. To Mike and perhaps some others her talk was sad for she seemed to have had such a fine time in her former inebriated state; it could have been the high point of her life, the only events in her bland existence that merited repeating even to a captive, interested body of listeners.

The next speaker told a tragic story. He was fired from his job at the Electric Boat Company in Groton; his wife walked out on him; his sisters and widowed mother wouldn't speak to him; in the end, he found himself strapped to a bed at the state mental hospital. After release, he fought a losing battle with booze, descending a bit each time, in and out of hospitals, friendless and with no hope until he met another alcoholic, a once-attractive, now ravaged Bethel, Connecticut, woman. She had entered the mental hospital to die in a bed rather than the gutter. They joined A.A. together and found new contentment.

The third speaker was a cultured woman in her early fifties, smartly dressed and attractive.

"My name is Helen and I'm an alcoholic," she began. "Unlike the other two speakers this evening, I didn't know I was in trouble. I had no sense of my life collapsing; in fact, I thought it was getting better. Before remarrying and moving to Branford, I was having a glorious time in Chicago as an account executive for a well-known advertising agency. I shan't mention the name because they still have a liquor account and someone might see a connection."

A sudden snicker bounced off the tiled walls.

"I did get the blended rye free but it was so rotten I gave it away."

Mike was interested in the speaker. Unlike the other woman, whose attempt to lighten her misfortune made it seem more tragic, this drinker was, obviously, sophisticated and she seemed to draw a bead on Mike's own problem. He somehow couldn't associate himself with the terribly flawed and devastated people who had preceded her.

"I think it might be interesting to explain how a person can get into alcoholism through the back door," she continued. "I came from a fairly wealthy Lake Forest, Illinois, family. I went to Vassar, then to the Sorbonne for a master's degree, married and was divorced within three years, and went to work for an advertising agency. Actually, I went with my father's tool and die account.

"Now everybody says that advertising people drink more than they should. Not necessarily true. My story isn't symptomatic of the advertising business, but it's one that's usually connected with certain jobs in large cities. You'll see why in a minute.

"At the time I joined the agency I didn't drink during the day. In the evenings I had a martini with my husband, sometimes two, but there was no dependency, no habit, not even a bare hint of alcoholism. Then I started going out to lunch with business clients and on these occasions I would take a drink. It didn't seem wrong because as I looked around the various restaurants, there wasn't a table without cocktails. In the beginning the lunches were two days a week and then they became five; my boss said it was part of business.

"Eventually I was drinking two martinis at lunch and three before dinner. Saturdays and Sundays became very difficult for me to get through because around noontime my body and mind would say it was time for martinis. I called up girl friends and we combined two-martini lunches with shopping trips and on

Sundays it would be one of the hotels that served brunch. It's important to understand that I didn't drink any more than two at lunch and three, possibly four, before dinner.

"Around this time a date and I were going up Lake Shore Drive one evening and a car driven by a drunken driver swerved over and hit us. True irony. I was thrown partially through the right front window and woke up in the emergency ward of a city hospital with eleven stitches and a minor concussion. It was about eight o'clock. Of course, I had missed my three martinis that night; it didn't bother me because they gave me a handful of pills and I slept until nine thirty the next morning, when I called my own doctor to arrange a transfer to a private hospital. He told me that beds were scarce and I would have to wait at least a day.

"About five that afternoon I began to feel dizzy and very strange. The intern said it was probably due to my head injury. He prescribed more pills, but by seven, it was much worse. I became disoriented and my hands started to shake. They rushed me up to X-ray and looked at more pictures and couldn't understand what was happening. The chief of service was called in along with the attending physician, a white-haired man who took one look at me and asked, 'You drink?' I nodded; he wanted to know how much, and when I told him, he said, 'You're suffering withdrawal symptoms.'

"The hospital had a general rule that all alcoholics or suspected alcoholics had to be sequestered on four north, the alkie ward. I protested and screamed because I was very frightened, but the orderlies strapped me into a straitjacket and I ended up in the foul-smelling crazy ward. They slipped me pills, tied me down to the bed, and all that night I sweated, hearing the yells of the poor helpless women around me who were nothing more than moaning, uncontrolled animals. It was a nightmare. When I was able, I called my lawyer and doctor and was transferred to a small, private, dry-out sanitarium. I joined A.A. and haven't taken a drink since.

"Later I learned that a good many people are addicted borderline alcoholics. Some progress, others don't, but *anytime* one's life has to be adjusted to alcohol, arranged around it, that person is in trouble. It can really get bad if the source is turned off for one reason or another—a hospital stay, camping trip, or a hundred other situations where alcohol isn't available. Finding out about myself the way I did was a terrible shock."

A stillness settled over the firehouse. It was a type of narrative that many of them had never heard because they had come to A.A. via the more normal route: "I've hit bottom, I'm as far down as I can go, help me."

The story depressed Mike; how did one know where the border was? But hell, he had his spooker with him all the time.

He had coffee with the "smiling man" and met everyone afterward. Then came the questions.

"What do you do, Mike?"

He was quick with his answer. "I'm in transportation."

"Railroads?"

"Trucking." He liked his little joke.

"Who are you visiting in Branford?"

"Friends."

"Who?"

"Friends."

He looked at his watch, put on a small smile, and briskly walked to the waiting taxi. He asked the driver if there was a bar on the way to the airport; the cabbie knew a good place and Mike told him to wait while he went inside and ordered an Old Grand-Dad. He was about to push the glass over for a refill, but he caught himself and instead waited till he got to the airport where he had his retarder: a bacon-cheeseburger with potatoes and two cups of coffee. A light rain had begun and when he landed at Danbury he was wet, cold, and tired.

This wasn't going to work.

He knew it as he went to the bar in the study of the Ridgefield house.

Just before his San Diego flight the following week, Mike drove over to a group in Stamford and between the two A.A. meetings, he experimented with his spookers. For five days prior to his trip he cut out the midmorning spooker, timing the rest of his intake precisely to a normal flying day. There were six and a half hours between the "Ellen" fill-up and the one at the Houston hotel and the pilot made it work. The first four days were difficult, but by the fifth day he didn't quite feel the nagging emptiness coming on between 10:00 and 10:30 in the morning.

On the day of his flight Mike stopped at Ellen's, but he didn't leave the cockpit all that morning. He wasn't ready for the afternoon withdrawal yet; however, when they left operations in San Diego, Jim said softly, "Getting ahold of it, Mike?"

"Damned right. It'll take a while, but I'm in the A.A. program now, cutting way back, Jim."

That night he and Pat dined at the Mexican restaurant in La Jolla; Mike had two drinks instead of four or five and he told Pat about the meetings, flying up to Branford and Stamford.

"Aren't you supposed to stop drinking? Isn't that the idea?" she asked.

"Honey, I don't want to stop entirely, I just want to drink less. *I'm* not an alcoholic in the real sense. You ought to hear their stories. Maybe it's smugness on my part, but I can't identify with those people. . . except for one woman in Branford who used to be in the advertising business."

Pat didn't know what to say, but she could tell he was easing off; perhaps the meetings were giving him some sort of undefined direction. He didn't take his usual after-dinner brandy, and when they made love that night he was gentle and sober.

The next few flights were routine. The holidays came and went without incident and Mike relaxed, knowing the worst was behind him. He didn't take the midmorning drink and it was on the third trip out to the coast without a problem that he decided to abandon the afternoon "spooker." The craving seized him before they got to San Diego.

Jim smiled when they left operations and said, "Good going," and Mike raced for the men's room and unscrewed the thermos. He didn't sip, he gulped, leaning back against the metal partition.

There was a beach party in Del Coronado that evening. It was the middle of January but the weather was fairly warm. Everyone dragged out hibachis and outdoor barbecues. Steaks, seafood, corn, and potatoes were cooking and as the party got into gear, Mike began to drink, too. He really had not wanted to go to the party since what he feared most was to be seen drinking the night before a flight and recognized entering the cockpit or on the PA the following morning. Pat roamed all over the beach saying hello to friends and by eleven o'clock that evening, Mike had had four stiff bourbons. He laughed and was enjoying himself, telling those clustered around the bar that he was vacationing for five days in Del Coronado. That excused his drinking but he hoped no one at the beach was planning to take the first outbound to New York the next day, IA flight 602.

A long way from the beach in Del Coronado, in IA's Dallas dispatch and central weather office, the night meteorologist was plotting the progress of a moderate low pressure located at 1200 hours central time over Columbia, South Carolina, and moving northeast. There was nothing unusual about the low and the construction of the frontal systems was almost classic: out to the north was the characteristic warm front, hanging off to the southwest the cold front, and in back of it cold air replacing warm air with a 1/100 slope range, meaning that one hundred miles into the cold air front the surface position of the boundary would be about one mile above the ground.

When the night meteorologist came on duty the barometric pressure appeared to be stable, but forty-five minutes later the teletype delivered new information. The ground stations in the Georgia, South Carolina, and North Carolina regions were reporting a deepening of pressure and a speed-up of frontal velocity. The meteorologist took an interest in the situation because it would, obviously, affect IA's operations out of their three New York bases the following day if the pressure continued to deepen. There were many weather conditions that could hinder landing operations: amount of moisture in the air, the stability of the air being lifted, the slope of the front, speed of the front, and moisture and temperature contacts between the air masses. As the meteorologist looked at the plots and the updated information clicking away on his machine, he sensed an empirical fog situation building along with the warm frontal precipitation.

The "prog" came up on the Dallas facsimile machine and it forecast acceptable but limited ceilings and visibility in the New York area valid until 1200 hours the following day. At that exact moment, as the Dallas meteorologist picked up his paper cup of coffee and began sipping it, Mike Hagen was into his fifth Old Grand-Dad on the beach in Del Coronado. The time was 12:15 Pacific, 2:15 central. Finishing his steak and lobster dinner twenty minutes later, Mike Hagen edged over to Pat, who was a little into it herself, and suggested they cut out.

"In just a minute, darling," she said.

That minute was an important one in Mike Hagen's life.

He went back and asked for a bourbon refill, and the salesman tending the oilcloth-covered bar poured the pilot a stiff one and Mike walked off toward the

tide line with his drink to kick his feet in the light surf.
Suddenly he turned around sensing that someone was
near him. The thirtyish woman wore bikini pants and
a halter; they talked for a while. Noticing her empty
glass, Mike offered to fill it and they walked back to
the bar. The pilot continued the conversation after re-
plenishing her drink and adding a bourbon to his own,
but the woman began to ask questions so Mike took
a big swallow, politely excused himself, and went off
to find Pat. He walked north on the beach, then south
until he found her. It was 3:00 A.M.

Things that go wrong usually start as granules,
minute errors in judgment that grow and compound
themselves; 602's extraordinary situation on January
16 began the night before on the beach in Del Coronado and in the weather-plotting room at IA's Dallas
facility. The low pressure by this time was picking up
speed, intensifying with the two associated fronts
branching out.

Mike Hagen went to bed at Pat's at 4:15. He was
not stumbling or wheeling about, but he was drunk.
They grabbed for each other in the dark but fell asleep
almost immediately because of the heavy drinking. Pat
woke at 8:00 with a bad head; looking over at Mike
Hagen sound asleep, she made sure that the alarm was
set for 9:30.

As she dressed she realized that she should not
have taken him to the beach party. It was a mistake,
the buzz in her head told her so, but there was an important client presentation that morning and her mind
was on her job, not Mike. She wrote a quick note and
left it on the kitchen table and left for the office.

Down in Dallas something else out of the ordinary happened. The night meteorologist who was
watching the gathering low pressure usually spoke to
his replacement, an elderly, complacent man who came
on at nine. Over coffee they would discuss the weather
pattern as it affected IA's routing, but that day the
young meteorologist went down to an all-night store to

buy his wife a carton of milk. Looking at his watch and realizing the replacement was already upstairs, he decided not to climb the three stories to the IA meteorological office and left. As he was driving home he thought about the cold front; maybe he should call the elderly meteorologist and tell him that the low might pick up, but then he thought that seemed presumptuous.

The alarm went off at 9:30. Mike rolled over, switched it off and when he finally opened his eyes and sat up, he knew he was hung over. It wasn't bad considering the amount of bourbon he had consumed, but he was a large man and his body was used to the spookers. The sensation that day was one of fuzziness, the out-of-sorts feeling he had experienced so many times. He leaned back on the bed thinking. Call in sick? No, as always, Mike rejected that one easy phone call. (A familiar story in A.A. meetings was the recounting of the murderous, paralyzing hangover when it was impossible to climb out of bed, much less turn up for a job—that wasn't him.) Mike's recipe for mornings like this was a very cold shower, the heavy breakfast, bigger-than-usual spooker, three Vitamin B-Complex pills, and a little oxygen when he reached the cockpit. This usually brought him around until spooker time.

It was seventy-five minutes to flight time. He wasn't going to make the hour sign-in, so he called Jim at the El Cortez.

"How are you, Jim?" he began brightly.

"Fine."

"Jim, I might be a little late. Tell them I had car trouble, but I'm definitely on my way. You go over a little early and work on the preflight, okay?"

Jim agreed and Mike pulled to his feet and stood still for a moment trying to decide how bad it was—about two from the bottom level, he calculated. He entered the kitchen, read Pat's note, put on the bacon, and returned to the bathroom to take an icy shower. The cold water woke him up, sending the blood rushing to clear his head. He dressed quickly, tucking in a fresh shirt, and after his usual "fat" breakfast, the shout in his stomach was capped. He went to the refrigerator, took out a tray of ice, and packed it in his plastic spooker bag; the pilot slid this into the thermos and poured in Old Grand-Dad, and then it was time for the vital lifeline spooker. He raised the bourbon and drank thirstily. Stuffing the empty bottle back in his flight case, Mike called for a cab, telling them to make it goddamned fast. The phone rang just as he picked up his bags.

"Mike, you on your way?"

"Yeah, cab's coming, Jim."

"I want your advice on something. We're going out at max allowable today."

"A lot of air freight?"

"Yeah, important shipment, they say. Of course, that's always their song. The MFP indicates we'll be over our Pittsburgh alternate with ninety-two hundred pounds of fuel onboard, but there's a warm front hitting New York with precip."

"What's the prog?" Mike asked quickly.

"They're forecasting limited ceilings, but if we take the company fuel contingency something else will have to go."

"How many people would we leave at the gate?"

"About twenty."

"Bump the cargo. We'll take the fuel and the passengers."

Fifteen minutes past check-in time, Mike walked into Operations after his usual dosing of Visine, Sen-Sen, and cover stick. The scheduling clerk looked up with obvious relief.

"Morning, Captain Hagen. I was getting worried."

"What about?"

"Covering the flight."

"Didn't Cochran tell you I'd be here?" Mike said with an unusual sharpness to his voice.

"Yes, sir, but it was getting hard to believe it."

Mike signed in for the flight and ambled over to the dispatcher.

"Phone message here for you, Captain."

He gave the pilot a slip of paper with Pat's number on it and Mike called her.

"How do you feel?" she asked.

"I'm okay. How about you, sweetheart?"

"I think I'm dying."

"That's 'cause you're an amateur."

"Darling, I'm sorry about last night. Really sorry."

"I had a great time. Good party, when's the next one?"

"I've been telling you to cool the drinks and look what I let us in for."

"Don't worry about it. I'm fine."

"You're sure?"

"Darling, please trust me. Okay?"

"You promise to keep up with the meetings?"

"Promise."

"Call me from New York, Mike."

"I will. Have to go now. Bye."

Mike returned to the desk to pick up his whoopee and the dispatch papers and then he walked to the weather boards, looking first at the prog, the surface charts, and finally at the winds aloft. He was satisfied with the situation as Jim had described it and hefting his bag, he walked out to the DC-8 that was being loaded by this time. Mike told Jim and the second officer to double-check the weight and balance sheets plus available fuel over the alternate. He wanted a good dose of oxygen without their knowing.

As the pilot climbed the steps to the aircraft the catering truck was backing up to the loading door. He said hello to Nancy, who was standing in the galley, and entered the cockpit, removed his spooker from the flight kit, and went to the first head to conceal it inside the flapped door. He returned to the cockpit, and as Jim and the second officer walked back toward Operations, Mike unfastened an oxygen mask and slipped it

over his mouth, holding it there so he could drop it to
his lap if one of the stewardesses happened to unlock
the cockpit door. (Cockpit oxygen on the DC-8 is a
demand flow. There are two functions on the switch:
normal and emergency. Mike hit the emergency side,
which is a forced flow, and the cool, rejuvenating oxygen rushed into his lungs and in a matter of minutes he
felt better.) The disturbing haze lifted from his head
and his neck was freed of the fatigue. He continued to
breathe the oxygen for a while longer and when he was
revitalized he put down the mask and stretched his
shoulders. Mike opened the cockpit door so as not to
arouse suspicion and shortly afterwards, about thirty-
five minutes before departure time, Jim Cochran returned.

"Checked out fine," he said.

The flight was boarded at 11:10. The cargo
hatches were closed ten minutes before departure time
and the stairs were pulled away at 11:27. The turbines were started, the air from the mobile starting
unit and DC lines detached; the lineman waved off the
flight and after ground control was contacted, N8695C
was on her way moving slowly toward the active runway. Mike was handling the plane.

They were cleared for takeoff at 11:38 that morning and the Stretch 8 lifted off routinely, climbed to
3,000 on a course that would take the flight to the
Blyth, California omni, then up to the Winslow station
in northern Arizona. The purity of the morning light
magnified the ground colors. Through the front windshield they could see almost a hundred miles—the rugged end of the High Sierras, the rough plateau country
beyond—and as they closed the first VOR station near
the Arizona border, the burst of yellow desert that
stretched before them, finally disappearing into the soft
horizon. The plane was on the autopilot, the passengers
were being fed, and Mike sat back feeling the first hunger of the day. He knew there would be two—one in
the morning, his 12:30 need—another about 2:00,

and he wondered if he could wait until 12:30 or if he would need a third, a goddamned third!

Jim looked over at the pilot; the reflected light filtering down on his face brought out the reddish glints in his eyes, which seemed pouchy and heavy that day. Jim knew why Mike had been late checking in. He recognized the signs of a hard night even through his ingenious cosmetic scheme. Twelve-thirty came at last and the pilot lifted himself out of his seat. Both heads were occupied; he waited along with an elderly man who entered the first lavatory when it was free.

When the second was free, the pilot stood at the water fountain and pretended not to see it. It seemed to take forever for the sign to switch from "Occupied" to "Vacant." The old man stepped out finally and Mike almost tripped over him as he entered, jerking down a paper cup on the way in. He recovered his spooker and lifted the cold bourbon to his lips; it tasted delicious that day, colder, nippier than usual, and he closed his eyes and saw the tawny liquid trickling down his gullet into his stomach, absorbed into his bloodstream, traveling up to his head to work the nerves. A drinking man should be made differently, he thought, with a watertight door in the top of his skull that could be opened and the booze poured in instead of going the long, slow route. He stood there for a minute, took a refill, and after he replaced the spooker and crushed the paper cup, he shoved a handful of Sen-Sen in his mouth.

When Mike returned to the cockpit, Jim had an enroute weather report. The situation at New York remained as forecast: 1,000 overcast, light rain, and two miles visibility.

It was now 3:40 in New York and the rain had started. The warm front connected to the low pressure was predicted to sweep through the area around 4:00 and the low pressure center had picked up considerable speed; it was already over the Atlantic and

deepening. Just as the young IA meteorologist might
have said, "she was a freaky low without a constant
rate of speed." Unknown to the crew of flight 602,
things were beginning to go wrong. The return flow,
the counterclockwise air coming around the backside
of the low pressure, was filling in and the New York
weather station observed a wind shift shortly after
5:15. The wind was from the northeast at 20 knots
with gusts to 30; the upper air currents showed a more
aggravated situation: at 20,000 it was 70 knots from
the northeast.

Those in the cockpit of N8695C weren't really
aware of the change until they reached their next
checkpoint, the Rosewood VOR southwest of Cleveland, just about the time Mike went for his second
spooker. The tiny thermos was almost empty after the
first paper cup; it went dry on the second. When Mike
returned to the cockpit, Jim informed him that Chicago wanted a call. Mike dialed the company frequency
and the chief dispatcher came on.

"Captain, we notice you're falling behind on the
check-in points."

"Affirmative. There's a bad head wind."

"How many pounds onboard?"

Mike asked the second officer, then answered,
"24,200."

"That's about what we show. Captain, JFK's
above minimums, but you can expect thirty to forty
minutes holding. That'll put you into your reserve."

"Roger," Mike said matter-of-factly.

"Would you elect Cleveland or Pittsburgh to take
on fuel?"

"I'll get back to you on that, dispatch."

Mike clicked off the button and leaned back in
his seat reading the airways chart. By the time they
opted for an alternate, were brought into the traffic
pattern, landed, took on the fuel and were cleared, at
least another hour and a half would have gone by; and
this time added to possible holding at JFK would put
Mike close to the "mean reds." He couldn't leave the

cockpit in Cleveland or Pittsburgh and shop around in his uniform for a bottle of liquor: he felt like hell; he needed a drink and he couldn't wait an extra hour and a half.

Then he made a mistake.

He called dispatch telling them that the flight would continue to New York.

Mike loathed himself. This was the *first* time that his decision-making had been affected by the spookers.

He was over the line now and he knew it.

The pilots had exchanged only a few words during the flight. Mike seemed to be in a bad humor and Jim wasn't going to invade his private hangover until he had done some calculations, but then he found they might be pinched into a low-fuel situation if JFK suddenly closed.

"Mike, I think we should file for Cleveland."

"Don't we have enough on board for the alternate?" Mike asked the second officer.

"Just enough, sir."

"Mike, I think we're playing this close."

"We're fine." Then he whispered, "Get the hell off my ass!" to Jim in a whisper low enough to outfox the tape.

In front of them stretched a deepening grayness, the remnants of the weather system; angry clouds were curling and sliding over each other. The passengers were contented; they had one and a half meals and plenty of drinks; the stewardesses had finished their work and were sitting in the jump seats reading. At 6:30 New York time JFK's ceiling was down to 500 on runway 4-Left where they were taking in traffic and the runway visual range was about 2,000 feet. Fog had already closed down MacArthur Field located farther out on Long Island and the weathermen at JFK were keeping a close look at the RVR. Flight 602 was nine minutes late at the next checkpoint, the Philipsburg, Pennsylvania, VOR. But they pushed on.

What was about to happen was not entirely

Mike Hagen's fault although Jim Cochran and the flight engineer believed otherwise. Many think, incorrectly, that the captain of an airliner is a singular god, possessed and ordained with supreme powers of decision making; not true. Although the captain does have total cockpit authority, his determination over the flight is limited by the Federal Air Regulations and two jurisdictions of the carrier: the central dispatcher and local dispatcher.

The mistake of not taking on fuel along the way was clearly Mike's blunder, but this was unknowingly compounded by the IA local dispatcher working the flight because he let the plane into the New York area when holding time was erratic. All that day as the fog drifted in and out, holding time alternately decreased and increased so as Mike circled and circled, things began to go wrong; he was behind in his fuel but he held on hoping. The dispatcher finally had to say, "Captain, you're going critical."

"That's affirmative," Mike answered with an ease that Jim Cochran couldn't believe.

"Name Philadelphia," the dispatcher ordered with an edge to his voice.

There was a pause.

"Philadelphia, it is," Mike said mechanically.

He made a PA. "Ladies and gentlemen, we have been diverted to Philadelphia, and we should arrive there in about twenty minutes. Once on the ground, we will attempt to keep the flight intact and return to New York as soon as conditions improve. We apologize for this inconvenience. Thank you."

Philadelphia International Airport is located on the Delaware River just south of the city and is equipped with four ILS runways, each designation following the magnetic heading. The two longest runways measure 10,500 feet and are marked 9-Right and 9-Left, meaning that if one landed from a westerly direction, the compass would read due east; if one approached from the east, the compass would read 270 degrees or west. By any standard, Philadelphia International is a well-equipped modern facility.

Mike knew they'd be over Philadelphia with barely enough fuel and combined with his self-disgust for not landing earlier, the fatigue that was creeping up on him, and his belly's futile scream for another spooker, he realized that he was in trouble. He said a small prayer to himself, "Get me the fuck down on that strip and I'll do anything! Just get me down!"

Jim Cochran noticed Mike's erratic movements. The cockpit was dark and the pilot's face was rimmed by the reddish glow rising from the instrument panel. Still, even in this dimness, Jim caught Mike's frequent hand movements about the instrument panel, fumbling over a frequency selector that didn't need an adjustment. The flight was descending routinely and the last of the fuel was being pumped up along the lines to the slowly revolving turbines. Each of the men understood the perils, but the sleepy passengers behind them were unaware of the problems, mechanical and human, that could affect their lives.

At 7:20 that night, as the DC-8-61 slipped through the scattered clouds northwest of Philadelphia International, the controllers were already taking in traffic on 9-Right via the ILS, the Instrument Landing System, which guides the pilots to the runway only.

They contacted Philadelphia approach control seventy miles away as the flight was out of 15,000 and descending rapidly.

"Philadelphia approach control, this is IA 602. We're with you northwest."

"Squawk ident, IA 602."

Jim pushed the button on the transponder and the flight was identified on the approach control radar in the tower.

"We have you, IA 602. Descend and maintain 8,000. Turn right to heading of 175 degrees."

Nancy unlocked the cockpit door as she often did and sat down in the fourth seat, prepared to enjoy a cigarette until the No Smoking sign flashed on when she would return to the cabin to make a final approach PA and check seat belts. As soon as she entered, she noticed something unusual in the cockpit. Ordinarily when she came there for a cigarette or to bring the trays up, she found a relaxed, easy atmosphere on the flight deck. Tonight the men appeared tense, their movements jumpy, and she sat silently for a minute before she asked, "Is everything okay?"

"We have a few little problems," Jim answered.

"What?"

"We can't go into it now, Nancy," Mike interrupted. "Please return to the cabin. Everything's going to be all right."

Mike's skull was pounding and he felt extremely uneasy over the situation that was building up on him. For a second he thought of asking Jim to take over, but Mike was stubborn and he had already decided this was going to be his final landing before running for help.

Landing a large jet is the point of flying when all parameters of speed, attitude, and sink rate—among other imperatives—must come together and corrections cannot be made as quickly as they can in a heavy piston aircraft. All the way down the alley Mike was sweating and when they broke out of the scud at the middle ILS marker, about 1,500 feet from the threshold, he was about fifty feet high and his target speed —which should have been around 140 knots—was reading 157.

"High and hot, Mike!" Jim yelled.

"There's plenty of concrete in here."

It was *clearly* a go-around situation but Mike continued, determined to stick it on.

"We're much too hot, Mike!" Jim yelled again as his hands reached out for the thrust levers.

"You touch those and I'll break your ass!"

They roared over the boundary and some 1,100 feet later they literally hit the runway. The noise sounded like an explosion; the plane bounced, preventing the spoilers from dissipating lift as they normally would. They were flying again, but this time they were fully committed to a landing.

It was *too late* for a go-around.

The runway lights whisked by in a trail of blurs; the needed concrete was slipping away, rushing by under them, and they were still in the air. Mike drove it on again.

This time the big plane stuck; the spoilers went up. Mike flipped back the reverse thrust levers, pushing down on the brake pedals as he saw the end of the 10,499-foot runway appear out of the soft, rainy mist.

"Shit!" Mike said to himself. "We're going off the end!"

They started to slow; Mike had the break pedals just about pushed through the floor. The reverse thrust screamed and Mike was silently screaming, too. Then they stopped, not forty feet from the fence. It was so close to the end that Mike figured if the plane had had its proper fuel weight aboard the momentum might have taken them off the runway.

They were on. Safe and stopped.

In the jump seat Nancy looked at the stewardess beside her and shook her head. "Wonder who made that one."

The passengers knew *nothing* except that it was a hard landing and most of them didn't appear to realize they had landed twice.

In a matter of seconds, as the big DC-8 turned off the last taxiway from 9-Right, Mike came on the PA. His voice was steady and he had regained his composure.

"Ladies and gentlemen, this is the captain speaking. We apologize for that rough landing, but we had wind gusts on the way down and as a safety measure we kept a little more power on to better control the aircraft. This routinely results in hard landings fully within the aircraft's operational parameters."

The PA sailed over everyone's head except those

in the cockpit; each knew the announcement was full of shit. The plane was too high and too hot. Had the landing occurred on a shorter runway they would have plowed off the end; it was only the structural integrity of the giant DC-8-61 that prevented the whole undercarriage from collapsing and spewing everyone out on the wet runway.

The plane and the passengers had survived the human factor. This time.

Mike taxied to the gate, then he slipped out of his seat and went to the head. He vomited and when he had washed and cleaned up, he saw what he never wanted to see again: a bloated face above the sweat-soaked collar with puffy red eyes and hands that trembled when he reached for the towel. He left the lavatory and went into the galley where Nancy was standing.

"New York's still reporting below minimums," he said. "We'll probably let the flight go here."

"Oh God, that means a limo."

"You got any of those little babies left?" he asked, indicating the liquor locker.

"Yeah, sure." She looked momentarily surprised. "I've already locked this one up but I think I can find a few. Just a sec."

Mike knew almost every stewardess had an incurable habit of dipping into the booze locker, concealing the little bottles in their bags. Nancy went out of the galley and returned in a few minutes, closing the curtain behind her.

"Here you go. Bourbon, right?"

She handed him four of the small bottles and he stuffed them in his pants pocket.

"Thanks, I'll take them to the Belvedere with me."

"You're staying in Philly tonight?"

"Yeah, I wouldn't get home before three. I'm tired of traveling. I just want to put my feet up."

"Don't blame you, Mike."

He went back into the head where he quickly drank two of the bourbons. He was bad off; he knew it.

At 8:50 that evening the flight was terminated and the passengers were provided with ground transportation to New York. On their way through the corridors of Philadelphia International Airport, Jim said he wanted to talk to him.

"Here?" Mike asked.

"Hell no!"

"I'm going to the Belvedere. We'll talk down there."

They rode in silence to the hotel on Broad Street where Mike checked into a room on the fourth floor. He ordered ice and poured himself another drink, and then slumped wearily into a chair waiting for the reprimand from his junior copilot.

"All right, Jim. Spit it out."

"I'm *not* flying with you anymore."

Mike had expected this.

"You said you were coming along, but you're not. This morning you looked like shit warmed over."

"Felt like it, too," Mike said, stretching his big frame.

"Mike, up until today I went along with you. I had respect for your flying and I thought you were really trying to lick the booze, but I'm not going to sit in the same cockpit with you again."

"I slipped up last night. I had a snoot full, got up hung over, had to take a couple drinks with breakfast, some during the flight—even bummed two off the girls after we landed."

"Jesus," Jim said.

"I'm caught in a goddamned trap, I realize it."

"I feel sorry for you, Mike, but you have to pull yourself out. When you do, let me know."

Jim turned and walked toward the door.

"Jim!" Mike called. "Will you help me?"

"Help you? I'm not a doctor, just a fool for riding with you. Mike, can't you see what's happened? For

godssake, I think you should get a doctor and quick!"
Jim's voice rose harshly.

There was a long pause.

"Jim, please." Mike crossed to him, put his hand
on the younger man's shoulder.

The copilot saw his bleary, pleading eyes.

"I've done enough, Mike."

"I'm not a bad pilot! I'm a goddamn good pilot.
Look at the job over Louisiana. My record is perfect.
You know that, Jim."

"It's not perfect. Drinking . . ."

"Goddamnit!" Mike thundered. "You drink, too.
Don't get sanctimonious!"

"Sure, I've taken drinks on layovers, but I
stopped. Why didn't we land at Cleveland, Mike?"

"Because my fucking spooker was dry. I needed
a drink. I couldn't wait another two hours."

"And that's why we stayed in the stack so long?"

Mike nodded. "There's a cheap, crappy bar in
Jamaica where I can load up. Don't you understand
what it's like? Haven't you ever desperately wanted a
drink?"

"Not that desperately and I hope I never do,
Mike. On that landing, couldn't you just have said take
it, Jim?"

"It was going to be my last landing until I got off
the booze."

"*Your* last landing! It could have been *my* last
landing, the last for over two hundred people. Christ!"

"All right. Quit preaching. It's over. Jim, just
don't say anything, please. That's all I ask. I'm sorry,
I know I've fucked up."

"Do everyone a favor. Go in and see Joe Barnes.
Take yourself off the line until you're straightened
out."

"I'll think about it, Jim. I will."

They shook hands and Jim left the room. Mike
stood at the window for a while looking out, then his
eyes slid toward the bottle of bourbon on the dresser.

* * *

Mike slept fitfully that night and in the morning he had his usual large breakfast, took two bourbons, and left for the airport where he deadheaded back to JFK.

When he arrived in Ridgefield the house was empty and he sat for a long time in the study trying to decide what to do. He decided to take the Waco up in the air just to prove something to himself and drove to the airport at Danbury. But when he had the biplane lined up on the runway for takeoff he suddenly retarded the power and taxied back to the hangar. He closed the door slowly, took a final look at the shiny blue bird, and ten minutes later, he was in the exotic flower office, his hand dialing the number of Doctor John Martinson, an icy G.P. who looked after the family. The nurse said the doctor could not see him for a week.

"It's an emergency," Mike said.

"Speak to the doctor, then."

"Hello, Dr. Martinson, this is Mike Hagen."

"What's wrong?"

"I have to see you right away."

"Have you chest pains?" the doctor asked.

"No," Mike said, "but I've got to see you."

"All right, I'll fit you in at two."

Mike entered Dr. Martinson's office, a wing of his large home on one of the better streets in the small town, and he waited for about twenty minutes until the nurse announced that the doctor would see him. Dr. Martinson was about sixty-five. Mike noticed how much he had aged since he had last seen him—four years before when Karen had appendicitis. The doctor went behind his cluttered old desk and he leaned back as his glasses fell along the thin, wrinkled nose. Straight out of a Norman Rockwell painting, Mike thought.

The doctor folded his hands over his starched white coat, and said, "What's wrong, Mr. Hagen?"

"Well, I'm a little embarrassed to tell you."

"I've been in medicine for almost forty-five years —very little I haven't heard."

There was a long pause. The doctor thought he knew what the pilot was going to say. He was probably having an affair—there had been a slip-up. "What is it?" the doctor said again.

"I drink."

"How much?" Many years of practice hid Dr. Martinson's surprise.

"Too much. I have to have booze during the day."

"How long has this been going on?" the doctor asked calmly.

"About a year or so—I mean, during the day. I don't get drunk or anything, but I'm, I guess you could say, sort of hooked on it."

"How do you stop when you have to fly? You're still a pilot, aren't you?"

"I don't stop."

"You drink while you're flying?" This time it was not so easy to mask the consternation in the doctor's voice.

"Yes."

"In the cockpit?"

"Well, I've been smuggling a small thermos aboard and I put it in the lavatory and, uh, go there."

"How often?"

"A couple of times during the trip."

"Don't you think you should stop flying until you get this thing cleared up, Captain Hagen?"

"I can't take sick leave without a lot of questions being asked."

"How can you physically handle the plane when you've been drinking? You realize you're risking passengers' lives as well as your own."

"I have copilots and autopilots, but actually, I never seem to get drunk like other people. In all the time I've been sneaking drinks it hadn't reached the point that it affected my ability or judgment until yesterday."

"Did you have an accident?"

"No, but we came damned close."

The doctor was silent for a moment, twirling a pencil around in his fingers. Then he said, "You need more help than a general practitioner can give you, Captain Hagen. I think you should see Court Jameson in New Canaan who's a specialist in drinking problems. He's an excellent man."

"Shrink?"

"Yes, but not a Freudian. He's a basic, no-nonsense guy. Played tackle for Cornell. I've referred quite a few patients to him and he's been able to help them all. I want you to tell Court the truth about everything and then do what he says. Agreed?"

Mike nodded.

"All right. He's going to ask for a complete physical. We can start some things this afternoon. I'll have to send you up to Danbury Hospital for a liver function test and X-rays. We can't handle that here."

"But I feel fine."

"That may be true, but Dr. Jameson will want to treat the whole person. There might be physical damage. Anyone who drinks constantly over a long period of time suffers some deleterious effects. A proven medical fact, Captain Hagen. I'll have my nurse call the hospital and make arrangements for you. Come back here—let's see, my last appointment is at five—say, five-thirty, and we'll go through an EKG, blood tests, urine, and tap a few places."

Mike thanked the doctor and walked out into the bright sunlight. An exultation came over the pilot for he had made a decision; he wasn't sure yet whether he could ever leave the spookers behind, or really wanted to. Down deep Mike didn't think he was an alcoholic—he never had blackouts, was abusive, or missed a flight because he couldn't get up in the morning. He could take one drink at a time and stop, so in his own mind he characterized his problem as alcoholic addiction, not alcoholism. Mike wondered about Jameson. What would he call it?

Mike came from an unsophisticated background where a psychiatrist meant something bad; either you were too weak to figure things out for yourself or too crazy, or both, and he was self-conscious about certain private things, like telling a stranger about sins or weaknesses.

As he walked around to the back of Dr. Martinson's office he saw the dark, wet earth and felt the sun on the back of his neck. January. How could it be January? It was like Florida after a rainfall when the dirt on the edge of the Glades turned ashy black. He remembered walking out Waldin Drive to the Catholic Church on Saturdays, hot Saturdays. It was west of Homestead and as he walked along, about 4:00 in the afternoon, he would be rehearsing his confession, trying to slip quickly by the lies, which he thought were major sins, and masturbation, which he was ashamed to tell the priest about. He could recall the Florida sky in summer—how the high cumulus developed over the Glades, towering puffs of pure white, and how the clouds floated out to sea or how they sometimes turned inky over the swamp, and you could see a slanting rainstorm miles to the west.

The church was always hot; it had been a Baptist meeting hall, gone to seed and deserted. There were so few Catholics south of Miami in the forties that the priest only came on Saturday afternoons in an old Chevrolet with a rumble seat that held his vestments and a cardboard suitcase of religious books and medals that he would sell after Mass. It was not a regular parish and as very few people came to confession, the priest felt duty-bound to spend a long time probing and lecturing each penitent. Mike abhorred those moments.

On his way back he would look at the clouds in the other direction, to the east, and he always liked that because his mind and conscience were temporarily free, at least, until the next Saturday; and he could see in the distance the biplanes landing and taking off from the dirt strips, loaded with spray for the groves to the north. On those long walks he knew he would like to fly among the clouds, and yearned to be old enough to fly with crop dusters and not have to spend part of each Saturday kneeling in a small box at the command of his devout, God-fearing father.

When he reached Danbury Hospital for the liver function test he checked into the clinic. Dr. Martinson's office had called ahead and a blue card was already waiting for the pilot. A cashier sat at the desk and asked how he was going to pay. He said by check and she asked which bank; then, his occupation.

"Airline captain, Intercontinental."

"Airline captain?" she glanced at him with a surprised look on her face.

"Yes, here," Mike said, pulling out his wallet and showing the woman his employee identification card from IA. She studied it very carefully.

"I'll have to ask in the office about the check."

She walked across the room to the office of another woman. Mike could see them through the glass whispering to each other. They both stared at him.

The cashier came back out.

"What's the problem?" he asked. "Don't you take airline checks? I have a local address."

The woman nodded, but she still looked disconcerted. Mike realized something was wrong. Suddenly, the tension which had been building up in him burst. He grabbed the card from the woman and said, "Let me see that."

"Please, that's not for the patient!"

His name was at the top and next to that, suspected condition, Acute Alcoholism. He thrust the card back at the woman. "Where's the nearest phone?"

She pointed to the hall and he ran out and dialed Dr. Martinson's number.

"I don't care if he is busy, get him on the phone," Mike demanded of the nurse. "Hello, Dr. Martinson, Mike Hagen. Is this your idea of discretion?"

"What's the trouble?"

"They have a card up here and it says I'm suspected of acute alcoholism. They asked what I did and I told them and now it's all over the whole goddamned place! I think we'd just better drop this right now. It's already going wrong."

"Hold it, hold it, Mr. Hagen. I'm terribly sorry. I have a replacement girl today. She must have copied it off my notes. I don't blame you for being upset. I'll call Admissions. Please, it's just one of those things."

Several minutes later Dr. Martinson called Danbury Hospital and told them that Mr. Hagen's records were mixed up with somebody else's. He was suspected of having infectious hepatitis.

"Thank you, doctor. I'm glad to know that."

The woman turned to Mike, "We're sorry, Mr. Hagen, you see. . . ."

"Never mind. I know what you thought."

During the long afternoon of the liver function test—swallowing colored dyes so his insides could be photographed, and going through a variety of other check-ups—Mike got the feeling that the two women in the office didn't believe the doctor. He wasn't sure but he sensed that the word had spread throughout the small, dingy hospital. He thought the X-ray technicians looked at him strangely and asked unusual questions, and he thought he saw them whispering, winking to each other. After a while, as the afternoon wore on, he didn't care; he just wanted to get out. It was spooker time. He needed it more than ever.

He drove down Route 7. It was almost four. He had a couple of choices: go home and drink, something he never enjoyed when his wife was there; find an "Ellen's Place" near Danbury where he wasn't known; or he could merely go to a liquor store, buy a pint, and have a private drink. He bought a glass at a roadside shop, found an ice machine nearby, and for fifty cents, a bag clunked out. Mike tossed it in the back of his car and with a bottle of Old Grand-Dad, he headed for the Danbury Airport. Two or three planes were in the hangar but his *Alice* was the finest plane there. (That had been the name on the first Waco he ever flew. He never knew who Alice was, probably some filly along the dusting route; maybe no one, but he painted the small name on his own Waco.) Mike had been offered fifty thousand for *Alice,* but he would never sell his love.

He went to the workbench right behind the plane, put ice cubes in the glass, and poured in the bourbon. He took his spooker, then another, and just sat there gazing at the beautiful plane. The pilot slid open the hangar doors, pulled away the chocks, and rolled *Alice* out into the warm afternoon. He got in, cranked over the old Jacobs engine, and the plane shook. He let her run for a while; then he taxied out, not to the runway, but past it to a place far down the field where the elms and oak trees bordered the threshold.

He taxied the old bird off to the side, pulled out the mixture knob, and the engine died. He got out and walked about fifty feet from the plane and felt the earth. It was wet so he sat down on a stone and looked at his plane. The pilot felt extremely low, thinking about his life, where it had gone; finally, the air became chilly so he climbed back into the plane and taxied her to the hangar and went home.

He called Dr. Martinson, "Lookit, I've had enough hospital stuff for today. Could we let the rest of it go until day after tomorrow?"

The doctor agreed.

Five

Like many stewardesses, Nancy Halloway lived alone
in the East Sixties of Manhattan. When she first started
flying, after two years of pounding a typewriter for an
investment banker on Wall Street, she had two room-
mates, also stewardesses. But as she grew older and her
patience thinned—the small apartment with girls coming and going, TV on all the time, and wash clogging
the bathroom—she changed to one roommate, then
none. When she arrived back in her apartment that
night after the Philadelphia landing, she was happy to
be alone. It was late, she was dog-tired, and she had
an early appointment the next morning. But she dug
the little bottles out of her suitcase as she always
did and fixed herself a drink while she got ready for bed.

She thought about Mike asking her for that
booze. Somebody could have seen him stuffing those
bottles in his pocket and that was one thing the airlines was rigid about: no liquor while in uniform. She
remembered an incident when she first started flying;
she had been unable to get the cork out of a cham-
pagne bottle and very innocently carried it to the cockpit for assistance. The captain, she forgot who it was,
practically threw her out.

* * *

A couple of days later Nancy trip-traded and went out on IA's flight 365, JFK/SFO with an intermediate stop in St. Louis. Her second stewardess was a girl who had been aboard 467 the day of the clear air turbulence, and she and Nancy rehashed the trip and talked about how scared they'd been.

On takeoff from New York they were again in the jump seat of a DC-8-61, the same equipment used for the San Diego service; Nancy happened to glance toward the lavatory door and the water fountain outside as they were talking and something that had been gnawing at her suddenly began to take shape. On that other flight they had taken off from the same runway early in the morning and she remembered Mike coming from the cockpit, taking a paper cup and going into the lavatory. She wondered about the cup then because the water inside wasn't for drinking.

But somebody had been drinking bourbon in the lav that morning. There had been a very strong smell of it. She concentrated, trying to remember the flight. They had only had eleven first-class passengers and she had been the first one up after the turbulence checking on the damage. She had gone to the lavatory to find out what the crash was all about and seen the little puddle, but none of the passengers had been in there. She was sure of it; the only one to use the lavatory up to that point besides herself and the second stewardess was Mike.

Then the Philly trip. That was what was bothering her. She had smelled liquor again in the lavatory, then her visit to the cockpit later, the guys nervous and that awful landing.

She was sick with what she was thinking. It couldn't be true; she decided to forget it, but the following day when she returned from San Francisco, it was still on her mind—Mike, the bourbon, the little bottles he asked her for. One minute she was convinced it couldn't possibly be true; the next minute, she was sure it was. She knew many pilots who drank lightly,

discreetly on layovers, and occasionally she had a nip
or two herself behind the closed curtains of the galley,
especially if it was a particularly bitchy trip. If Mike
Hagen was sneaking a few on the job, she could almost
understand it; she'd heard his home life was falling
apart and he was seeing some girl in San Diego. Mike
was a cautious, skilled pilot—the best; look at the way
he'd handled the CAT incident. But still she had that
gnawing feeling.

During her long career Nancy had had several affairs with IA pilots and she had gradually become dis-
illusioned because the affairs were always the same:
one-sided. The guys were usually Catholic, she liked
Irish captains, and divorce was impossible "until the
children grew up." Her relationship with Mike Hagen
was different; there had never been any sex between
them, but they had developed a strong mutual liking
and respect for each other over the years they had
flown together. Mike had covered for her several years
earlier when she had missed a flight, the worst possible
infraction of rules, automatic grounds for dismissal.

Now she was in a position to clobber the guy.

If it were true, they'd fire him on the spot, and
she didn't want to be the one to blow the whistle on
him. On the other hand, what she suspected was a *pattern* of drinking and that meant trouble for everybody.
She had a responsibility to the people who would
climb aboard one of Mike Hagen's flights. If she didn't
mention this and something terrible happened one day
when Mike was drinking and at the controls. . . . She
was positive now that they had been in more trouble
than she realized on the Philly trip. It wasn't only the
hard landing—anybody could "drop one in"—but Mike
had probably been drinking pretty heavily. There had
been something different, unnatural about Jim and all of
them that night.

What might happen next? As a matter of fact,
she was scared for herself; she flew with Mike more
than anybody. Maybe the best favor she could do him
would be to bring things out in the open so he could

get professional help. Rationalization. Rat on her friend, screw his life up for good.

What she would like to do was lay the whole burden at somebody else's feet. But whose? Her supervisor, a company-minded freak, saw everything in terms of black and white. Perhaps she should tell Joe Barnes. In Nancy's eighteen years with the airline, she had never heard of a stewardess reporting a captain. But the same little scene kept playing over and over in her mind like a small piece of film looped end to end and repeating itself every few minutes: Mike taking the empty paper cup into the lavatory, the pungent smell of the bourbon, Mike asking for booze in the galley that night. Nancy decided she had to talk to someone. It was driving her crazy.

She decided to tell Gloria Esposito. Gloria had been a supervisor of cabin attendants at La Guardia for about five years now, and at one time when she was still on the line, she and Nancy had been very close. They were still good friends and when Nancy called, Gloria told her to come right over.

"Christ, what's the matter?" Gloria said, opening the door to her East Forties apartment.

"Offer me a drink, will you. That's what I want to talk about."

Gloria poured them both Scotch and they sat down on the white leather couch. Nancy began in a low voice to detail the December 10 flight, the turbulence, the landing in Philadelphia, finally her growing suspicions about Mike Hagen.

"You mean, he's drinking in the head?"

"I don't want to think so, but when you put it all together, that's what it adds up to."

"Shit, that is a problem. I wish you hadn't told me."

"I wish I didn't know. Gloria, Mike is the one who saved my hide that time in San Diego. Remember Paul, the Navy pilot stationed at Miramar? I used to stay over in his quarters when we had a date; well, one night I didn't make it back, missed the return flight.

Mike covered for me with crew schedule, the other girls, everything. He invented a long story about how desperately ill I was. Christ, they were about to set up a fund for me."

Gloria laughed and got up to make a fresh drink.

"Anyway, as far as I'm concerned, he put his own job on the line for me. Not only that, the guy is a damned good pilot. I just don't know what the hell to do."

"Are you making it with him, a little affair maybe?" Gloria asked.

"No, no, nothing like that. He's a very open, friendly sort of guy, kind of country-boyish. Everybody likes him, but I *owe* him."

"Well, it's a bitch. I can understand how you feel but if the guy is drinking, somebody higher up ought to know. I have an idea. I'll check-ride out on 467 next time Hagen's on and sit up front where I can see everything. If we catch him doing it again, we'll just have to report it."

"Where?"

"I don't know yet," Gloria said. "That's a bridge to cross when we come to it."

"Is it any of our business? I mean, there's something else I thought of. If this is going on, surely the copilot and flight engineer must know. Why don't they say something?"

"You know how goddamned close mouthed they are; they protect each other. We may be worrying for nothing. Let's be sure first; I'll set it up and get back to you."

In the cab riding home Nancy thought: goddamn it, why did it have to be Mike, and why did it have to be me who saw him.

Mike passed his physical. There was no liver damage; his blood pressure was slightly high, but that had to do with his weight, and he set up an appointment with Court Jameson for the following week. Mike had spoken on the phone with Jim Cochran three times after the Philadelphia incident and he told the younger man about taxiing the Waco into the hangar until he got hold of himself and the trip to the doctor. Jim agreed to fly with Mike again and on a cold day in late January they both showed up at JFK Operations for 467.

Dr. Martinson had told Mike that he should start by cutting down on his drinking immediately. The pilot only took two drinks the night before, but driving out to JFK during the final miles, he felt the old hunger grip his stomach, and the aching feeling, so he pulled off the highway and drove the Nova toward Ellen's Place. He put on his El Al mechanic's jacket and went inside promising himself that he would tell Ellen to make it light, but when the fat woman pulled out the bourbon and the shiny glass, he didn't say anything. He touched the icy liquor to his lips and felt the first bite of the fluid running down to do its work. He thanked Ellen and drove to Operations.

Once again, the pilot looked at himself in the mirror of the car. His eyes were okay this morning; his nose didn't need the makeup, so he hoisted the captain's hat slightly higher on his head and walked into the old hell. He put his flight bag down, looking around, getting used to the bright, harsh lights, and saw Jim Cochran at the weather desk.

"Morning, Jim."

The younger man studied the Captain and after a pause, he said dully, "How are you?"

"Fine. How's the enroute weather?"

"Looks good. No turbulence reported, unlimited all the way to Houston. Some scattered to broken at 15,000 for the second leg. Very easy for a change."

Jim handed the captain the MFP, the terminal and area forecasts for Houston, and Mike walked over to the desk looking at the prog, winds aloft, and 500 millibar chart. There was nothing much of interest. The weather fronts, lows, and the jet stream were far removed from 467's flight path; one shallow low was located over Jacksonville, Florida, and another was stalled along a Duluth, Boise, Idaho line.

Mike was looking at the undulating curves when Gloria Esposito came up behind him.

"Captain Hagen."

He turned around quickly, not recognizing the voice. Gloria didn't think he looked like a lush, but the redness and puffiness were not too apparent that day.

"I'm Gloria Esposito, check-riding first-class."

"Oh, sure. Well, looks like we'll be having a smooth flight. Nothing much I can tell you."

She smiled and nodded. Nancy, standing on the far side of Operations, never looked up.

Before boarding the DC-8-61 Mike took Jim Cochran aside and they leaned against one of the large curving windows in the corridor.

"You know, Jim, Pat took off at me in San Diego."

"Really?" Jim acted surprised.

"Yeah, she said if I didn't get help, it was all over."

"Mike, I'm glad you put the Waco away and went to the doctor."

"He's sending me to a specialist, and I took it easy last night."

"Great, Mike. I hope you didn't mind me sounding off the other night in Philadelphia. You have *too much* going to fuck up."

"I know it and I just wanted to thank you. I'll be taking one or two probably. I don't have the cure yet, but it's coming."

"I understand. No problem, Mike."

"Thanks," the captain winked and slapped the younger man on the shoulder.

Mike boarded the plane twenty-five minutes before departure. He took his thermos from the bag while the flight engineer, a new man, was checking the undercarriage. The pilot left the cockpit for the first lavatory and slipped the thermos up under the disposal bin, Gloria Esposito was sitting in 1-B where she could see the forward head and the cockpit door. She was pretending to read *Vogue,* but over the pages she watched the Captain enter and close the door. She looked around and eyed Nancy, who had also seen Mike.

After stowing his spooker Mike left the lavatory and returned to the cockpit; the door was open and Gloria could see him take off his coat and hang it on the rack directly aft of the jump seat. He lifted himself into the left seat and began the pre-flight cockpit check. Gloria crossed to the galley.

"He didn't take a cup."

"Look inside the head. Go over everything," Nancy replied as she took the trays from the catering jack truck resting beside the open galley exit.

Gloria entered the lavatory. It smelled sweet, having just been perfumed by the cabin service personnel. She studied the lavatory carefully, feeling the paper towels storage rack, then she returned to the galley.

"Nothing different," she told Nancy. "No smell or sign of booze."

The flight was signed off the gate on time. Jim contacted ground control and ATC cleared 467 along their old and accustomed route to Houston. They were third for takeoff and Mike was handling it. He swung the DC-8-61 onto the centerline of runway 31-Left, pointing the nose directly down the 14,572 feet of concrete; beyond was a clear, blue sky. The wind was light, 9 knots, and a few high cirrus clouds rested on the far horizon.

"IA 467, cleared for takeoff."

"IA 467 cleared for takeoff," Jim responded.

Mike fed in his takeoff thrust and the big plane began to move quickly under the surge of power rushing from her Pratt & Whitney JT3D-7's.

"110," Jim called.

The centerline was rushing past in a whirl.

"125."

"140, V-1."

"V-R, and we rotate."

Mike eased back and 467 raised her nose; lift occurred and she was in the air, climbing out easily, effortlessly. The second officer went through his after-takeoff checklist and Mike pulled the plane into a climbing left turn, looking down, across, and up; he always searched for traffic, something every man who flew with Mike learned. As they climbed out heading for the "Coyle" intersection over New Jersey, Mike gave the ship to Jim and he sat there a minute glancing over his panel; satisfied, he brought his hands behind his neck and pulled at his muscles. He was quite well rested, having had a good night's sleep, and the usual dull fuzziness in the back of his head was hardly noticeable today.

He picked up the microphone and pressed the button. "Good morning, ladies and gentlemen, this is Captain Hagen. Welcome to our early-bird service to Houston. Good to have you aboard. We're anticipating a smooth flight all the way. Our cruising altitude will be 31,000 feet and our trip today will take us down west of Washington, over Knoxville, Chattanooga, Jackson, Mississippi, and then into the Houston terminal area. Our flight time will be approximately three and a half hours, and the temperature in Houston is 56 degrees with broken to scattered clouds at 10,000 feet. Sit back and let our beautiful IA gals serve you."

The meal service was started as soon as they reached cruising altitude and about two hours in the flight, just as they were passing west of Birmingham, Alabama, the cockpit door opened and Mike Hagen stepped out. He did not look aft or notice Gloria Esposito in 1-B. Almost mechanically, his hand reached toward the dispenser; the pilot snapped a paper cup down and entered the lavatory. Gloria's eyes were fixed on Mike as the door slammed and the "Occupied" sign slid over.

Mike looked at himself in the mirror and pressed closer trying to see the red rivers on his left cheek; they were lighter, maybe some of the bloody network had disappeared back into his face. He wondered how he would feel and look when he stopped the spookers. But it wasn't time yet, not quite yet; a little time was left and he reached into the disposal locker, felt his baby, and carefully pulled the cold thermos through the flapped door. He unscrewed the top and poured the bourbon into the paper cup. He sloshed it around and smiled.

"You fucking little shit," he said half under his breath. As if to start his own therapy program, the pilot poured a small amount back into the thermos and swallowed the rest.

He loved the feeling. It started deep inside him, then rose as if a soft, heated blanket were sliding over his naked body.

As soon as he came out, Gloria glanced at her watch; she wrote down the time he went in and the time he came out. He'd been in the lavatory four minutes, ten seconds. She immediately went in. Nothing unusual. No smell of liquor.

"Nancy, I just saw him take a cup into the lav," Gloria whispered as she stepped into the galley, eyeing the second stewardess who was serving midway down the aisle.

"Smell anything?"

"No."

"I want to check myself."

Nancy entered the first lavatory. Gloria was right. No odor.

On the last leg of the flight, the pilot went to the lavatory once when they were over Arizona, and that evening at dinner in San Diego, the girls began to quickly discuss the Mike Hagen routine.

"He does the same thing each time," Gloria said, "but I noticed something on that last leg. When he came out to use the lavatory, the first one was occupied; the second lav wasn't, but he waited until the first one was free."

"You think a bottle's hidden in there?" Nancy said.

"Possibly, but I swear, Nancy, I searched that place thoroughly." She sighed. "Maybe he's just carrying a couple of miniatures around in his pocket; he's such a big guy, you'd never notice it. I'll try to look for that tomorrow."

"Maybe we won't find anything," Nancy said hopefully. "I'd like to think I was wrong about the whole thing."

Fifteen miles to the north Mike Hagen sat across from Pat in the small Mexican restaurant; he was unusually silent, only drinking one bourbon; hurrah for A.A., she thought.

"I want to tell you something," he said slowly. "Almost called, but then I decided I'd rather see you."

"Must be heavy stuff. You look so serious."

"I tried A.A., Pat, but it wasn't for me. Those people seem to enjoy getting up and telling the whole world about their boozing. I just couldn't do it. I'd be embarrassed."

"You only went because of me, didn't you?" Disappointment showed in her voice.

Mike nodded his head. "But something happened last week. I made some mistakes on the flight back to New York."

"Oh God, I knew it! That party. It's all my fault."

"No, it wasn't your fault. I *shouldn't* have been in the cockpit. Our burn-out was more than calculated head winds. We should have landed at an alternate to take on fuel, but I didn't. JFK's weather was marginal; we held too long, fuel ran low so we put in at Philly. I made a sloppy one-bounce landing—came over the fence high and hot. I was scared, Pat. First time in twenty-one years of flying I was pissing green and the next day I was going to fly my Waco. I couldn't. I just rolled it back in the hangar."

"Why didn't you land and refuel?"

Mike paused and looked down at the red tablecloth. "My bourbon was gone."

"Oh, Mike," she grabbed his hand.

"I wasn't thinking straight. Anyhow I went to the doctor at home, had a medical checkup, and next week I'm seeing a shrink."

"You're not fooling yourself anymore, are you, Mike?"

"No, I'm in trouble, I know that."

"You shouldn't be flying until this is all over. It's dangerous."

"Well, I've cooled it quite a bit and I wanted to tell you. I know now what I have to do, Pat. For me. And for you."

She thought of the potential disaster in Philadelphia, the plane full of innocent passengers and she couldn't wipe it from her mind; maybe this stubborn man was convinced now. But were there others like Mike? It was beginning to haunt her; she was glad the restaurant was dark because she didn't want him to know how frightened she was.

The flight back was a long one with very little push from the westerly winds, but the skies were still clear, the air quiet. The plane was on autopilot most of the way and the numbers ticked off in the window of the DME. Mike went to the head twice, and after his final visit, about four hours and fifty minutes into the flight as 602 was over western Pennsylvania, Gloria Esposito followed the pilot into the lavatory.

Bourbon!

The supervisor bolted from the compartment and signaled Nancy with her finger. Both women entered the lavatory.

"Do you smell it?" Gloria asked.

Nancy sniffed and did not answer until she was sure. "Yes," she said. "That's bourbon—very faint, but it's bourbon."

"We both agree then that we smell bourbon in here."

"Yes, it's not as strong as last time. Then it was stinking up the place. We'd better get out of here before the passengers start thinking there's something wrong with us."

They landed at JFK twenty minutes late. Mike got into his Nova, turned off the expressway, and headed down a side street toward Ellen's Place. He parked in back and sat in the car for a minute or two.

"Shove this fucking place!" he said aloud as he started the motor again.

He drove home.

It was the first time in almost five months that he reached Ridgefield without the kick of a spooker. He felt a small pride.

Mike's elation heightened because during the next two days he was able to cut down a bit and he thought he looked better. Then it was time for the drive to Dr. Jameson's in New Canaan; he dressed carefully in an old suit and applied just a hint of the cover-up stick.

"Where the hell do you think you're going?" Jean said as he walked through the kitchen on his way to the garage.

"Have to see someone."

"Who?"

"Insurance fellow down in Stamford."

"We can't afford any more insurance and you're supposed to be at the office today. Mrs. MacGregor is behind on all the orders; we'll have to fire that bag. Go over and light a fire under her."

"Have a little patience, she's an old woman."

"Patience, shit. We're running a business."

"At least she doesn't steal. The last two were light-fingered. I wish we could find someone to steal the whole business," he added.

"Beautiful. And I wish I had married a man with ambition instead of a lazy, boozy flyboy."

"Get off my back, you bitch!"

He continued to the garage and as he drove into New Canaan, about nine miles south of Ridgefield, he saw a bar and he wanted to stop. The anger was churning his gut and he could hear his heart pounding.

"Fucking bitch!"

Dr. Jameson's office, like Martinson's, was in his home, but this house was much larger, a restored eighteenth-century colonial with a manicured lawn reaching out in all directions. In the crushed bluestone driveway were two new cars with Connecticut M.D. plates, a Lincoln and a Mercedes. The man must be good if he could afford all these cars, Mike thought, or maybe he was just expensive. He sat in his Nova for a minute looking at the white door to the side of the house and the polished brass plate that read: COURT JAMESON, M.D.

For a split second he considered bolting, but he remembered Philadelphia and walked to the door. He pressed the buzzer and a pleasant, smiling woman in her thirties appeared.

"Good morning. You must be Mr. Hagen."

"Yes, hello."

As Mike sat at the desk giving the woman his address and other information, he began to look at the closed door on the far side of the comfortable waiting room.

He imagined a pompous, stiff man in a white coat sitting on the other side. The secretary, or nurse—Mike didn't know which a psychiatrist had—told him about the fees and he nodded without saying anything. Finally, she took him across the room and opened the door.

"Dr. Jameson, this is Captain Hagen."

Dr. Jameson was sitting with his feet up on the desk; there was a hole in his shoe about the size of Adlai Stevenson's famous one. Court Jameson looked much younger than Mike had envisaged; maybe it was his smooth, Ivy League face, the kind that immediately tells you there's plenty of money and a long family history someplace. His voice was tinged with a New England accent and he wore a blue-buttoned-down

Oxford shirt with a regimental striped tie. Mike was relieved. There was no beard, no couch, and the doctor
got up immediately and shook Mike's hand.

"Glad to meet you, Captain Hagen."

A comfortable-looking red leather chair faced the
doctor's antique desk and on the paneled walls were
sporting prints and bookcases filled with everything but
medical books.

"Have a seat," he said.

The doctor went behind his desk, but instead of
sitting down, he rolled the chair out in front and sat
alongside Mike, placing his feet up on the desk again.

"We're kind of informal around here."

"That's good," Mike answered.

"Do you mind if we use first names?"

"No."

"Call me Court—dumb name," he said, flashing
a smile that Mike picked up.

"Well, how do we begin?" Mike asked.

"We already have. You're here. And Dr. Martinson has filled me in."

"I told him everything. Did you ever know a pilot
with the same problem?"

"No, but I doubt you're the only one in the history of aviation. Let me ask you a few questions,
Mike."

"Shoot."

"Are you committed to licking this thing now,
whatever it takes?"

"Yeah, no choice. I didn't think it was affecting
me until I sort of screwed up a landing the other day.
That's some fucking admission, isn't it?"

"Well, you're here now because you want to work
it out. So let's get started. I'm not going to tell you all
the horror stories, but the liver can only take so much
and the booze eats away the brain cells, can even cause
impotence. It's progressive and you just have to catch it
or it'll wreck you. And it's a bad way to go down."

"I know."

"We want to find out *why* you drink, Mike, that's

most important, and how best to wind it down. This is a *treatable* disease and I can help you get off the booze, but until we find out what's behind it, you'll always be fighting the same losing battle."

"I understand."

"There's three ways we can pull you off the stuff: A.A., they do a great job; then there's the hospital where we detoxicate you under medical supervision. It's a real tough five days; you'll probably have delirium tremens and convulsions; it'll scare the shit out of you but the results are guaranteed and it's safe. Also expensive. The third option is to set up your own program of withdrawal, cutting down a little bit each day. We measure it very carefully, scientifically."

"Might as well tell you. I'm an A.A. dropout. It's not for me."

"Okay. If everyone could be cured at A.A., a lot of psychiatrists would be out of business."

"What does the hospital cost?"

"Five hundred a day, but it's a top staff."

"Maybe I could borrow it from the Credit Union, but what do most of your people do?"

"Depends. Everyone's different. A number of them try A.A. If you really have willpower, you can wind down yourself. It's cheaper than the hospital and we can always move on to other ideas if it doesn't work. But it's not easy."

"All right. I've already cut down a little so I know I can do it."

"I have a little plan that you're going to laugh at, but it works," Dr. Jameson said.

He got up and moved behind his desk; he brought out a shot glass ringed with different colored lines.

"You'll have to buy a jigger, a four-ouncer. I want you to take some waterproof oil paint and make five circles: red, four ounces; green, three ounces; blue, two, and pink, one. Yellow, the last circle, is a half ounce. Will you do that?"

"Sure, why not."

"Next thing. Here's a small diary with a page for

each day and the hours. Get one of these and a box of stars like the kids have for spelling."

He took out a small box and spread the "paste-up" stars on his desk. Mike laughed. "Haven't seen those for years."

"I know, kiddie stuff, but you didn't like the other two choices, remember?"

"Okay. What do I do with them?"

"You match colors; red star, red line. You're drinking on board the plane by hiding the thermos in a lavatory, Dr. Martinson said."

"I have industrial glue on it, goes in the disposal bin. Took me a damned long time to get it right."

"From now on, you measure how much you drink. Keep the jigger with the thermos, rubber band maybe. Begin by drinking just as much as you normally would. If you have three or four a night—is that about your level?"

"About."

"Then record that. I want to see how much you're really drinking. Do you think it's a fifth a day?"

"I don't think so."

"We'll find out. *Don't cheat!* Don't let up tonight or tomorrow just because you're keeping score. Write down your exact intake. Here's the way we measure it. Pour your drink, whatever it is, into a glass, then into the jigger, back into the glass again. Day after tomorrow I want you to drop down one ring on the jigger. If you start on the red, go to the green. Spend three days like that; then we'll move to the blue for three more days."

"How far do we go?"

"That depends, Mike, but the only way this is going to work is with total honesty. I know you probably think it's crazy, pasting the goddamned little stars in the book, but I want the record to be accurate. If the stars get clumsy, buy some small colored pencils —anything to keep track. One more thing, if you feel a withdrawal attack coming on after you've stopped for a period, take two pills which I'll give you a prescription for. They're strong tranquilizers. One final unorthodox bit; you can see I have my own thing going."

"You sure do."

"It works if you work. Half of psychiatry is bullshit; it's the other half that's important. I want you out of here and well as fast as possible, and I use a blend of psychotherapy and psychoanalysis plus some chemotherapy if it's indicated. Rather than have you come into the office week after week and tell me your whole life story, I'm going to ask you to write your history in three installments: boyhood to teens, teen years through early twenties, and adult life. This cuts down time and the way you write, how you put it down, what you leave out, different emphases, tells me quite a lot."

"I'm not much of a writer."

"That doesn't matter. Don't try to impress me with style or tell me what you think I want to hear. For instance, you could start with your family background. What was your father like? Your mother? Were they rich, poor, did they drink, how did they treat you? Did you love them, hate them? Don't be afraid to express your emotions."

"Tell it like it was."

"Exactly."

"How do I know what's important?"

"If you fell down one day and scraped your knee and your mother put a Band-Aid on it and the cut healed, that's not important, is it?"

"No."

"On the other hand, if your mother said she didn't want to waste a Band-Aid on your bleeding knee, that's different. What I want are the substantive facts; it's up to you to choose what's relative. Like a court trial, under the rules of evidence, they only allow relative testimony to establish a point."

"Can I tape it?"

"No. I used to do that but some patients fell in love with their own voices and rambled too much; others were tongue-tied. Write it out. You type?"

"Hunt and peck."

"Then type it and deliver installment number one to my secretary the day before your next appointment. Will you be able to take a little time off initially until we have a handle on this?"

"Yeah, I'm finished for the month, not scheduled out again until early February."

The doctor stood. "Good luck, Mike. Don't cheat; that's all I ask. If you do, it's just a waste of my time and your money."

Mike drove very fast to the center of New Canaan and ten minutes later he was in a phone booth in the rear of a stationery store, having just bought the diary and colored stars; he dialed Pat Simpson's number.

"Where is she? Louise's? Do you have a phone book? Yes, it's important. Let me get this down, hold it."

Pat was eating with a friend at Louise's, a small restaurant near the advertising agency, when the head-waiter came over.

"Miss Simpson, you have a long-distance call."

Pat rushed to the phone thinking it might be her mother in Los Angeles who had been suffering from a minor heart ailment.

"Hi, it's Mike."

"Are you all right?"

"Yes, yes."

"Scared me," she said, drawing in a deep breath. "I thought something must have happened."

"Sorry. Just came back from the psychiatrist's."

"You *did* go, Mike."

"Yep."

"I was praying you'd keep the appointment. Tell me about it."

"Well, he's a nice guy, a little Ivy League, but okay. Gave me a lot of homework, but he said my thing was treatable."

Mike went on to tell her about the stars, the diary,

the jigger with the colored bands, and the three-stage autobiography.

"I've never heard of this sort of approach."

"I know, but if it works, it's great."

"The important thing is that you went for treatment. I'm so proud of you, Mike, and please do everything he asks."

"I am, Pat, believe me. I'll call you later tonight."

"Thanks for letting me know, darling, I'm so pleased. Talk to you soon."

She put down the phone. She had not been this happy for a long time.

Six

The travesty was Irene Monihan. She was the head supervisor at IA's New York base, an obnoxious Irish spinster broken down by booze and bad love affairs; she took it out on the girls. In turn, they called her the "fucked-out, boozy bitch" or the "FOBB." She was the biggest known alcoholic on IA's New York payroll and about the most disagreeable person the carrier ever employed. How she continued without being fired was a mystery. Some said she threatened the line with discrimination as the women's movement went forward, but that was only a rumor and no one could prove it. The FOBB had a way of tearing into a young girl that either brought tears, anger, or both and always hate. She began as a stewardess long before the jet age, then graduated, if that's what it was, to a supervisory post. IA's policy before the civil rights bill was passed was to retire the stewardesses at age thirty-two when they could become secretaries or supervisors. It was not a problem normally at IA because by the time the border year rolled around, most of the girls were married and home raising families.

Irene was one of the exceptions; she went from base to base as a supervisor and the older she got, the more she bore down on the young, bright-eyed girls fresh from the carrier's Houston training school. The word reached Marketing Vice-President Peter Hanscom, and the FOBB was moved permanently to La Guardia as chief supervisor of cabin attendants. That way, she could only make life miserable for the five supervisors under her instead of the two hundred and eighty inflight cabin attendants stationed at the New York base. Both Gloria Esposito and Nancy Halloway had had run-ins with Irene. There were very few who hadn't.

After flight 602 arrived in New York, Nancy and Gloria went to Nancy's apartment for drinks and decided they would have to go through regular channels in reporting their suspicions about Mike. And that meant Irene. They had decided to report the incident together, partly for moral support, and to share the blame for what might happen. As far as they knew, nothing like this had ever come up at Intercontinental; or if it had, the carrier had hushed it up. Irene, they felt, would simply walk across the aisle at La Guardia and tell Joe Barnes.

Perhaps she would force them to go in and tell him. Nancy feared that because she knew that Barnes and Mike Hagen were good friends. Where would it go from the chief pilot? His superior was another pilot, Cliff McCullen, vice president and head of the flight department, and he reported directly to Fitz. They knew who McCullen was, but they had no idea if he was close to Joe Barnes or not; it was too many levels above them.

The following morning Gloria picked up the phone at her desk in JFK's operational office and called the FOBB.

"Nancy Holloway and I have a very important matter to discuss with you."

"Shoot me a memo, sweetie," Irene said.

"No, we need to see you," Gloria replied.

"Honey, shit, I'm busy. Tell me over the phone."

"I can't; it has to be in person. Nancy and I want to come over; if you can't see us, we're going to Fitz."

There was a lengthy pause. The FOBB's tone changed. "That important, huh? Okay, eleven o'clock."

Gloria called Nancy and told her to be at the FOBB's later that morning. All the way out to La Guardia in the cab, Nancy felt rotten. Perhaps it was all a mistake.

Gloria was already sitting in Irene's office located to the left of a pool of secretaries. They could see at once that the head supervisor was ill-tempered, probably had a bad night, which was going to make matters worse.

They related the story. The FOBB said nothing, listening without a change of expression. When they finished, she said, "Do you swear everything you've said is true?"

"Yes," Nancy said. "I swear it."

"We're not accusing anyone; we're just telling you what we saw and what we smelled in the lav," Gloria added.

"Like shit you're not accusing anyone. Do you realize what it means to fuck up a captain's career!"

"I have a pretty good idea," Gloria said.

"If you're wrong, both of you will be out looking for jobs."

"Irene, we're as upset as you are over this, and the last thing I would ever do is dump on Mike Hagen," Nancy said.

"Well sweetie, I hope you know what you're doing because Joe Barnes is a tough old bastard."

Nancy's heart sank. "Irene, would you tell him?"

"Oh no, you can't get off that easily. He's going to call you in when he hears this, so we might as well get it over with. Come on, ladies."

The FOBB got up from her desk, crossed between the clacking typewriters, and pushed open Joe Barnes's door. Nancy and Gloria followed slowly. The FOBB and Joe had little conversation with each other;

they reported to different departments on Third Avenue. But he knew the woman was usually sullen or angry, so he stayed out of her way.

"Want to hear a horror story, Captain Barnes?" the FOBB inquired.

"Don't bother me with your cabin people's problems, Irene, I can't help."

"Sweetheart, it's one of your very own."

Joe stiffened. The insulting bitch, he thought. "What about my pilots?"

"It seems one of them drinks on the job."

Joe laughed. He thought it was a bad joke until he looked at her avid eyes; then he was suddenly very angry. "What the hell are you talking about?"

"There's a supervisor and a stewardess here with the goodies. Shall I bring them in?"

The way she said it, Joe suddenly had an uneasy feeling. "Yeah, I'll listen."

He knew Gloria only slightly but he recognized Nancy Halloway from the hearings in San Diego. "Sit down, girls. It's all right. I'm not half as bad as Irene," Joe said with a big grin on his chubby face.

They relaxed a little, but no one spoke. Finally Joe said, "Irene said you had something to tell me."

"It concerns one of our pilots," Nancy said. "Captain Mike Hagen."

"Best man at this base. Wrote a memo to Mr. McCullen telling him how Mike handled that clear air turbulence. What's the problem?"

Nancy eyed Gloria, drew a deep breath, and said in a low tone, "I'm afraid he's been drinking on the plane."

Joe Barnes laughed. "What put that in your head?"

"He goes into the lavatory during flight and takes a paper cup. I've smelled liquor in there."

"I can back Nancy's story up. I was check-riding one of their flights and saw the same thing. Here's my notes."

Gloria passed the paper to Joe Barnes who took it, read it, and tossed the paper back to her.

"All this tells me is that Mike went to the can several times; you went in later and smelled bourbon. A lot of people nip in the heads. They bring flasks aboard. You know that."

He paused, no longer pleasant, and pointed a finger at the girls. "Did either of you ever actually *see* Captain Hagen drink?"

"No," Nancy said.

Gloria shook her head; she knew the stewardess wouldn't tell Joe Barnes about Mike asking for the bottles in Philadelphia.

"Then you're accusing him on circumstantial evidence. You know the consequences of something like this?"

The FOBB sat far back in her chair, her skinny legs crossed and a slight smile on her face. She was enjoying the delicious little drama, one of the few that came to her dull office routine.

"Maybe you girls got something against Captain Hagen."

"Of course not," Gloria replied.

"Then why are you doing a number on him!" Joe thundered at Nancy. "You been going out with Mike? This a personal grudge?"

"No, no," Nancy cried.

"This guy probably saved your life during that turbulence and you march in here with this bullshit. Christ Almighty!"

Nancy jumped to her feet suddenly. "Damnit, I'm tired of being the heavy! I happen to like Mike Hagen very much but I did see this thing and you have an obligation to check it out."

"Easy, honey," Gloria said, putting her hand on Nancy's arm. "Captain Barnes, I think perhaps we should take this up with McCullen or Fitzsimmons."

Joe Barnes said sternly, "You girls don't have to threaten me about going downtown."

"If you don't believe us, we have no choice," Gloria said.

"I didn't mean to imply that I didn't believe you;

it's just that I want you to be absolutely sure you know what you're saying. Mike Hagen is one of our very best pilots. And you are making a goddamned serious charge."

"I realize that. Don't you think it was a difficult decision for me?" Nancy replied. "Mike and I are very old friends."

Joe's head was rumbling with thoughts. The memo on Mike Hagen had gone out, and Cliff McCullen called saying how goddamned happy Fitz was. He wanted to take Mike to lunch; Cliff had even suggested that Mike might be management potential, and Joe was basking in the reflection of Hagen's good work. And now this had to happen. Jesus Christ, what a fucking bad scene.

"Nancy, Gloria, of course you did the right thing by coming here, and I want you to know I appreciate it. I guess I just got a little upset because I know Mike Hagen very well."

Nancy nodded her head.

Joe went on. "I want all of you to promise me you won't mention this to *anyone* until I have a chance to investigate. That means boyfriends, girl friends, the man in the supermarket. Will you do that much?"

"Yes, certainly," Nancy said. Gloria and the FOBB agreed.

"Now, I want you girls to listen closely. First of all, you can be *assured* that this department, myself personally, will check this out immediately. There have been pilots before who drank . . . a bad personal situation can happen to anybody, death in the family, divorce, financial pressures. This is a wild story," Joe said. "I never heard anything like it around the business. I'm not saying it *couldn't* happen; I'm not even positive it hasn't happened before. But for Mike Hagen to go off like this surprises me and to tell you the truth, I very much doubt that he's sneaking into the head for bourbon. But we'll sure find out and quick!"

"Would you let us know what happens, Captain Barnes?" Gloria asked.

"Yes, as long as you promise me this stops right here. That's the deal."

"All right."

The FOBB spoke up. "Sorry we ruined your weekend, Joe."

"You did that. Oh, one more thing. Gloria, would you mind leaving me those notes you took."

She hesitated for a moment, then smiled and held them out, "Sure, why not?"

"Thanks. I appreciate it."

The women trooped out of the office and Barnes closed the door after them.

"Whew! Sure hope you're right, sweetie," the FOBB said, blowing out a long breath as they moved toward the corridor. "The guy looked as if you'd just told him his mother was a whore."

Nancy nodded miserably.

"Didn't you know how he felt about Hagen?" Gloria asked the FOBB.

"How the shit would I know? That's a different department; I don't hobnob with those apples, hardly talk to Barnes. We just happen to share some of the same office space. I'll tell you one thing, though, there's going to be plenty of trouble over this— Hagen, if it's true, you, Nancy, if it's not. Because, sweetie, your file already stinks."

Seven

It was 11:45. Joe sat in his office looking straight ahead for almost ten minutes after the women left. He was too stunned to concentrate; he didn't even hear the roar of the jets taking off from runway 22. Then, forcing himself to think about what the stewardesses had said, he convinced himself that it wasn't true. How could Mike Hagen be drinking in the head, for Christ's sake. Mike had just told him on the way back from San Diego that he didn't touch the stuff in the daytime. Yet if it did turn out to be true, it would rock the entire flight department. He would have to tell Cliff McCullen. Fitz would know. All the way up.

Joe opened the door and looked across the secretaries' desks and he saw the FOBB talking on the phone. Couldn't trust the bitch, he thought; she was probably already telling somebody about it. He walked downstairs and over to the restaurant on the roof of the main terminal building. At a table he ordered a double Scotch on the rocks, something he didn't ordinarily do during working hours, and a chef's salad. His mind was still clogged. Slowly, he began to sort things out in sequence. Who to tell? McCullen? No. Should he call Mike in and confront him with it? Not yet. Joe had to be sure.

There was Dr. Silverman downstairs. Should he work with him? Naw, the guy was a joke. No one took him seriously and Mike certainly wouldn't. It was a rule that each base had to have a permanent doctor on staff. In addition to giving the annual examinations, semiannual in the case of pilots, and attending to the medical needs of all personnel—mostly colds, flu shots, and menstrual cramps—his chief duty was to "clear" flight crews after they had called in sick and were ready to go back on the line again. Since most of the sick calls were from stewardesses who either wanted out of a trip to keep a new date or recuperate from a previous one, he wasn't exactly compelled to deal with life-and-death matters. When the girl was ready to fly again, she went in to see Silverman with some made-up story and he gave her a little white slip that she presented to Crew Schedule, signifying that she had the doctor's permission to go back out. If he did work with a doctor it would have to be an outside man, Joe decided.

He picked up his second drink and thought about Mike's copilot, Jim Cochran; Joe was sure Jim wouldn't reveal anything, even if he suspected a problem.

By the time Joe finished lunch he had decided what to do. He'd call Larry Zanoff, a check pilot in Los Angeles, Larry was an old buddy. They had started in DC-3's together and worn down a lot of seats. Joe would ask him to request a temporary New York assignment.

Back at his office, he dialed McCullen's number. "Cliff, Joe Barnes. I'm a little tight on the check-ride schedule. All right if I bring Larry Zanoff in from L.A. just for a couple of weeks?"

"Sure. Want it in writing?"

"Not necessary. I'll call Fred and tell him you cleared it."

Joe contacted LAX headquarters and told Fred Fisher, his counterpart on the West Coast, that the head of the flight department had okayed a transfer for Zanoff to the East temporarily.

"No problem. Larry loves your side of the country. He's on a ride at the moment. Due back tonight."

"Leave a note. Tell him I'll call him at home about seven your time."

By midafternoon Joe was hard at work on the next part of his plan, which involved crew schedule. They were the fellows who handled the big sheets, made sure all the trips were covered, took sick calls, phoned the reserves, and assigned all the flights connected with New York's 720 inflight personnel. It was not an easy job, especially when the weather or equipment delays caused cancellations and rerouting. There were IA crew schedule counters at La Guardia, Kennedy, and Newark Airports; it was the department at JFK that would assign Larry Zanoff to Hagen's flight sequence.

He knew one man out there, Gordon Terrell, who had been studying flying for some years hoping to move into IA's flight department, but the going was slow and Joe felt the young man would never make it. He picked up the JFK tie line and asked Terrell to come in that afternoon.

"Wanted to see me, Captain Barnes?" Gordon Terrell stood at Joe's office door, a nice-looking young man with hair rather longer than Joe remembered or liked.

"Come on in, Gordon, have a seat. How's the flight training coming?"

"Pretty good—four hundred hours now. I passed my IFR ground and I'm almost ready for the flight test. That's what the instructor says."

This surprised Joe. "Well, I'm proud of you. I had two reasons for calling you in."

The young man was nervous, and he slid around in his chair. "Yes, Sir?"

"First, I wanted to make sure you were still flying. I'd like to see you in the cockpit one day. I like men with ambition. Of course, right now we have a lot of guys on furlough."

"I know, sir."

"I need a little confidential favor from you, Gordon."

"Anything, Captain Barnes."

"You heard about Mike Hagen and that turbulence on 467 last month?"

"Sure."

"Hagen did a great job and Fitz thinks maybe Mike could help update our S.O.P.'s. We want to take a closer look at Mike Hagen."

"I understand."

"Now, if we just put a check pilot in, Mike would become nervous."

"Of course."

"So, Mr. McCullen had a very special idea."

"Oh," Gordon said, knowing McCullen was the vice-president of the flight department.

"Yeah, McCullen picked out a man from our L.A. base. He's really a check pilot, but no one knows him at this end."

"What's his name?"

"Larry Zanoff. I used to fly with him years ago. Larry also has an engineer's ticket, which he's kept up to date. I want him assigned to Hagen's trips."

"No problem. He's senior man and he'd knock the other guys off anyway."

"No one must know except us."

"Sure, Captain Barnes."

"Of course, McCullen and Fitz are in on it, and a couple of guys in L.A."

"I've got the message. I won't say anything. The bid sheets are due back in a couple days and when I get Hagen's, I'll just assign Zanoff to his trip. No one will ever know."

"Any complications, call me. Otherwise, I'll assume everything is OK. If anyone asks who the new face is, tell 'em he's from L.A., temporarily in here because his mother in White Plains is sick. Got that?"

"Yes, Sir."

"When he arrives, I'll send him in to see you with the transfer slip and papers."

"Fine, Captain Barnes."

The young man left with his first major assignment in six years with IA. Joe realized how stupid he was. IA's S.O.P.'s on turbulence had been established years before. The young man should have known that.

Mike bought a jigger after searching through five or six stores. A four-ouncer was difficult to find and he spent the afternoon at the office painting colored lines around the glass. It had begun snowing around three and Mike stood at the window of his office watching large, white flakes blot the small main street of the New England town. He felt good, so good he went to the icebox and poured himself a spooker. He was just about to drink it when he remembered the jigger, the stars, the book.

He poured the bourbon back into the jigger—three and a half ounces. Mike decided not to split ounces. Should he pour more in or some out? What the hell, he poured a bit of the gleaming liquid back into the Old Grand-Dad bottle, the rest into his ice-filled glass. He was at the green line. He chuckled out loud as he took the box of stars and pasted a little green one next to the 4:00 line in the diary. He put the whole kit back into his drawer and returned to the window and drank, laughing as he looked out.

"Is that you, Mr. Hagen?"

"It's me. Funny things are happening."

"Oh, I thought I heard someone laughing."

"I'm seeing stars, Mrs. MacGregor, colored ones —red, blue, yellow, pink."

"Have you been seeing stars very long?" she asked seriously.

"Just today. I started seeing my first colored stars."

"That's nice, Mr. Hagen. I hope they'll always be colored."

"I'm sure of it, Mrs. MacGregor."

He returned to his own desk and opened the drawer once more to look at his first entry—a green star for three ounces.

"What games," he said under his breath.

He took out a piece of white typing paper and rolled it into his old Remington. The pilot sat and looked at the blank paper, then at the white snow falling past his window. He didn't know where or how to begin; he vaguely remembered something his old English professor at the University of Florida once told him: "When you write, come to the point in a very few sentences. Write a topic sentence, then go from there. Organize your work . . ."

CHAPTER ONE
MICHAEL HAGEN—A beautiful baby

He took that out, realizing he was going to quit on the first line.

MICHAEL HAGEN
Years 0–16

I was born on January 8, 1933, at Mercy Hospital, Miami, Florida, the second of two children. My brother, Tom, was born four years earlier. My grandfather and grandmother came from Galway, Ireland, in the late nineteenth century, settling first in Portland, Maine, and then, a few years later, they moved to Washington County, Maine, near the Canadian border. They bought a sixty-acre potato and blueberry farm where my father was born in 1900. He had four brothers, all of whom worked on the farm. My father also worked in the lumber business and in 1925, he was selling lumber for shipment to Florida.

The hotel building boom of the twenties was in full swing and, apparently, my father got a job moving down the coast on a schooner bound for Miami where he was to be the representative for the Maine lumber dealer. He made quite a lot of money because he was able to buy a small citrus farm on the outskirts of Homestead, Florida.

He married a girl he met in Miami whose father ran a restaurant, and they started citrus growing and lumber jobbing, turning out doors and other stock items for the hotels.

The Florida building boom was over when I was born and we had a difficult time during the early years. My brother and I worked and we were able to get by since we grew our own food and my father took odd jobs as a carpenter. He was a very religious man and we always attended Mass. My mother was a convert. I remember my father used to drag me in front of the priest telling the man that I was masturbating, and that was a mortal sin. The priest told me often that impure thoughts were the work of the devil, all that sort of 1942 Catholic propaganda. I think I felt guilty all the time and I was shoved into the confessional almost every Saturday when I was growing up.

Nothing much happened that was too unusual when I was a kid, except that I took up flying and I was spraying groves at sixteen. My brother was killed at Inchon, and I remember that my father went into a state of shock. Had a lot of friends around Homestead, played on the high school baseball team, but flying was my whole life. I received a partial scholarship to the University of Florida at Gainesville; the other half I paid for by crop-dusting. I started at the university in September, 1949, four months before my seventeenth birthday.

End of Chapter One.

Mike was tired of writing and he reread what he had typed. He knew it was inadequate but he made a few corrections in pencil and dropped it off at Jameson's office.

Larry Zanoff called Joe Barnes that evening and Joe told the West Coast check pilot what had happened.

"That's something," Larry said. "Think it's true?"

"No, but I have to find out. I don't want this going up to McCullen."

"Don't blame you. I'll take a couple of trips with him. If he's putting down a few, Joe, we can sure as hell find out. You can only hide so much on a plane."

"I agree."

"How does his medical record look?"

"I had it pulled late today. A little overweight, that's all."

"How the hell can a guy operate when he's drinking on the job? Wouldn't someone know?"

"His copilot might, but sure as hell he's not telling me."

"I'll bet on that. My wife knew a guy in her office who would have a couple before work and he'd drink all day on the Q.T. It went on for some years before they found out. Some guys can just put it away and it doesn't show."

"Larry, we have to look into this and quick. Can you imagine this getting out?"

"It would blow a few minds and the newspapers would be sure to pick it up."

"Do you think we ought to simply call Hagen in and put it to him?"

"Maybe. But let me fly with him first. You have to be damned careful about accusing anyone."

"I know. One of the brass over on Third Avenue came in a couple of years ago and claimed he saw an IA captain drinking in uniform. Turned out he was wrong, but the poor bastard almost got fired. The flight department doesn't like that kind of thing. It's a captain's world, you know."

"That's what it is."

Mike Hagen kept the little notebook with him all the time and he faithfully pasted in the stars. At first they were all green, almost nineteen ounces a day, just under a fifth. Then he moved to the blue, which

dropped it down to sixteen ounces. He felt the same but
slept a little longer in the mornings. He took his first
spooker of the day bfore leaving for Ridgefield; there
he would sit in the warm upstairs office smelling the
perfumed plastic flowers with his eyes fixed on the
clock. By 11:00 he desperately needed another spooker, the "mean reds," as Holly Golightly called them,
getting to him.

He had them today. He had to get out of the
office, so Mike drove to the airport, where he saw Jerry
Clurman, a Pan Am pilot with a rebuilt Stinson on
the field. He had often flown with Mike in the Waco
and handled the heavy tail-dragger like a pro.

"Mike, how the hell are you? Christ, I never see
you anymore. They say all you do is taxi that beautiful bird of yours around the field."

"Like hell."

"How about a flip?"

"Sure. I was going to take her out since the snow's
let up," Mike said.

"Front cockpit or back?"

"I'll take the back."

Mike wondered why he hadn't thought of this
before. He could have been flying *Alice* around with
Jerry, a man he trusted implicitly. A blushing yellow
sun was sitting low over the Danbury hills. The plows
had been down the two runways and a couple of planes,
training flights, were already doing their touch and go's
on the east-west runway. They opened the hangar
door, unchocked the wheels, and rolled the big, powerful beast out upon the snow, which crunched under the
pressure of the massive tires.

In their fur-lined jackets and goggles, the two airline pilots taxied the old plane out and lined her up
with the runway. They lifted off and the bare trees slid
by under them. The fresh air revived Mike as he felt
higher than God just being back in the plane once
more. The sky was opening up. Large patches of blue
broke through. Then the sun, a pale wintry sun, came
out and it felt slightly warmer as the crisp wind shot

over the Waco. Being cold, feeling it, was all a part of the excitement, Mike thought. They climbed into the world of 5,000 feet and saw the last dove-gray clouds of the short winter snow squall resting someplace west of the Hudson, which came up like a bright silver streak cutting through the patchy white landscape. Far to the south there was a smudge, the skyline of New York City. They put the biplane into a long, lazy circle and left the coast around Rye, flying over Long Island Sound, which was speckled with white cakes of ice near the shore. The beautifully tuned engine roared on, but as soon as the sun slipped down it became very cold, so they headed up along Route 7, and Mike guided the plane over his house.

They landed at Danbury Airport and the plane was rolled back into the hangar. They started the belly stove and wiped dampness from the cloth wings and dried the tires. Mike had not felt so good in a long time. Still, there was a big knot of emptiness inside him.

The following day Joe Barnes picked up the medical and flight performance records on Mike Hagen and Jim Cochran, and at 3:00 he was driving toward Newark to meet the arriving Larry Zanoff.

Joe hadn't seen Larry Zanoff for almost a year. Larry never changed in Joe's mind; he remembered him in their Atlanta days as being prematurely gray, but the light spots in his crew cut never increased. Even in his twenties, Zanoff had a pocked, hard face like so many other Poles coming out of western Pennsylvania, and he never aged. Twenty-seven years since they met, and Joe had gained twenty pounds and his face had turned jowly and wrinkled; but Zanoff walked straight, and his eyes were young and bright blue even though he was now over fifty. With 26,000 hours in his book, Larry was one of the youngest, finest captains IA had on the line.

Arrangements had been made for Larry to stay with the Barnes's in Englewood, a family reunion.

However, the job to be done was extremely unpleasant for each man and Larry had thought about it all the way east. They didn't discuss the matter during the first twenty minutes driving up the Garden State toward the Barnes's home; finally, Larry asked, "Have you found out any more?"

"No."

"Is there any reason for the girls to lie about this?"

"Don't know. Hagen and this stewardess have been flying together a long time, I found out. Wouldn't be the first time a guy got rapped by a jealous broad."

"I know you don't like this sneaking around behind his back. Better than jumping the gun, I guess."

"Damned right. I'm hoping to squash an ugly rumor before it goes too far," Joe said quickly. "I'm not taking those girls' words for this. Shit, they lie all the time about other things, calling in sick when they're not, pinching bottles off the plane!"

"It's getting to you, Joe."

"Well goddamnit, how do you think I felt when they prissed in there with their little notes. Have you ever heard of a pilot nipping on the job, Larry?"

"Nope, but that doesn't mean anything. With over fifty thousand airline pilots in the world, the law of averages says it could happen."

"Not this guy; he did a helluva job with that clear air turbulence."

"How good is Hagen, Joe?"

"Damned good. Started in Ag flying, excellent record with Northeast. There's his file."

Larry Zanoff picked up a tattered folder from the seat, studying it as they drove. "High-timer, isn't he?"

"Probably has the highest amount of logged time for any man his age on the line."

"What about Cochran, the copilot?"

Joe pointed to a second folder and Larry picked it up. It was some time before he spoke again.

"Don't like this, Joe."

"What's the matter?"

"He has under 5,000 hours, only 850 in type."

"I saw that—about average. He had a proficiency check two months ago. F.A.A. first-class medical four months ago."

"I'd rather be in the right seat just in case this guy really is slopping it up. If anything should go wrong, I want to be near those controls. Nothing against Cochran, but I don't want some low-time kid in there."

"Hagen might suspect something."

"Same story—mother sick in White Plains—only I'm a West Coast captain in here instead of an engineer."

"Don't blame you; this is delicate stuff."

That evening after a steak dinner, Joe called Mike on the pretense of setting up a lunch with Fitz and Cliff McCullen. Then, the chief pilot said casually, "Oh, by the way. There's a Larry Zanoff in here from L.A. Do you know him?"

"Heard of him, I think."

"Mother's quite ill; I arranged a transfer east for a few weeks. He's supposed to go out on 467 with you. Hope you don't mind. Cochran's assigned to reserve."

Mike Hagen felt an immediate alarm, but he steadied himself and calculated that he was doing so well with his booze wind-down that he would be able to cover up.

"Fine. I'll see him in Operations Tuesday morning."

A few minutes later Mike went to the downstairs study and called Jim Cochran.

"Jimmy, did Joe Barnes phone you?"

"About an hour ago."

"He mention anything, you know, about—uh—the spookers?"

"No, he told me there was a West Coast crew member coming in—Mother was sick or something. I'm on reserve. Don't mind since we're putting in an upstairs room."

"That's *all* he said, huh?"

"Nothing else." Jim paused, then said, "How are you doing, Mike?"

"I'm seeing a psychiatrist; no phony baloney though. Straight guy, and he's already got me drinking less."

"That's the way to do it, Mike. You planning to take the thermos aboard with this new guy?"

"Have to; might not need it on the second leg, but it's a security blanket and I want it there just in case."

"You sound good, Mike."

"Yeah, think I'm finally on the right track. The doc's okay. Believe me, Jim, just going was half the battle. Well, say hello to Betty for me."

"Will do. So long, Mike."

Eight

Mike wasn't exactly easy about his second visit to Jameson's office; it was not the first kind of nervousness, wondering what the guy would be like, but Mike knew he had done a poor job with the autobiography. Still, he had faithfully kept the drinking log and he felt he was slowly, successfully coming off the booze. As soon as he entered the office, the doctor looked at his notebook.

"Everything accurate?" he asked Mike.

"Down to the ounce," the pilot said proudly.

"You drink a lot, but not quite a fifth."

"I think I was up to a fifth at one time."

"How do you feel, Mike?"

"Not too different."

"Good. When are you supposed to fly again?"

"Tomorrow."

Court Jameson brought his chair around the desk once more, put his feet up, and Mike noticed the same hole in his shoe. The doctor took the page and a half that Mike had written.

"I was surprised at this."

"Well, I was sort of embarrassed writing about myself."

"You didn't write about yourself. You wrote

about your father. It's the shortest first chapter I ever received."

"I'll tell you the rest."

"When you started talking about masturbation, I thought you were going to open up. But suddenly, there was a case of writer's cramp. What about your early sex life?"

"Not much to tell. Got laid the first time when I was in high school. Thought it was great. Broke up with the gal, found another. Better as a matter of fact."

"You mentioned a priest . . ."

"My father was a religious nut. When I got to the university, I decided not to go to Mass."

"Do you believe in God at this point?"

"Yeah, I do. My daughters attend St. Mary's in Ridgefield. I go with them every now and then."

"Does your wife go?"

"No."

"Growing up in Florida during the forties—I want to talk about that part."

Mike told the doctor about his walks to the church, his strict father, his flying, and a few other details. And when he had finished, Court said, "You liked Florida, didn't you?"

"It wasn't the Florida you're thinking of—hotels, beaches, pools, all that. Right behind Miami or just south of it was a really wild kind of place full of gaters, snakes, swamps. Christ, I got so I could pick up a big old diamondback without those spitting fangs touching me. We all could. There was always a water tower with the name of the town painted on it for the crop dusters who'd come in for the spraying season. The railroad went past us down to Key West. It was a big steam job, sixteen wheels on tracks—hell of a whistle. Still hear it, and the whines of those crop dusters. We had to start 'em with cranks. They'd whine faster and faster and we'd snap 'em in. We'd sit under the shade of the wings—hot as hell down there—drinking Dr. Peppers, eating Moon Pies. Cold Dr. Peppers and Moon Pies. I liked those people. Each guy had a story. Some were World War I pilots—at least that's what they said; others were busted because they drank too much or piled up mail planes. It was special, the Florida I remember. Of course, most of it has changed now, but I liked growing up down there."

"You told me quite a bit. Not about Florida but about yourself."

"I did?"

"Yes, the way you put it—your love for the outdoors."

"When I bought my own plane, I made sure it was an outdoor kind."

"When did you take your first drink?"

"At fourteen. But everyone thought I was sixteen. Big for my age."

"Where was this?"

"Near the Ag field where I learned to fly."

"Did they all drink? I don't mean Dr. Peppers."

"Almost every guy had a flask. They were tough, hard drinkers—sort of flying cowboys. That's what they were called, flying cowboys."

"So you never associated anything wrong with drinking and flying?"

"Never did, up to a point. I saw a couple of cowboys go in. One was killed, but each time the goddamned engine cut out—nothing to do with bombing it up. They could drink damned well. You were judged on how well you could drink and fly—not separately—together. Those guys in the forties were a very close group. A lot of 'em were dropouts from the war, but they had their own thing going. They flew their own equipment, followed the crops and did what they wanted. Back then a guy could bring in about four hundred a week over expenses.

"Half of them would sleep in the back of the hangar and every night they'd get 'bonkered' at the 'Gator Hole'—goddamned lousy bar, but they had country music on Wednesday and Saturday nights and good chili for twenty cents a bowl. There were always a few hookers around, gals who got dumped from the Miami Beach hotels—first-class hooks. One time when I was fourteen they said, 'Let the kid come along.' I was their mascot and they were going to get me laid. The bitch didn't show so they got me drunk instead. Never forgot."

"And you wanted to be an Ag flyer?"

"I didn't want to be, I *was* one. Flew all the way through college and earned a hell of a lot that way."

"Did you continue to drink at the Gator Hole?"

"That or others. Each Ag strip had a Gator Hole. Bartenders knew the flying cowboys were loaded and they all drank. Almost every one could play the harmonica. They taught me, but I haven't practiced in years. Do you remember Woody Guthrie? The flying cowboys used to collect his seventy-eights. A couple of them told me they met him out in Joplin or someplace along the dusting route. That was a whole other world."

Mike spoke in a nostalgic, affectionate way as if the old crop dusters were still down on the Ag field and the Woody Guthrie seventy-eights were spinning as always in the Gator Holes of the South. Mike was living in the forties, Court Jameson was certain of it. The wistful man in front of him was far away in a place that no longer existed if, indeed, it ever did exist exactly the way Mike imagined.

The man inside the burly pilot quickly emerged in the doctor's mind. This pleasant drinking man was right out in the open and his emotions and loves ran close to the surface for everyone to see except himself. Mike was not nearly as complex or intricate as the usual corporate executive who came to see Court Jameson. In that sense, Mike was a pleasure as a patient. His values, his needs were basically simple—as if they were hitched to a more innocent time—and Court tried to visualize Mike's old life: the Florida of Dr. Peppers and Moon Pies, of hard-drinking, hard-flying men piloting old planes along rows of crops under a hot sun.

It was a unique world of flying Mike had talked about.

One had to know the land and the air and where they came together; the subtle boundary between life and death. Too high and the fertilizer spread in the wind; too low or too near, death. Court realized that Mike Hagen must have had the qualities he talked about. Packed in his words was an old love and respect for wide-open spaces, big fields, and big skies.

He was a cowboy and probably as good as they came.

"I was thinking about you the other night," Court said, "asking myself what it takes to be a really good pilot. Is there a perfect pilot? Does it mean going by the book?"

The word "book" turned Mike on and he came to the edge of his leather chair, staring hard at the doctor. Finally, he got up and walked to the end of the room.

"The book is here," Mike said, thumping his chest.

"In your heart, huh?"

"I'll tell you about the book. Half the people who write them don't fly. All they know is numbers, not feelings."

"But there has to be a book," the doctor said hastily.

"When I started in DC-3's the book was small. They told you how to get it going, the rest was in here," he pointed again to his chest. "We didn't have a checklist."

"Is it mind or heart?" Court asked.

"Both. We wrote the book each day. The DC-8 handbook is over five hundred pages."

"But the equipment is more sophisticated—bigger, more powerful."

"You asked me what it takes. It's not in the book, it's judgment—knowing what to do and when. And what *not* to do."

"I find it interesting that you talk about judgment."

"I knew you were going to say that. I drink in the air. That's *not* good judgment, but let me tell you about judgment—the way I see it."

"I wish you would," Court Jameson said, as he reached for his yellow pad. What would that be, the definition of judgment by an alcoholic airline captain? Somehow, Court felt the pilot would be truthful. That was half the battle. When he couldn't get through the lies, his work added up to nothing more than listening, sending out bills, and buying expensive cars.

"In all the years that I've been drinking and flying, I never thought I was taking a chance. They say if you drink while you're driving, you're apt to hit the accelerator. Not me—I compensate, I've always been aware of how many spookers I could get by with. I realize my reactions in the air are slowed down by the booze so I studied accidents, it became my hobby. I've always thought about the perfection of flying, even wrote away to the F.A.A. for accident reports, trying to get an idea of what went wrong. That's all you ever get—the facts, never the sense. I have a whole disaster library and I think I know more about accidents than any captain on the line. What did I learn? Two basic things: sometimes there were accidents that the pilots couldn't control—like mid-air collisions—but looking at the whole spectrum, accidents with no pilot connection account for only a few 'knuckle-breakers.' The rest: pilot error. What's the pilot error? Very seldom does it have to do with fast reflexes; I figure that pilot error is ninety-five percent judgment. Big equipment does take numbers—book flying—but once in a while, that doesn't help. When you're on the shoulder, say, an ILS approach into a marginal field, maybe a field without ILS, that's when judgment comes in. What to do? Land, go to your alternate, or come in with the margin?

"A guy can get a plane through all sorts of shit

that the passenger doesn't know about, handle turbulence, in-air mechanicals, the works, and because he lays it on heavy, drops in too fast and there's a bang, all within limits, the pilot gets shitty looks from his crew, maybe a few complaints by passengers who jerk out that little form letter. Most pilots don't know the value of margin, which means altitude and speed.

"Another thing: imagine a classic situation in which all the autopilots are out, the crew has to fly by instruments accurately hour after hour. Few guys can do this unless they practice like hell. I can hold a better course and altitude with severe turbulence in IFR than any pilot at IA. There's more to weather than numbers; it's a sense of the pattern, knowing the boundaries; just recently, I saved a bunch of people because I felt we might hit clear air turbulence."

"You know, Mike," Court Jameson said. "There's a flaw in all this. The Philadelphia landing you said you screwed up—what happened there?"

The pilot paused as he slowly punched his fist into the cup of his other hand. "Guess that's why I'm here. Ninety-nine times out of a hundred you'll get by with a few spookers; but it's that one time that counts, when lives are riding on the line."

"How serious was the situation?"

"Might have been a disaster. Don't know."

"But, you must have made hundreds of instrument landings."

"It's hard to explain. There's a lot to think about when you're putting a heavy plane down the glide scope. I was nervous, my mind was jammed. We were high and hot over the threshold and the copilot was screaming to go around." He shrugged. "But it was my decision. I put her on. I was craving bourbon like a crazy addict."

"Mike, I want to make sure you realize you *cannot* fly while continuing to drink the way you have. It has to impair judgment and reflexes."

"I know."

"Why didn't you ask the copilot to land?"

"Too proud. He was making me mad. He even touched the throttles. Anyway, there was no need."

"You might have killed everybody onboard," Court said.

"But I didn't. I handled it all right."

Mike was still rationalizing; even as he admitted a potentially catastrophic mistake, he ended up by saying that he had pulled it off. Court felt Mike didn't distinguish between a no-option situation and one involving pilot skill and judgment.

"Do you really want to stop drinking?"

"No, I don't think so."

"That's what I figured."

"But I *want* to get it under control," he said forcefully.

"Okay, we had a good session. Remember, one more day on the blue, then we'll go to the pink. Don't get overconfident; you'll slip once in a while. Don't worry about it or feel guilty."

When the pilot had moved his bulky frame from the office, Court Jameson drew in a deep breath. A borderline alcoholic airline pilot was frightening enough, but he was beginning to wonder if this one was blind as well.

Nine

Mike woke up a little later than usual that morning; a grayish light was filtering through the downstairs window. He dressed and cooked his eggs, and with his notebook and the ringed shot glass packed in his heavy black flight bag, the pilot began the drive toward JFK. He had taken two drinks the night before, each two ounces. He was at the fourteen-ounce level for the last time; tomorrow the pilot would reduce it to twelve ounces, the next plateau. His addictive feeling was less intense that morning and he knew he could drive past Ellen's, but Mike realized the ten o'clock area would be sweaty, so he decided to have one ounce at Ellen's while she refueled his thermos.

He handed her the jigger and said that he had been seeing a doctor in Boston; she did not react one way or the other. Jeez, she thought, if everyone had a doctor, her morning booze business would collapse and with the price of eggs and bacon—

You could barely see the one-ounce of bourbon: a tiny brown puddle circling giant icebergs. He brought it to his lips and in a second it was gone. He hardly felt the bourbon as it disappeared inside him. Another one, he thought? No. There were thirteen ounces left for the rest of the day; the pilot wanted to stretch them out, leaving a good reserve for his night with Pat.

He took a page from the back of his book and charted the day:

6:30 A.M.—1 oz. at Ellen's
10:00 A.M.—2 oz. in flight
1:00 P.M.—2 oz. lunch at hotel
   (no drinks on afternoon leg)
Evening—three 3-oz. drinks

The big change in his old pattern—the one he wasn't sure he could handle—was the afternoon segment over the southwest. He might have to go to the lavatory, but he planned to take his meal and two ounces at the hotel as late as he could, pushing the 12:00 Houston spooker to 1:00; that would be just enough time before checking into Operations at 1:15 for the next leg. Yes, he would slide the schedule around so his addicted body wouldn't need a refill at the wrong time.

The pilot gave himself a final check in the car mirror—eyes, cheeks better this morning—and he gobbled the Sen-Sen, threw his mechanic's jacket in the trunk, and walked across the lot to Operations. Inside the room, Mike put his flight bag down with the others, and adjusting to the fluorescent lights and hollow banter, he crossed to the crew schedule counter and signed in. He asked the guy behind the desk to point out Larry Zanoff.

"Over there, Captain Hagen."

Mike looked across at a tall man with a pepper and salt crew cut studying the winds aloft chart. He walked over and as the man turned his head, he was surprised to see his age. From Joe's phone call, he had figured Zanoff was a copilot.

"Mike Hagen."

"Hello, I'm Larry Zanoff. Nice to meet you."

"Joe said your mother was ill."

"Yes, I'm staying with her in Westchester. Guess we'll be flying together for a few trips."

When Larry Zanoff brought his arm up on the

counter, Mike noticed the four stripes; on his lapel were the tiny red dove wings, IA's thirty-year service insignia. He was a senior captain, obviously, and for a minute, Mike was confused. Larry noticed this and he said, "I'm in the right seat today. Just picking up time while I'm here."

"Sure, Joe didn't say you were a senior captain."

"He must have forgotten. We started out at the Atlanta base together. Hell of a guy, Joe."

"One of the best," Mike said. "Are you on the line now?"

"I've been a check pilot, then I went on the overseas routes."

"How's the weather going south?" Mike asked, looking at the prog sheet.

"Minor frontal situation on a St. Louis-Birmingham line. She's topping out at 24,000."

"Jet stream?"

"Way north of us this morning."

"Are you accepting the MFP?"

"Yes, it looks fine," Larry said.

"Hagen—Captain Hagen, there's a telephone call on three."

Mike walked to the far side of the crew scheduling desk and picked up the phone.

"Mike, this is Court Jameson."

"Oh," Mike said, surprised, "checking up on me?"

"In a way. You know, I've been thinking since our last talk—maybe you shouldn't take any flights out at all until we wind this thing down some more."

"Well look, I cooled it last night and everything's okay this morning. Only had one ounce, so small I could hardly see the stuff in the glass."

"How do you feel?"

"Good. Slept well. I have a new copilot today, a senior captain in here temporarily. So there'll be two senior captains on the flight deck, a second officer who flies, and two autopilots."

"All right. You have the pills?"

"Right in my pocket."

"Mind calling me when you get into San Diego?"

"Not at all."

"And take it easy out there, Mike. Keep on the schedule."

"I will. I'm doing fine—better than I thought. Coming off isn't too tough."

"Talk to you later," Court said.

As Larry was filing the flight plan, Mike walked over to his bag. He knelt beside it with his back to the rest of the room and slipped out the thermos with the jigger attached to the side under broad rubber bands. He pushed his coat over it, closed the flight kit, and stood waiting in the narrow corridor for Larry Zanoff.

Larry Zanoff resented his task. There exists between pilots a rare allegiance, for the men who fly the big jets are a unique breed just like those that flew the airmails before them. To sit in the left seat of any airliner is a job of utmost trust and each man on the flight deck must rely on the other, knowing that the giant plane operates solely on a federation of practiced skills and standard operational procedures. Because of this rare camaraderie, pilots will help each other and in so doing, they maintain and strengthen the impeccable standards of flight personnel all over the world. They will cover for one another and stick together until a certain line is crossed. Jim Cochran, for one, realized that his captain was on the far side of the boundary. The copilot had lain awake many nights agonizing over what he had to do.

With Larry Zanoff, it was different; he was ordered to fly with Mike Hagen. He could have refused but regardless of who investigated Mike, it was going to be a painful experience and Larry approached it with uneasiness. One captain spying on another was a sensitive matter in their tight world; yet Larry knew it had to be done, for if it were left alone, unattended, lives might be sacrificed and pilots will not compromise with safety.

As distasteful as the check pilot considered his

temporary assignment, he nevertheless was convinced that he could find out about Mike Hagen if, indeed, there was anything going on. He was a professional cockpit investigator, recognizing the small clues, the tiny tell-tales that index a pilot, but Larry didn't know how well a large-bodied Irishman who had been drinking since fourteen could handle his booze and still perform. The check pilot had no idea of Mike's flying ability when his head and stomach weren't being attacked by a murderous case of the "mean reds." Ironically what Larry Zanoff was to observe on that morning's takeoff from JFK would be something he wished he could see in every pilot on the IA line.

Like many long-time heavy drinkers, Mike Hagen was a highly proficient actor. He knew how to assume an outward calm that could fool anyone. As they walked along the cavernous halls to gate seven about forty minutes before departure time, Mike joked with Larry Zanoff, who noted his subject's apparent ease; his manner was not that of a man under the pressure of alcoholic addiction, squeezed between the last drink and the one coming up.

As they stepped into the cockpit of the DC-8, Mike placed his coat over the left cockpit seat, back-handed the thermos, and was out of the cockpit and into the first lavatory before Larry Zanoff knew what was going on. Mike worried that the piggyback spooker with its attached shot glass wouldn't fit into the disposal locker, but it just did. As a further safeguard, the pilot edged it far back into the upper corner of the bin with a hooked wire that he had carefully stowed up his sleeve. Thirty seconds later Mike was back in the cockpit.

Meanwhile, Larry had been rifling through Mike's flight kit and his overcoat, and just as the pilot returned and was sliding into his left seat, Larry accidentally brushed against him. He could neither see nor feel the bulge of small bottles and he felt Mike couldn't have hidden a bottle in the lav in such a short time.

Larry felt better, for, of course, he was hoping not to discover anything.

Mike went through his flight deck workload with care and efficiency. He checked the load figures on the MFP and studied the dispatch papers, noting the route that would take the plane over the high altitude airways southwest into the Houston area. According to the load data on the computer print-out, the flight would be very light that day—almost 91,000 pounds under the JFK and Houston allowable weights.

"Reduced thrust," Mike said with a smile.

"Guess so," Larry answered.

Mike checked the outside temperature twice and scrupulously went through the calculations of the second officer and Larry Zanoff noticed this.

When their paper work was finished, the challenges and responses of the "before engine start" completed, Mike slid out of his seat and stood at the cockpit door greeting the last of the oncoming passengers with his big, congenial smile.

"Good morning, nice to have you with us."

"Good morning, Captain."

"Hello, welcome on board."

"Will it be smooth today?"

"Very smooth. Good morning . . ."

Since the days Mike flew DC-3's for Northeast he felt it was important to establish a personal contact with the passengers, not for the airline's sake, but rather to ease the fears of the few first-timers and those who flew because they had to, not because they wanted to. Mike figured just the sight of a confident captain walking slowly up and down the aisle was enough to reassure people, but as jet flying developed pilots were ordered to the flight deck to work behind locked doors. This was because of the possibility of unexpected turbulence and, of course, hijackings. The only time the passengers saw the pilots was at the gate when the cockpit door was open, and then usually they saw the backs of two heads and the profile of another. Mike made up for this by chatting with the passengers a few minutes before and after each flight. Larry Zanoff had only seen one or two other pilots do this, but he thought it was a good idea from a company point of view. That was a plus mark for Mike, and who could be cheerful with a blistering hangover, Larry thought?

The flight was pushed from the gate on time, the turbines started, and ground control directed the Stretch 8 to runway 31-Left; they were seventh in sequence for takeoff and Mike made his usual "you can smoke until we go" PA. The weather was cold, 34 degrees, and the sky was remarkably clear with only a few cirrus clouds hanging on the far western horizon. They moved up and Mike flipped on the No Smoking sign, the "Before Takeoff" checklist was read by the flight engineer, and responses called back; and finally, they heard, "IA 467, you're cleared for takeoff."

Mike fed in his thrust with an easy movement of his arm and his meaty fingers parted and curled around the lever knobs; he took the four throttles forward just enough for the Pratt & Whitneys to give them the necessary speed and distance for takeoff—about 8 percent under full power. (The average passenger cannot tell the difference between the reduced thrust takeoff and the full thrust because the noise reduction is imperceptible.)

The purpose of the reduced thrust takeoff is to increase engine life and reliability while conserving fuel. When it was first introduced, pilots had problems accepting it; they said, "We have all this power. Why not use it?" Some argued, and still do, that it is risky to reduce power on takeoff, but the F.A.A. sanctions it up to 10 percent when other conditions such as weight, runway length, and temperature are met. Those who argue for it claim that the reserve power is a tiny bonus that can be restored if needed.

Mike felt it was safer to employ full power, but when he was being checked or flying with a suspected "company man" like Larry Zanoff, he used the reduced thrust takeoff.

When they reached V-R, Larry called it, but Mike left the bird on a couple of seconds for a touch of extra airspeed. It was an old habit growing out of his biplane days when a little extra speed was often the difference between life and death, but this flying philosophy has little linkage with big-jet operation.

Mike held his airspeed needle right on V-2 plus ten knots, the former being takeoff safety speed or the aircraft's stall speed if the flaps were up. They climbed to 1,500 and Mike started his left-hand turn which brought them over the old Floyd Bennett Field They cleared the Long Island coast at 3,000 feet to allow inbound traffic to runway 4-Right to slide in under them.

Larry quickly added up the points in his head. On the plus side Mike looked good; his cockpit procedures were correct and business-like. His passenger contact was approved, so was his reduced takeoff decision. His ground handling was expert, his course holding and transitions right on the button. On the minus side was Mike's decision to delay the rotation.

Departure control was swinging the jet high and southwest of the airport, allowing the incoming traffic complete freedom of approach at the lower altitudes. They were handed off to New York Center and the controller saw the parallel blips come up on his scope. The Stretch 8 then began her southwesterly course climbing into the high world of 20,000 and then to their cruising altitude of 31,000.

Larry Zanoff was satisfied with Mike Hagen He knew a professional high-timer was in the left seat and he was almost certain the man wasn't nipping in the lavatory. But there were many miles before them and Larry continued to observe the pilot out of the corner of his eye.

Flight 467 took its usual route west of Washington, Chattanooga, and Birmingham. Around 10:00,

Mike stood up and excused himself from the cockpit. Nancy, who was in the galley making coffee, saw the door immediately when it opened.

Something different.

The pilot went directly into the head without taking a paper cup. A bit perplexed, she noted this on her seat chart taped to the bulkhead.

Inside the lavatory Mike hooked his baby with the five-inch wire and pulled it toward him. He grabbed the thermos and poured two ounces into the ringed jigger and drank slowly. When it was gone, he took out his little notebook and carefully marked it in pencil. (The star would have to be put in later.) The pilot refastened the jigger and pushed his bourbon far back into the darkness of the disposal locker. Planting and unplanting the spooker was a full-time job, Mike thought.

Nancy slipped into the lavatory as soon as he left. She sniffed the air. No smell of alcohol.

A few minutes after Mike returned to the cockpit, Larry slid from his seat and left the flight deck. He had observed Mike carefully; the captain did not stop by his coat or flight kit to pull out a small bottle, nor were there bulges in Mike Hagen's pockets. The check pilot was certain Mike wasn't carrying bottles, so if he were drinking the bottle would have to be hidden someplace in the lavatory. It was a small area, hardly twenty-five square feet, and Larry knew he could find the booze if, indeed, it was there. Nancy, who had been briefed about Larry Zanoff, waited for the check pilot to exit the cockpit and she approached him quickly.

"He used the first lavatory," she said, "but there was a change this time."

"What?"

"He didn't take the paper cup with him."

"You sure?"

"Absolutely."

"I'll go in and look around anyway."

"I just did. No odor."

Larry heard the edginess in Nancy Halloway's voice and knowing that the woman had made a difficult decision provoking this whole appalling search, he nodded reassuringly and entered the lavatory. Larry was methodical; he started on the left side of the counter and moving slowly, carefully, he pulled up every panel that could be removed, taking out the tissues and small soaps and dipping his hand into every opening. He even applied pressure to the bulkhead panels to test their security. Larry was just about to leave when he noticed the disposal flap door. He stooped down to look in, but he couldn't see anything. Then he stood and poked his hand inside as far as it would go; he felt nothing. Larry came out, shook his head at Nancy, and hunching his shoulders, he reentered the cockpit.

They landed at Houston on time and Larry noted the ease and precision with which the pilot slipped her on. Again, Mike went to the head; he came out a minute later, his black raincoat concealing the thermos. Larry went in and ripped open the disposal locker; there were no bottles buried in the trash. When they reached Operations Larry suggested they have a bite to eat, but Mike said he had a luncheon date with someone at the hotel. Feeling awkward, Larry followed the pilot staying quite a bit behind him. He saw Mike register at the front desk, take a key, and walk to the elevator carrying his bag. Larry crossed the lobby to the counter.

"A friend of mine, pilot for IA, just registered."

"Oh yes, Captain Hagen, room 409."

Larry waited a few minutes and then went up to the fourth floor where he passed room 409 and took a position at the far end of the hall. He realized that if Mike Hagen were drinking on the plane, he'd certainly be taking a few in the hotel room, a very private place.

Inside 409, Mike was holding back on his next spooker. After a hot bath, he rested on the bed watching TV. At the last moment he picked up the phone and called room service. Ten minutes later a young waiter with a small tray knocked on the door and entered the pilot's room. When the bellboy came out, Larry approached from down the hall.

"Son, I need a little help. I'm from the airlines—routine check," he said, showing his official IA identification card. "What did you just take the man in 409?"

"Swiss on rye. He has the same thing all the time."

"Any drinks, like liquor, beer?"

"No, sir."

"Ever see any booze around the room, or bring him some?"

"No, sir."

"What about ice. Ever bring up a bucket of ice?"

"Nope. Say, what is this about anyhow?"

"Routine." Larry pulled out a five and handed it to the waiter. "Have you ever noticed any women or a particular woman go in there?"

"No, he's always alone—just reading or watching TV."

"How long has he been checking in here?"

"About two years."

"Always the same room?"

"No, usually on this floor or the one above, though. I cover both floors."

"Is there an ice dispenser on the premises?"

"Nope, you have to get it through room service —me."

"Thanks, son. Don't mention our conversation, okay?"

"Sure. Thanks for the bill."

Larry was satisfied that Mike wasn't sitting around the hotel room drinking warm booze. But why did he lie, say that he had a luncheon date in the hotel when he didn't? Why did he take a room at these prices? Larry could understand it if the pilot were meeting someone, but that didn't seem to be the case, unless a girl was slipping in without the waiter seeing her.

Larry stayed down the corridor where he could

watch the door from a distance. No one entered Mike's room, and a few minutes later the pilot came out and went for the elevator. Larry didn't have much time so he hastily approached the door and tried the handle. Locked. In the distance he saw the maid's cart and ran down and told her that he had left something in his room. She unlocked the door and let him in, but she stood outside watching.

Larry entered the bedroom and opened closets. No sign of a woman. The bed was mussed up so he must have taken a nap. There was no smell of bourbon and no empty bottle or miniatures in the trash basket. Then Larry crossed to the bathroom and saw that one of the two glasses had been used and he smelled it. It had the unmistakable odor of Lavoris mouthwash.

Larry returned to the cockpit fourteen minutes later.

"Where were you?" Mike asked.

"Oh, I met someone I used to know."

"I don't like late check-ins," Mike said crisply.

The check pilot was stunned and then Mike smiled.

For the first time in his life, Larry Zanoff felt just a trifle dirty.

The afternoon segment was routine, autopilot almost all the way. The delayed lunchtime spooker helped Mike and he got through the rest of the flight without leaving the cockpit, although his baby was stored just in case. His thirst was beginning to surface as he walked out of San Diego Operations and took a cab to Pat's advertising agency. He arrived at her office around 4:00 and they left immediately in her Jaguar for Coronado. It was not to be the Mexican restaurant that night; Mike's decision to fight the bottle was occasion for a celebration and Pat was cooking his favorite dinner at home. But as they drove south, the pilot felt that lust for the bourbon as if alarms were going off deep in his belly, in his head. It was not imagination. The signals were *real*.

* * *

Larry Zanoff rode over to the El Cortez in the crew limo with the girls and flight engineer. When they reached the registration desk at the hotel, he called Nancy aside.

"Would you mind stopping by my room for a few minutes?"

"In about half an hour?"

"That would be fine."

Later she arrived in Zanoff's room.

"He never left the cockpit this afternoon," Larry said. "But if he's drinking, it must be stowed somehow in the lav."

"He always goes in the same one before and after the trips."

"I searched that head, almost pulled everything apart. I didn't find anything."

"You don't think he's carrying it in with him?" she asked.

"No, I pretty well managed to check that out."

"Captain Zanoff," Nancy said diffidently, "maybe I jumped to conclusions and acted too fast."

"You said you smelled liquor in there."

"Gloria Esposito and I both did—very faintly."

"Okay, you did what you thought was right under the circumstances. I'm going to call Joe Barnes. I want to try something different tomorrow. I think I know how we can be sure about this. If he's hiding booze in the first lavatory and if he's a real alcoholic, he'll have to get to that head, won't he?"

"I guess so. It's a long flight."

"After he comes aboard tomorrow and goes into the first lav, I'm having the mechanics turn off the valves so the toilet won't flush. You put up a sign and if he tries to enter the head just tell him it overflowed. If he makes a lot of noise about using that head instead of the other one, we'll know he's got something in there and we'll tear it apart when we get back to New York. If he's casual about the whole thing and merely uses the second lavatory, then I think we can be pretty sure there's nothing to worry about. You agree?"

Nancy nodded her head slowly.

Pat prepared a festive meal that evening and Mike drank his remaining nine ounces; it wasn't enough, but he had promised Jameson and when he considered the other two choices—standing up in the A.A. meeting or blowing a wad on an instant dry-out—he decided to stick it out if he could. And tomorrow would be rough—his first twelve-ounce day.

While Pat was making coffee, he plotted the next twenty-four hours. The flight left at 11:30 A.M. He would take his first three ounces in the morning before departure. He scribbled:

9:00 A.M. PST—3 oz.
2:00 P.M. PST (in flight)—3 oz.
Ellen's—3 oz.
Ridgefield—3 oz.

He put the notebook away and went in to call Jameson. It was late, but the doctor said he was glad to hear an affirmative report. Mike was holding on. Later that night Mike showed Pat his book with the stars. At first she smiled, but when she caught the earnest look on his face, the small glint of hope, she grabbed his hand.

"I'm proud, very proud of you, Mike."

"You know," he said with a rueful smile, "I'm more scared of the ground than the air."

"What do you mean?"

"Oh, this thing—the stars, the book. When I get to the point when there are no more stars in the book, then what? Something has to change. I've been drinking to escape, like everyone, same old story. But there will come a day without stars and I'll see it all. Pat, I keep asking myself, do I really want that? It's so fucking awful."

"Your wife?"

"Yes, and everything else. That oppressive upstairs plant shop. I hate it! The smells—it's enough to drive anybody to the juice."

"I know, but it's more than the plant shop."

"I don't like my life, any of it, that's what scares me. There's nothing I like about it except you. Coming out here is all I have except for my daughters, and Jean is even drawing them away from me."

"Darling, now I have something to tell you. About two months ago, I sent my portfolio to a New York advertising agency."

"I thought you didn't like the big city."

"I was there years ago as a scared little kid. Things are different now, Mike. I want to be with you."

She had told him often she would never go back to New York. It was a bad memory.

"Are you doing this for me?"

"Both of us. I'm sort of trapped here. If I get the job back east, then we can talk about another kind of life."

"Do you really mean it?" he asked, brightening.

"Yes, I'm coming east, Mike."

They embraced and made love. She knew things were going to be different for both of them.

Ten

Larry Zanoff arrived at IA's San Diego maintenance office at 8:00 the following morning. They had instructions from Joe Barnes to do anything Captain Zanoff requested that didn't conflict with the FAR's.

"It's only a stop valve," the man told Larry, "but I never heard of such a thing. It can be turned off, but why do you want to screw up a toilet?"

"There's a good reason."

"Yeah, well, okay, the first head on 9086."

"I'll walk out with you," Larry said. "Do you have some of that steel tape in the shop?"

"Strapping tape, you mean?"

"That's it."

"Sure."

"Give me a roll and I'll need some heavy scissors."

The plane was hauled to a position near the gate an hour and twenty minutes before the 11:30 departure. Catering began at 10:40; they started pumping on the Jet 1-A, and everything was completed by 11:05. When Larry Zanoff was certain that the forward head didn't work, he left the cockpit and walked along the corridor toward IA Operations at the far end of the Lindbergh concourse. He was fifteen minutes early and he asked for the MFP and looked at the

weather situation. There was a rapidly deepening cold
front on a Boise, Salt Lake, Amarillo line associated
with a deep low near Denver. Another fast-moving, but
minor low pressure was over Detroit topping out at
27,000. According to the MFP, they would divert
slightly south of the usual route and the flight would
take a gentle bend over Albuquerque and gradually
work north over Wichita Falls, Texas, south of the
frontal disturbance.

Winds aloft were swift this day. At flight level
330 on the southerly course they ran well over 160
knots, not far from the jet stream. It would be a fast
flight if the winds held their velocity and direction east
of the Mississippi.

Mike was right on time and Larry saw him coming from a distance; the captain walked smartly,
straight, not the pace of a man heavily pressed by
booze. Larry was certain by this time that the girls
were wrong, but the test today would probably put an
end to the whole embarrassing matter. Larry was glad
because he knew it was just about destroying Joe
Barnes.

Mike entered the first head and stowed his spooker. He had already taken three of the allotted twelve
ounces and he pasted the small pink stars in his notebook. It was going to be a tough day and he patted his
pocket to make sure he had the plastic bottle of tranquilizers.

The flight, always popular, was the earliest San
Diego-New York nonstop out of the West Coast city
and even though it arrived late in New York, 7:30 P.M.,
it usually went out at about 70 percent load factor.
The flight was never late because it was a "first out" in
the morning.

At precisely 11:31 A.M., flight 602 was away, her
four turbines started; the two captains waved at the
line crew and they were on their own. Mike taxied
the ship to the single San Diego runway where they
were second for takeoff behind Western's 807 for San

Francisco. They saw the puffy kerosene trail of the Western flight disappear into the strong morning light and Mike swung the DC-8-61 onto the runway and as he did, their clearance came. He pushed in power for a full thrust takeoff and the jet picked up speed. Their rotation had been calculated at 151 knots; Larry read it off and Mike rotated. The gear went up; the flaps curled back into the trailing edge of the wing, and twenty-three minutes later, they reached their assigned altitude of 33,000 and trimmed the ship. Mike pressed his "bingo-bungo" as he called it: the number on the flight director that would take the plane to their first VOR station along the high altitude airways, the "Buckeye" Omni in the torrid Arizona desert. Mike made his usual cheerful good-morning PA, and then he settled down, looking at his watch. Spooker time was two hours away. Two hours of boredom. He wished he could stick his head out the window and feel the wind, yell. Anything.

Nancy Halloway had taken the strapping tape and covered the first lavatory door as if it held a tiger gone mad. She even went one step further: using a piece of IA stationery, she made a sign:

> LAVATORY CLOSED. TOILET INOPERA-
> TIVE. WE ARE SORRY FOR THIS IN-
> CONVENIENCE. PLEASE USE OTHER
> LAVATORY.

She tacked this on the door and went back to start her breakfast service.

Mike began to feel it when the flight was fifty miles west of Tulsa. First the hungry sensation; he asked for a breakfast, which always softened his body's initial cry for the booze. But past Tulsa, the shriek came again. It wasn't time.

Their ground speed now was over 660 miles per hour. Thank God, Mike thought. It would be a fast trip and the wind, that beautiful westerly airflow that Mike sometimes cursed, would blow the giant DC-8

into New York. He looked at his expensive chrono-
meter again and changed the hands to central time.
They had a little over three hours left in the air. Now
it was ten minutes to spooker time and the ache, the
want surged through him, but he stuck to his schedule.
Five minutes, three minutes.

Time.

"Piss call," he said, slipping out of his seat.

As he did, Larry reached across the instrument
panel, his hand casually sliding past Mike's pocket. No
little liquor bottle.

When Mike stepped from the cockpit, he was
looking down the first-class cabin and he didn't notice
the tape and note on the lavatory door. Nancy, coming
out of the galley, stopped, put down a tray, and crossed
to the magazine rack on the bulkhead near the galley.
Then Mike saw the paper on the door and a bolt of
fear tore through him. He was aware that Nancy was
watching him and brought out a mock smile. "God,
what did you have, a flood?"

"A little one."

"Why didn't you call the flight engineer?"

"I was going to, but we've been busy."

He smiled again to cover his surprise and fright.
He moved to the second head. He went inside, uri-
nated, and came out again with the pills in his hand.
Nancy was stuffing magazines into the rack. Mike took
a paper cup, filled it with water, and stepped into the
galley. She followed him.

"You ever have hay fever?" he asked her.

"No."

"I've got it back again this year."

"What do you take for it?"

"Doc gave me a prescription, better than drugstore antihistamines."

He drank the water and returned to the cockpit,
his stomach flip-flopping. The stark panic resulting
from his severed umbilical cord was combined with the
withdrawal jitters. The doctor had said the pills would

work. What if they didn't when he began to get the shakes? More pills?

The gnawing hunger switched to pain. He was *starving!* Then he became slightly light-headed. His vision seemed to be affected. He felt as if he were floating. Mike looked at the instruments, and they swam back into focus again.

"Our next checkpoint?" he asked Larry, hoping to get his mind off the panic.

"We're one hundred forty miles off the Nashville VOR."

"Good push today."

"Almost a record."

Mike shoved his hands to the left side in case they started to shake. "The head's busted," he said to the flight engineer.

"No one told me."

"Better take a look."

The engineer left the cockpit but returned in a few moments. "The girls have it taped—not many in first anyway. Doesn't matter."

"Take a look anyhow. The water might be leaking down on the electrical circuits."

The flight engineer left the flight deck again and he returned in about five minutes.

"Fix it?"

"No, the flush button is out. No water leakage."

"Okay, make a report. Was it on the sheet last night?"

"No, nothing is written up."

Twenty minutes later Mike was beginning to feel the shakes. He thought of the story he had heard in Branford and he tried to remember what he knew about the D.T.'s. Would he have hallucinations, see pink elephants, go into convulsions? Maybe he was far enough into the "cure" not to have full-blown D.T.'s. More pills? No, he would hold out as long as possible. Jameson said they were strong. As the flight was rapidly closing the distance on the Nashville VOR, being

pushed by the strong high-altitude flow, Mike began
to feel different, calmer as the heavy tranquilizers entered his bloodstream and went to work. He kept checking the instrument panel; the numbers were still sharp-
edged, but the pills made him tired and sluggish. He
wanted to slip off into a long sleep. He looked over at
Larry who was studying a chart in his lap; his eyes
crossed to the DME. The heavy, lethargic feeling continued and Mike ordered coffee and began to talk with
Larry just to keep awake. The older man spoke about
his days with the Eighth in one war; Mike responded
with a story about a later conflict.

Mike could feel the butterflies in his stomach
again and his eyes fastened on the DME as the numbers clicked off minute by minute. Questions were
spinning around in the pilot's mind: what if there were
an inbound traffic delay at JFK and they had to circle?
Would he fall into a stupor or get the "mean reds"?

The drugs were worse than the drinks. Shit, what
would have happened if the head had broken down before he had the pills, before he met Jameson? In his
mind he saw himself rushing to the galley, closing the
curtain, and dumping all the liquor bottles out as the
girls looked on petrified. What would happen now if
Larry Zanoff were to slump over the wheel suddenly?
The guy must be fifty-three. Could he get the plane
down with a flight engineer whose ability to help with
the giant aircraft was limited?

Mike feared the unexpected. If he only knew what
the pills would or wouldn't do. The coffee seemed to
help. He felt more awake, but quite strange—as if there
were another person living inside him. His vision was
still good and he asked Larry for the chart.

"Right here," Larry said, pointing to a VOR forty
miles west of Baltimore.

Where had the minutes gone? Was he losing his
sense of time and perception? "We'd better pick up the
JFK weather," Mike said. "And you take her in,
Larry."

"Very good."

Mike looked far below. It was a clear night and he could see the speckled lights of the farmlands; above, the moon was playing with fast-racing cirrus clouds high overhead. Mike felt all right for a while and near Philadelphia, Larry's hands reached for the throttles and he eased back on the power; 602 began her long descent into JFK. Mike watched the air speed. The altimeter began to slowly unwind. Suddenly, without warning, the apprehension and anxiety came back again; he felt as if he were going to explode and Mike knotted his fists and prayed, fumbling around in his pocket for the pills. He grasped two from the little plastic container and picked up the intercom.

"Do you have a drink back there—Coke, maybe?"

"Be right up. Anybody else want one?"

"Anybody want a Coke?"

They shook their heads.

"Just one," Mike replied into the handset.

The second stewardess brought the drink to the flight deck. Mike took a swallow and quickly slipped the two pills into his mouth and washed them down with the liquid. The out-of-sorts feeling continued but after a few minutes he felt drowsy and drugged. The thought that JFK was near eased his terror. The flight was out of 17,000; more lights could be seen on the ground as they streaked over the Jersey coast. He would make a PA. It might keep him going.

"Let me have that weather," he said to Larry.

Larry handed him a slip.

"Contact approach control. Let them know we have information Delta."

Larry contacted JFK for his inbound instruction. They had already heard via the tape broadcast from the New York VOR station, information Delta, that inbound traffic was using 22-Left; approach control told them there would be no inbound delays and their traffic was a National 727 at eleven o'clock, holding 10,000.

Mike pressed the button. "Ladies and gentlemen,

we're presently over the New Jersey coast. The lights to your left are Atlantic City. We're at 12,000 letting down for JFK; we don't expect any inbound delays and we should be on the ground in about fifteen minutes. The weather in New York is clear, temperature 33 degrees, wind 18 miles an hour from the southwest. Local time in New York is 6:50. Because of strong high-altitude westerly winds, we've picked up about thirty minutes. I'd say this was one of the fastest eastbound trips we've had in quite a while. On behalf of the cockpit crew and all the girls, we want to thank you for flying with Intercontinental and we look forward to serving you again in the future. Good to have you aboard."

He snapped off the button. "Shit," he said to himself. "If those people only knew. If they only *knew*. Oh, shit!"

Mike looked from his window, down and back. "I have the National on visual," Mike said. "1000 below us."

Larry again noticed how the pilot was always peering from the window, but this time it was only to cover a deep yawn.

"That our traffic?"

"Must be," Mike answered.

Mike fixed his eyes on the panel; the rims of the instruments had not gone soft, but his head felt as if it were wobbling loosely on his neck and he was sweating under the heavy uniform.

Five minutes later they switched frequency to 119.1 and Mike said, "This is IA 602 with you."

"You'll be landing 22-Left. Wind two four zero at eighteen. Altimeter two niner, eight niner. Your traffic is a National 727."

"Thank you. We have him."

Mike fed in his first flap increment as the flight was out of five thousand for four. The seat belt sign went on and as the National jet swung around for her short final, Larry ordered full flaps and the airspeed fell off. Mike thought Larry was climbing up a little close on the National inbound.

"Slow her up just a hair," he said.

"I was just about to," Larry answered a bit pee-vishly.

The gear was down-locked and they went through their final before-landing check. National was on and rolling out; they were cleared and Larry put her on easily.

Mike said a small private prayer of thanksgiving. Almost eight hours without a drink. But Ellen's Place wasn't far away. He would call Dr. Jameson immediately, Ellen's Place or not. Should he try to enter the lavatory? That was another acute problem which jammed Mike's head: what if the clean-up crews discovered the thermos in the bottom of the bin? Would they forget it? Think it belonged to a passenger, or would they connect the spooker with a crew member? Trying to rescue his liquor when the lavatory was inoperative would be dangerous. These were too many fears for Mike to handle at once, so he temporarily forgot the thermos; he could always buy another one if he had to. Mike edged off his cockpit seat and things seemed just a bit blurry, not too bad, but the hard edges were gone; the throttles looked like an impressionist painting. He stood at the cockpit door saying good-bye to the people. An elderly woman with two children approached.

"I've been promising my granddaughters they could shake hands with the captain."

"How do you do?" Mike said, as he took their hands.

Nancy watched Mike laughing with the children. She felt terrible, and shortly afterward, when Larry came from the cockpit, he shook his head slowly, but happily.

As they walked across the concourse, Mike told Larry he had to make a phone call and they said good-bye.

"Nice flying with you," Larry said.

"Thanks. Say hello to Joe for me."

Mike was glad Jim Cochran hadn't been aboard. The older, more experienced man had given the pilot a certain sense of security. Mike entered a phone booth, took out a handful of quarters, looked at the number in his wallet, and dialed, telling Jameson's answering service it was very important. They said the doctor would call right back and the phone rang in the concourse booth almost immediately.

"Mike, are you all right?"

"I think so. The head broke down on the plane. Haven't had a drink for eight hours. I started to feel it up there and took the pills."

"How many?"

"Four."

"That's a lot. Where are you now?"

"At JFK. Just landed."

"Now Mike, listen carefully. Don't take a drink under any circumstances. I don't think you should drive either. I want you to leave your car down there and take a taxi to the hospital. I'd like to put you under observation for tonight and tomorrow. You can't come off this fast without supervision. This is a critical time for you."

"What will I tell my wife?"

"Say you're spending the night in town, pilot's meeting or something in the morning. I'll meet you at the hospital. You'll be signed in under another name, Robert Brown."

He gave the pilot the address of Silver Glen, the private mental hospital in Stamford.

"And don't walk in with your uniform on. Do you have a sweater or something?"

"Yes."

After calling his wife, who seemed a bit foggy herself, Mike caught a cab outside. His eyes were so heavy that he dropped off to sleep once or twice. The cab took a long time to find the hospital, a once private estate in the hills outside of Stamford. He paid the driver, placed his coat and hat in his bag, and took out a sweater. He rang the doorbell and a woman answered.

"Mr. Brown?"

"Yes."

"The doctor is waiting in the office."

Mike walked into a comfortable paneled room and they shook hands.

"How do you feel?"

"Drugged, goddamnit!"

"You *are* drugged."

"What happens here tonight?" Mike asked, looking around.

"I'm going to give you a quick physical—blood pressure, heart—a light supper, and a shot that'll really make you sleep. In the morning, try not to have a drink, just the pills. When your condition is stabilized and you're awake, we'll have a session here."

"When can I leave?"

"Maybe tomorrow evening, possibly the next day. We might be able to break down the withdrawal symptoms very quickly."

"I was scared, damn scared."

"You had a right to be. I shouldn't have let you fly that trip, but it's past now and I think we're going to lick this thing."

Eleven

Joe Barnes had been partially relieved by Larry's phone call from San Diego the night before, but he waited with a certain amount of anxiety until the check pilot reached Englewood. He met Zanoff at the door.

"Does he or doesn't he?" Joe asked, letting out his poor joke.

"No, *he* doesn't. But *I* do. How about a drink?" Larry was smiling.

They went to the sun porch where Joe fixed his friend a stiff drink and took one himself.

"I guess you want everything?" Larry said.

"You're goddamned right everything! Christ, I haven't been able to sleep thinking about this."

"Well, first of all, he's a good pilot, just as you said. His technique was flawless except that he left it on the concrete a little too long in New York, and then again in San Diego this morning."

"I know, I know. He always did—carry-over from his DC-3 days."

"Okay, but it isn't good. I don't like innovators in the cockpit doing things their way, not ours."

"All right. I agree, but it's not serious. I know he can fly. What else?"

"Mike checks into a motel on the Houston lay-over."

"It's only two hours."

"I thought he might be drinking in there but the waiter claims he's never seen liquor or carried him anything from the bar, not even ice. And who drinks warm stuff except the British?"

"Especially bourbon. That's Mike's drink."

"Then I figured it must be a gal."

"No, he's serious about some chick in San Diego. Mike doesn't whore around."

"I checked the room after he left trying to figure out why the hell he was paying twenty bucks for such a short stop. There was no woman, no booze. Nothing. Joe, he *wasn't* drinking in that room, I'm positive."

"Does he do this every trip?"

"I think he must. The bed was messed up. He had ordered a sandwich, so maybe a private meal and a short nap are worth the money to him."

"Did you follow him in San Diego?"

"No, I felt my spying had gone far enough. I'm no Mannix."

"Yeah, sure. What about going into the head?"

"As I mentioned over the phone, he went to the head once during the morning leg yesterday, but Nancy said he *didn't* take the cup. On the afternoon segment Mike didn't leave the flight deck. Today you know we taped the first lav shut. According to Nancy, Hagen just looked at it and entered the second one. No problems. He came out in thirty seconds—a short piss. He then took a cup and swallowed two pills, allergy medication he told her, hay fever or something."

"*That's* why he's been going to the head," Joe said with a sigh of total relief. "Of course. Why didn't I think of that?"

"Could be. I sort of brushed by him checking his pockets several times when he left the cockpit. I'm sure he *wasn't* taking anything into the head, and I searched the place thoroughly before the flight and after we landed. Joe, there wasn't a bottle hidden in there. I poked every place. That head was empty."

"He didn't appear to be drunk at any time, even a little?"

"No. I'll take one more ride with him next week, just to make sure, but I'd say it's all a mistake, a bad one."

"Thank God."

"One more thing," Larry said, "Nancy. She's very upset. She feels she started one hell of a fire."

"She did."

"I wouldn't take it out on her, Joe."

"Do you think she really believed Mike was drinking?"

"Probably. She kept telling me she was only reporting what she saw and smelled."

"But there were no liquor smells this trip?" Joe asked, just to make sure the verdict was unequivocal.

"None."

"I feel a lot better, Larry. Christ, do I feel better! Sorry to have to put you through this."

"We *had* to know, right? You think you could arrange for Mike to take out 15 next week instead of his regular trip? It would give me a good six hours in the cockpit with him, and if everything is okay, we'll forget this whole business."

"I should be able to fix it up. Let's see, ordinarily he would be going out again in five days—"

"Eight days would be better for me," Larry interrupted, "if it's possible. I notice he has a very light schedule this month. I don't think it would cause him any problems."

"Okay, I'll see what I can do."

It was 9:30 when Mike awoke the next morning. His head was fuzzy as a nurse entered with a bright good-morning and lifted the blinds. It was sunny outside and Mike noticed the windows had no wire mesh. The room was decorated in orange and yellow with a Winslow Homer print on the wall. The rug on the floor was plush, expensive.

"How are you today?" she asked.

"Feel sort of funny—musty."

"You'll get over that. Take these two pills. Here's our breakfast menu and *The New York Times*," she said, placing the paper on the nightstand.

Mike obediently swallowed the capsules.

"Incidentally, you have an appointment with Dr. Jameson at eleven. We have a gym with a pool and an indoor tennis court. I've scheduled you for a massage later, if that's all right."

"Yes, thank you." A massage would be great, Mike thought. He checked off bacon and eggs and gave the menu back to the nurse. In the private bath he took a shower and shaved. He felt considerably better and the events of the previous day seemed like a far-off nightmare.

Mike walked out of the large manor house toward a new brick building. It was a clear day and he felt good; no morning drinks. He was back across the line. Inside the building was a small gym where several men were going through exercises. They were obviously wealthy, middle-aged businessmen on the dry-out run. Farther on there was a solarium, a small hot whirlpool, and a small swimming pool beyond that. Mike introduced himself to the chief physiotherapist, who showed him around. He took a swim, then went to the steam room, and later he rested upon a table as a big, burly masseur worked him over. At 11:00, Mike was back in the main building waiting to see Court Jameson.

"You didn't have a drink this morning?" the doctor said.

"Just pills."

"Mike, I made a bad mistake in letting you take that flight out. Coming off the booze is often worse than being on it."

"It would have been okay if the head hadn't broken."

"I was going to ground you, but last time after that dissertation about your flying judgment I thought you could make it. Anyhow, you're going to have to drink something today. I think we can drop down to six ounces. If you can get by today and tomorrow at that level, we're in good shape. I want you to go out and buy another jigger, just like before, and keep up your log entries."

"Do I fly next week?"

"When next week?"

"Monday."

"Five days? Well, if I can get you stabilized at six ounces, maybe less, without anything during the day, you can go. If not, then call in sick."

"I think I can do it, I'm sure I can."

"Okay, then. Let's get back to your autobiography and pick up where we left off. You're a licensed pilot now. You have a scholarship to the university and you're crop-dusting."

"Right. During my freshman year my mother died of a heart attack. I was quite broken up and my father seemed to age overnight. The fifties' land boom in Florida was beginning and we sold off sixteen acres at a good price. But it was all too much for him, losing a son in the war, then my mother. In a way, he gave up. He just sat on the porch; in fact, he died sitting on the porch. That was the year I graduated—1953."

"Good marks?"

"Not bad."

"Did you fly in the service, Mike?"

"No, I never went in. At the time I was spraying soybeans during the famine years in India, so I got out of it with an agricultural dispensation."

"What did you want to do after you graduated?"

"Spray crops, just like I'd been doing. I had this idea of organizing the sprayers into a co-op, upgrading the equipment, maybe buying into a fertilizer plant someday. By that time I was married to Jean."

"We haven't talked much about that, have we?"

"She was very pretty, the sexiest woman I ever knew—she could blow your cock off. I told you I met her on an Ag field. We were married and for a while

I loved her very much, but slowly it began to come apart."

"What happened?"

"Well, when the sex let up, when it wasn't new anymore, there was nothing behind it. She just spent money like crazy and criticized me for flying."

"If you wanted to be a crop duster, how did you end up with the airlines?"

"That's a long story and not a very happy one."

"I'd like to hear about it," Court said, taking out his pipe and settling down more comfortably, bringing his feet further on top of the desk.

"As I said, I really wanted to spray crops. It was high-paying outdoor work and I liked low-level precision flying. The guys along the spraying routes were a bunch of tuned-up characters. For instance, during the War there were guys in their sixties laying down the fertilizers, old beat-up drunks who couldn't make the air force, and a group of kids too young for the draft. I just fell in love with it. After we were married, I continued spraying. I took Jean along and we hit all the country towns up in tobacco land. I had my own plane, a Stearman. Damned nice job. Well, Jean would drive along from town to town in this cranky old Chevy station wagon we had and meet me wherever I would land to load up on spray.

"We didn't have a real home except for an apartment back in Fort Lauderdale; most of the time was spent on the circuit and we lived in motels. I remember a tobacco job, hell of a lot of acreage up near Winston-Salem. I'd been spraying for about twelve hours a day and one night Jean told me the big bird was on the way. I wasn't surprised because we spent most of our time in bed drinking—spray and screw, spray and screw, spray and screw—not a bad life, I figured. I was bringing home about five hundred a week after expenses—clear—five hundred a week. I was twenty."

"I thought you said you graduated from the University of Florida," Court interrupted.

"That's right. I went when I was sixteen. I sort of skipped the fourth grade. Well, I didn't really skip. You know, it was one of those rural schools and they figured they had to have at least five kids for a teacher below the eighth grade. I was the only one going into the fourth grade so they just didn't have a fourth grade that year. It didn't matter because they could have cut ten grades out and it would have been all the same. The teachers were so old and tired they didn't give a shit, so most of the time we just fooled around.

"I graduated from the university when I was twenty. Anyhow, Jean was knocked up and I was pretty happy about it. I sort of wanted a son. Well, this night in one of the Gator Hole places she said to me that I'd have to settle down. It got to me. Our first blowout. I thought I was settled down. Hell, how many guys twenty have their own fifteen-thousand-dollar plane, a college degree with a lot of Ag courses, 3,900 hours in their log book, and a damned good client list along the crop-spraying route? I was thinking about a second plane—making a real business out of it.

"Jean said we couldn't raise a kid in motels and Gator Holes. I knew she was right about that, but I figured she could go back to Lauderdale and I would fly the dusting season, come on back for a long sugar cane and citrus season. I'd base the ship in Lauderdale and just be out for the soybeans and maybe a little cotton in southern Georgia. I told her I'd forget the Carolina tobacco.

"She just wouldn't listen. There was another problem. She saw one of the guys go in. The pilot lost power on takeoff from New Bern, North Carolina, and the fool tried to come around. He spun in and the plane exploded. Jean was sitting right there and saw it. She said it would happen to me someday. I told her I was a much better pilot than that. She said if you love me, you'll settle down. I got kind of pissed off and asked her what the hell I was supposed to do. I'm a pilot. That's all I know.

"She suggested I go to law school or learn a profession. Now what the shit would I do in law school? I didn't care about a fancy profession, I already had what I wanted. I was never anything but a rural kid who loved Florida and planes. I had a thing about dusty roads and big clouds and I thought crop spraying was the greatest thing in life. Still do.

"Then, Jean says maybe I should fly for an airline. When she first said that, I laughed, laughed my ass off. Me in a uniform flying an airliner. Do you know that up to that time I had only flown in a closed cockpit three times? I was an open cockpit guy. Shit, I sat outside with goggles and felt the wind and smelled the goddamned oil in that big old radial up front of me, and goddamnit, I'd know every change in the engine. That was my life—sniffing hot oil, seeing the rows drift by, pulling up at the last moment when I came to the end of a row. I'd pull that stick back and feed in the power. I never missed a tobacco plant. I knew what I was doing. Half the clowns would miss plants on the section line.

"But she kept on my ass. We began screwing less, arguing more. Finally I said fuck it and I gave up a cotton job in Alabama and we returned to Lauderdale. I remember flying through a rainstorm somewhere south of Athens, Georgia, on my way back to Florida and suddenly I wanted to go into a right bank and fly away. Forever."

There was a long pause and Mike stared at Court Jameson.

"Forever? What do you mean?"

"I should have flown away, right there in that rainstorm. I sensed trouble coming but I didn't know what kind—a screwed-up marriage. I kept on going, though, and that night I landed at Lauderdale and decided to have it out right there."

"Were you angry?"

"Goddamned right I was."

"What was your solution?"

"It wasn't law school, maybe the airlines. I just didn't know. But then Jean said she had spoken to her mother about it and that was all I had to hear. In the end I gave in and told her I would investigate the airline situation.

"The next day I flew down to Burnside-Ott Aviation in Miami, one of those factory flight schools. They told me I could enter their program and get my instrument and ATR rating in about six or seven months. They showed me some placement requests from airlines, said I would be making about eleven thousand to start. Hell, I was already making over twenty; I figured that would cool Jean off but it didn't.

"Her father picked up the phone and called a friend at Eastern who told him a captain was getting well over twenty-five thousand and it was going up. I signed with Burnside-Ott to get my ATR and Jean went back to work for that fake flower plant in Lauderdale. Then came the second blowup; who was going to pay for the course? Five thousand dollars. I needed time in a DC-3 and that cost $190.00 an hour; we had a little money saved but I still owed something on the plane.

"I wanted to keep that bird. I really wanted to keep her just to fly around in and I asked Jean if her father could lend me the money. With a steady airline job I could pay him back, but she said, 'If you think I'm going to ask my father for money, you're crazy!' I stood there on the edge of the field one day and watched some strange guy climb into my Stearman and fly away and it just about broke my heart. I didn't sell an old biplane, I sold myself.

"Anyhow, I went to flight school every morning and worked like hell to pass the ground courses. I had more time than half the instructors so I made it out of there in four months with a fresh ATR. Matter of fact, I rather liked sitting in the cockpit of the DC-3. I

felt like a lord, someone kind of special and I liked instrument flying, so that part of it was okay.

"Then came time to find the job. There were a lot
of Korean-trained pilots around so the job market
wasn't exactly red hot. I wanted to fly for a southern
airline and I tried them all, the large carriers like
Eastern and National, then Piedmont and Southern.

"Finally, the placement department at school
called asking if I wanted a copilot's position with
Northeast. I'd hardly heard of Northeast and going up
there didn't interest me. Jean said she wanted to try it,
so up to Boston we go. I started flying DC-3 equipment. They had their own school in Boston and we
lived in a small apartment in Cambridge. That March,
Jean had a miscarriage. I think she always blamed it
on me. Right after that, I went on the line. It was wild
flying—little fields, worst goddamned weather, wings
icing up half the time."

"Did you like it?"

"Yeah, I did."

"If your whole orientation was crop-dusting, the
South, I can't imagine you flying for Northeast."

"Well, I was surprised frankly. Boston was a great
place and the airline was small, kind of informal. It
was really beautiful flying over Vermont, landing in
Rutland, Concord, a lot of little towns, especially up
in Maine. When the spring came, I could look down
and see the crops starting to grow. Then we'd fly
down to Nantucket and Martha's Vineyard in the summer months. I got to know some of the regular passengers. It was long before sky-jacking. We used to
come out of the cockpit and talk to the people. Then
we bought this house in Needham—nice little place and
life was okay. After about two years with Northeast, Jean and I had another one of our little talks.

"She didn't think I was making enough money, wanted me to fly jets for a major carrier. I told
her Northeast was my kind of airline. I loved it by
then. It was beautiful in the fall and I began to know

the routes, the landmarks. All the station managers became friends. Somehow, I thought I was really doing something important. The railroads has gone bust in New England and we provided about the only service for a lot of people. When we'd land at Franconia, it was an event, the coming of the plane was the outside world dropping in. Jean had spoken to her father again and he told her that Northeast was in financial trouble. Hell, they always were so that was nothing new.

"Jean was pregnant again by this time so I applied to some larger lines. In 1957 I was hired by IA to fly copilot on their Convair equipment—short routes, Indianapolis, Cleveland, Buffalo."

"Were you drinking?"

"Yeah."

"How much?"

"Couple of drinks a night."

"Against the rules?"

"That's right, but I never flew hung over."

"What was IA like compared to Northeast?"

"All the difference in the world. It was a big, highly organized carrier—forms to be filled in, all the chicken shit. We moved into the Ridgefield house and things began to sour up. I made my transition to jets when the 727's came in and the money was much better, but the bills were bigger, too. Almost from the first year we were in Ridgefield, I knew I wasn't going to like it. Then I realized the marriage wasn't going to last or if it did, it would only be a front for the children."

"Let's see, you have two daughters, sixteen and thirteen."

"That's right. Jean and I started arguing all the time—fighting. We usually made up in bed. She still liked her sex, but we haven't slept together for some time. Then I took a job teaching at Danbury Airport. It was great getting up in the morning and going over there and talking to the kids. Sitting around the hangar bull-shitting."

"Like Florida in the forties and early fifties?"

"Yeah, like the old Homestead Ag field. At least, I was close to planes and flying, but there's no money in instructing and I realized we weren't going to stay on top of the bills. About that time my wife decided we should go into the plastic flower business. The gimmick was the flowers smelled. They didn't smell, they stank! We did fairly well and our product line grew, but I hated every fucking goddamned minute!"

"Were you drinking during the day at this time?"

"Yes. I used to have one or two before lunch. I bought this small refrigerator. I remember the first drink in the morning. It was at home. I just needed it somehow. Then it became a habit."

"How long ago was this, Mike?"

"A couple of years, I guess."

"And did it progress? Did you eventually need several to get going?"

"No, I stayed at the same level."

Court Jameson looked down at his yellow pad. "Let's backtrack for a second. You liked flying the DC-3's . . ."

"Yeah, because it took some piloting just to find out where the hell you were. You couldn't push a button, letting some electronic device take you to the VOR station. At IA our equipment became more and more sophisticated—more paper work and company bullshit that took up more time than the flying. It all got too big. Autopilots for the autopilot. What the hell was I? I began to think I wasn't needed or maybe I was nothing more than a Greyhound bus driver. He doesn't even have an autopilot."

"So the job changed around you?"

"That's right. I tried to get some of the old feeling back by restoring the biplane and doing some instructing in Cessna 150's."

"When did you meet the girl you mentioned—Pat Simpson?"

"About three years ago."

"Are you in love with her?"

"Yes, I am," Mike said emphatically.

Court got up from his chair and walked about the large room that had been the library of the private estate. Mike watched the thin man framed against the light of the big bow window. He sensed the next question.

"If you weren't in love with your job or your wife, why didn't you do something about it?"

"I did. I drank."

"If you had all the options in the world, if you could do anything you wanted, had all the money, how would you change things?"

"I'd like to marry Pat. We talked about it, oh, maybe a year ago and it was sort of mutually agreed that we'd wait until my daughters were a little older so they could understand the situation, but the tension, our constant bickering—the kids know something's wrong and it's hard on 'em. Maybe a divorce would be better for everybody than living in the middle of a squabble. Debbie's the one I was worried about. She's a solemn little kid, but I think she'd be okay. She's almost fourteen now and she's got a good head on her shoulders."

"Assuming you work your personal relationships out satisfactorily, what about the job, your work?"

"I'd like to buy a couple of Ag planes and develop a route through the crop counties starting in Mississippi with soybeans, moving along to cotton, sugar in central Florida, finally winding up the loop in the deep citrus country. Then it would almost be time to start back in old 'Miss' again. I think I'd go into a fertilizer plant of some kind, organize the pilots into a co-op. In fact, I've talked to quite a few of 'em. They say the idea isn't bad. Even if I didn't start a fertilizer factory, I could at least set up a distribution point— buy wholesale, make a couple of cents a pound. It wouldn't be bad."

"Do you have the money for that kind of operation?"

"I've saved some. I could sell my Waco if I had to—she'd bring in forty thousand, maybe a little less."

"And that would make you happy?"

"Yes."

"You'd be giving up a high-paying job with the airlines."

"I'm not going anywhere this way. I want to make a break."

"As soon as we pull you off the booze, Mike, you'll have to come out the other side with something new, something else to look at, hope for. Without it, you'll be back on the juice in a month."

"Yeah, I know, but I'll tell you something—I'm not going to let it get to me again like it did."

"Good."

There was a lengthy pause. Mike seemed to be trying to say something and Court thought he knew what it was.

"Where was I heading?" Mike finally blurted out.

"How far down were you going?"

"Yeah, where was the end?"

"There're two endings, Mike: some die and are buried; others die and go on living. There are bums on the Bowery who have been drunk for years. They should be dead; their livers are nothing but fat, but the men still go on functioning. Pride collapsed before the body in those cases."

"You don't really think I was going to end up that way?"

"Not exactly. Most alcoholics can't drink. You could and, as we said, that was part of your problem. Your system handled it very well to a point, but sooner or later, something had to happen because nobody can drink constantly, progressively, without running into trouble."

"Philadelphia?"

"Exactly. Mike, you do realize how lucky you were?"

"I came damned close, I know."

"If this had gone on much longer, we would have had a more difficult job."

Mike told the doctor about Pat coming east; he

thought that might be the first step. In the long run Mike had to make a decision and that time was coming up fast. During the rest of the wind-down period, the pilot was told to report to the hospital daily on an out-patient basis, and they would continue to talk. To get his mind off the withdrawal symptoms, Court suggested that he swim each day and perhaps try some tennis on the indoor courts.

The day after the trip Joe Barnes called the stewardesses into his office. Nancy was thoroughly shaken and Joe saw it, but a heavy burden had been lifted from the chief pilot's back and he could afford to be magnanimous.

"First of all, you did the right thing. It's obvious that Captain Hagen isn't drinking in the lavatory. He was taking some kind of pills for an allergy. I'll talk to him about this when I see him at lunch this week. I want to thank you. Don't be afraid to come to this office any time. None of us will mention this again. It's over."

That's all there was to it. The girls went to the FOBB's cubicle. The senior supervisor spoke softly for the first time in years.

"I'll add my appreciation—it wasn't easy coming to me. I know what was going through your minds," she said. "Thanks very much, both of you. Don't worry about anything."

The week went well. Mike bought another small thermos—for safety's sake, he told himself—and again painted the rings on a new jigger. He continued to paste in the stars; there weren't too many now. He was down to the six-ounce level and holding. It was the third day in a row that he had reached 5:00 without taking a drink and he rolled open the hangar at Danbury. He started the old bird and flew her around the pattern one time.

It was his special victory flight.

Mike had been told that once in a while the

spooker need might catch up with him and he should take a drink if he had to. During the late afternoons of that week he felt the urgency and wondered if he would ever be able to get by the cocktail hour without a drink. But he had come a long way and he was proud of himself. The day after he flew *Alice* around the Danbury Airport, Mike took the limousine to pick up his car at JFK. It was the day he was going into the city to meet the brass.

They ate at the Harvard Club—Joe Barnes, Cliff McCullen, Fitz, and Peter Hanscom. They talked about inflight procedures, the chances of the December 10 incident happening again. Everyone ordered drinks before lunch. Mike decided on a dry sherry, not to impress the others; he was out to impress himself, but when the sherry came, he thought it was much too dry and only took one taste, which Joe Barnes noticed.

As they stood in front of the Harvard Club, Fitz came over to Mike.

"Did you ever think of management, Captain Hagen—moving over to Third Avenue?"

"Not really."

"Well, if you ever do, give me a ring. Plenty of good opportunities on the management team. There are a lot of challenges ahead and we always need men who can think, who know airline operations."

Mike smiled and thanked the vice-president, but running through his head was a small laugh. If they only knew how little he cared about airline management—the books, memos, manuals—a treadmill of trivia from which the pilot was desperately trying to extricate himself. He shook hands with the clean-faced, immaculately turned-out executives; they went east on Forty-fourth Street and Mike walked west. He didn't know why but he went the other way.

Twelve

Mike sat in his study, contemplating the changes in his life. Much of the clutter and chaos had begun to clear. As fewer stars were fastened into the small black notebook, a new lucidity came to him. But something Jameson had said began to gnaw at him: "When you come off the booze, there better be something to replace it." The pilot was in that soft gray area where the blackness of a long tunnel begins to lighten just before it washes into the stark brilliance of the open air—hard reality. There were new verities far removed from his half-drunken dreams of the forties and fifties: the shade of old biplane wings, the cold Dr. Peppers and Moon Pies and big Baby Ruth bars for a nickel, the banter of tough-edged cowboys who flew the groves and drank at the Gator Holes listening to Woody Guthrie sing about a country that was on the way out.

Those things were gone. The pilot was certain that the old planes were in junkpiles or museums, or in hangars like the one in Danbury—refuges for ancient Wacos. Maybe everything was on the scrap heap. It was easy to sit in a psychiatrist's office and jabber on about a rural Florida youth, but to return to those times, a way of life long gone, was a pathetic, whimsical goal.

Mike was intelligent enough to know that his beloved daredevils were no longer sliding glued-up biplanes into dirt-strips. They had been replaced by
young, highly trained men flying sophisticated, expensive equipment—even choppers—and, too, the spray
business might have gone big-time too.

Chucking in the towel on a $55,000-a-year cap-
tain's job for a crop-spraying venture appeared more
and more frightening, but what were the options? He
could report to Third Avenue and become an executive, although that new life might evoke the same old
problems; there was instructing at maybe $10,000 a
year; or flying with a third-level carrier. He'd have to
develop a plan.

Mike noticed something else as day by day the
craving for spookers lifted; he saw and smelled more,
as if he were looking at a complicated painting and
suddenly discovered hidden details and colors in the
shadows. The branches on the maple tree in his front
yard seemed larger than he remembered. Could they
have grown?

Had he been away that long?

Things at the Danbury field began to look different: the hangar for old *Alice* seemed smaller and
the brutish Waco's color seemed brighter now. The office, the fucking upstairs world of fake exotic flowers,
was worse than he imagined; his house seemed sloppier.

The pilot slammed the doors shut and walked out
into the yard. It was a rather mild, wet afternoon and
a flight of ducks were laboring overhead disturbing
the silence. The rain soaked through his heavy Irish
wool sweater, which smelled of new moisture. He
plodded around on the soft earth looking back at the
huge house that seemed to have grown during his
spookers. He knew, as Dr. Jameson said, that it was
decision time. If he continued with the airlines in the
same job, the upstairs flowers, the heavy financial
pressures of suburban living with a woman he no
longer knew, he would be back at Ellen's Place in no
time.

But could he change everything at once? First, he had to tell Jean that it was over. Then, away from the large house and the flower business, he would be with Pat and perhaps, he might call Fitz and say he would consider the executive job. They could take an apartment in New York; put *Alice* in a hangar at Teterboro and fly her on weekends. That was a realistic goal; the vice-president had offered him a job and not many pilots received that sort of treatment from senior management. Then, while he was collecting his checks at Third Avenue, he would investigate the crop-spraying business.

He told Jean he had to talk with her. They sat in the study and she looked a little bored, as if she knew what was coming.

"Jean, I guess you know our marriage is over." There was no other way except to come right out with it.

"Darling, it's been over for some time," she said. "Hadn't you noticed?"

"No sense in dragging this out."

"There was no sense in getting married in the first place, if we get right down to it."

"So how do we do it without hurting the girls?"

"I don't know," she said, getting up and moving to the bar. "We could get lawyers and fight like everyone ⌐ but I don't think we need that. You, obviously. ⌐ve someone."

"Yes. '

"Maybe I do, too, I don't know. I want a lot more than you can give me, Mike. I'm enlarging the flower business, moving it to New York."

"I see. I might go back down South and spray crops again. I'm not sure of how much support I can muster up," he said.

"Well, I haven't told you yet, but I obtained some new financing for the business and a partner in New York. He's a lawyer. I might marry him. Also, I've spoken to a few real estate dealers about the house.

They think we might get an offer of $140,000 with the price of land around here as high as it is."

"That much?" Mike was very surprised at the figure and felt a burden lifting. Perhaps it had been a prudent investment. They only paid $65,000 and the mortgage had been reduced considerably.

They sat talking calmly for a while and it was the most sympathetic and rational conversation they had had in years.

Mike called Pat that evening and the following morning he drove out to JFK to meet her. They put the bags in the car and went directly to Ellen's Place.

"Where are we?" Pat asked.

"I thought I would come back here—for the last time."

"What is it, a bar?"

"One of the snappiest, and the best hidden. When I was going out in the morning, I'd stop by here to fill up my thermos and have a spooker. I want to say good-bye to Ellen and to a lot of other things. She thinks I work in Boston. I'll tell her you're my wife, which you're going to be."

Pat understood the significance of the visit and she entered the grimy, dark place that smelled of stale beer. She could not imagine Mike coming here to drink and she was overcome with pity, but when they slipped into a booth and he told Ellen he wanted a Coke, she knew he had won. Pat had a glass of milk and finally, Mike stood, and a big smile bloomed on his face as he crossed toward Ellen.

"Ellen, I'm being transferred and I won't see you anymore. Good luck."

"Sure, good luck—whatever you do."

Mike walked out of Ellen's Place forever and they drove north to the Hilton Inn in Rye where Pat checked in. During dinner he told her about the talk with Jean, and Mike finally said, "Would you like to be the wife of an airline executive or a crop sprayer or something?"

She smiled and leaned over and kissed the big, red-faced pilot.

"Anything you want, darling."

"I'm just about off the booze now, down to four ounces, but I want a new life. I'm not trapped any-more."

They talked about living in New York. She was going for an interview with an advertising agency, and the pilot kept thinking about working on Third Avenue. Other people did it and with Pat there, maybe he could survive.

They slept together that night at the Hilton Inn and early the following morning he took her up in *Alice*; they flew over his house, and then he pulled an inside loop, and Pat screamed, partly from joy, partly from fright. Everything seemed perfect then; he had made it.

The next morning Joe Barnes called asking Mike to take out 15, the JFK-LAX nonstop, with Larry Zanoff flying in the right seat. Mike agreed and for the next three days he wondered whether or not he should carry the spooker aboard. Perhaps he should, because it would be a long trip, six or more hours, depending upon the head winds. Every once in a while, just as Court Jameson had predicted, he felt the need for a few ounces.

"Coming off completely is difficult," Court had told him once. "The last few ounces, the bottom lines on the jigger glass are the worst."

But Mike still didn't know if he wanted to leave it all behind. He liked a little booze and he knew his limits now. He had his final session with Jameson just before the nonstop to Los Angeles.

"Is this graduation?" Mike asked.

"I think so, but when things begin to go wrong, and they will from time to time, don't be tempted into reaching for the bottle. Come back and let me help you. You've proved that you have self-control, Mike, and that's the most important thing."

"I want to really thank you."

"You did it yourself."

Mike left Court's office that day a confident man.

It began as a light snowstorm, a low pressure off the Carolina coast that deepened as it raced across Virginia and then out into the Atlantic. The forecasters predicted a limited fall. That was changed to a heavy snow warning as the low veered toward New York, leaving five to eleven inches of downfall behind. By 9:00 on the morning of Mike's scheduled departure for Los Angeles, the snow committee at JFK had been called in. At 10:00 the first few flakes appeared, blown by a sharp wind from the southwest. What had begun as a light fall suddenly intensified and large flakes were hurled through the air as a snow cover began to spread out along the JFK taxiways and runways. Shortly before noon on February 20, everything was white and the snow committee closed two runways for plowing, 22-Right and 31-Left. At that time the wind was gusting 14 knots.

Mike was planning to take a cab out to JFK; he had a three-ounce drink at lunch and then went into Pat's room at the Hilton and slept for a few hours. When she woke him, it was 4:00 P.M. and he looked from the window and saw the snow. It was already a heavy accumulation and the pilot picked up the phone and called IA Operations.

"This is Captain Hagen. I'm taking 15 out tonight. Do you have an ETA on the inbound equipment?"

"Just a minute. Yes, it left L.A. on time—1000—no delays enroute, but we have half-hour inbound delays now."

"What about outbound?"

"No delays yet; snow's not too bad down here. They're plowing; I'd say at the worst 15 will be away from the gate maybe twenty to forty minutes late."

IA had two nonstop dinner flights to the coast that usually went out at 80–90 percent load factor.

Flight No. 1, a 747, was their traditional red-carpet service, a 6:00 P.M. departure with an arrival in L.A. around 8:30 P.M. Pacific time. IA's second nonstop of the evening was flight 15, the 7:30 departure, which usually took the spillover from 1. It also catered to those who could not leave their offices in time to make the earlier flight. Fifteen was DC-8-61 service and the plane that had been on the route for almost four months was N4962C, a Stretch 8. The F.A.A. certified the equipment airworthy in July, 1969, and it was delivered into the IA fleet on a long-term lease from a Chicago bank the same month.

The plane was configured exactly like N8907C, the equipment used on 467, with 28 first-class seats and 175 tourist. The plane's maintenance log showed that the required 180-hour special inspection had been carried out two weeks earlier. The front brakes were checked for wear, also the nose steering, which had been written up as difficult. It was noted in several write-ups that the left landing gear was slow in retracting and during the 180-hour inspection it was found that a strut bolt on the boggie trim cycling unit was out. This was replaced along with two main undercarriage tires and two tires on the nose wheel assembly as required by the F.A.A. parameters: 49 landings for nose wheels; 86 for main undercarriage gear; and 209 landings for brake assemblies. On February 20, the tires were Goodyear, the brakes, Bendix. The plane had shown no chronic maintenance problems in the three important areas: airframe, systems, and power plant.

The equipment was on the daily JFK-LAX route, spending each night in Los Angeles, and when 14, the inbound service, landed in New York at 6:25 P.M. on February 20, no one on the flight deck entered a maintenance report. The trip was thirty minutes late arriving at JFK and 15 was set up to go out at 8:30 P.M.

It had been a difficult week for snow removal operations at JFK. Several frontal systems had pushed through and the snow committee, composed of pilots from various carriers along with airport officials, had been called in three times to work out a plan of attack so the airport's snow removal manpower and equipment could be used to best advantage. The residual accumulations around the airport that hadn't melted because of persistent below-freezing temperatures measured a total of twenty-two inches from the three snowfalls. On the afternoon of the 20th the snow committee was called in again to assess runway conditions, but they only had two runways, 22-Left and 22-Right, to consider now, for the wind had accelerated to forty knots, sustained, which meant the other runways couldn't be used because their headings were too divergent from the prevailing wind direction to permit safe takeoff and landing operations.

The crews had worked for five straight hours plowing and blowing a six-inch accumulation off the two actives, but by 3:50 P.M., the snow had turned to rain and the temperature had risen to about thirty-two degrees, forming icing conditions on both runways.

The snow committee was watching the situation closely. Continuous aircraft operation and wind often make a runway patchy so that one part of it may be slick while another section remains rough; this can affect an aircraft's braking.

Twenty-two-Right opened to traffic at 4:20 that afternoon while they plowed the parallel runway, 22-Left. The rain continued, the temperature hung around thirty-two degrees, and traction was almost impossible to achieve without constant sanding. All that afternoon and evening they alternated runways, closing one, operating the other.

Mike and Pat left for JFK at 5:00 P.M., allowing themselves extra time for traffic delays. They arrived at the employee parking lot at 6:15 and Mike brought Pat inside the green doors to see Operations. As soon as they entered the impersonal, dingy, airless room, she understood why Mike detested it. Captains leaned against the counters studying maps and harried men walked around gathering dispatch papers for the outbound crews. The stewardesses sat in clusters, polishing nails and chattering. It was noisy and confusing but it was here that every airline flight was born. Entering Operations totally sober was another victory for Mike, like drinking a Coke at Ellen's Place, or flying old *Alice* around the Danbury pattern.

Mike and Larry Zanoff discussed the flight in Operations after Pat left to purchase her ticket; there wasn't much to discuss. The computer had told them where to go.

"The front is beyond us," Larry said. "Some turbulence up to nine. After that it should be relatively easy. Situation's local."

Just after 7:00 the sign was posted at gate six on the left concourse:

FLIGHT 15—DC-8 NONSTOP SERVICE
TO LOS ANGELES WILL DEPART AT
8:30 P.M.

In addition to Larry and Mike, there were seven others in the crew: the flight engineer and six cabin attendants, five female, one male. IA's flight 14, the inbound equipment, was always operated with a Los Angeles-based crew that stayed overnight, picking up the first West Coast outbound in the morning. The two nonstop evening departures from New York were covered by local personnel.

The flight engineer on 15 that night was George Gibbons, twenty-eight years old with 3,890 hours as a second officer, 2,200 in the DC-8-61. He knew the plane well, having served on the West Coast route for almost a year and a half. George was typical of most flight engineers; he totally comprehended his board and he was thoroughly interested in the power plant he helped monitor and control. He was devoted to his turbines and all he wanted was to graduate to the 747's on the overseas routes where his flight pay would jump from $26,500 a year to $38,000—top bracket for a second officer.

George came up and identified himself to Mike, who was studying the winds aloft chart. The pilot had never flown with Gibbons before.

"We have a high-velocity westerly flow tonight," Mike said. "Better take on another 8,000 pounds. What are we loading?"

"1-A," George answered.

"Okay, rework your load calculation and update the computer."

"Yes, sir."

"How near gross are you ordinarily?" Mike asked the flight engineer.

"Within 20,000 pounds."

"That heavy, huh?" Mike said.

Among George's pre-flight duties was an inspection of the exterior of the aircraft, a series of visual checks involving the turbines, control surfaces, and undercarriage.

Louise Conners, a pretty blonde of about twenty-nine, came up to Mike and introduced herself as the senior stewardess that evening.

"This weather's local," Mike said. "We shouldn't have too much trouble once we're out of here, about twenty minutes or so into the flight."

Louise smiled and thanked the captain. She had never flown with Mike Hagen; at least, she didn't think so and he had the kind of handsome, outdoors face she'd remember.

At 7:22 that evening Larry filed the MFP. The routing was not unusual for JFK-LAX nonstops, a heavily traveled and cluttered piece of airspace slanting a little southwest out of New York, north of Pittsburgh, below Chicago, to the "Bradford, Illinois vortac"; there the flight would lock onto "old J-64," the preferred high-altitude jet route that would take them across a dozen VOR stations, generally on a heading of 258 degrees magnetic, and down into the Los Angeles terminal area.

Louise and her cabin attendants left Operations together and walked along the jammed concourse toward gate six on the left side of IA's terminal. When they reached the gate, it was more packed than usual and they groaned when they saw the passengers bunching up around the check-in counter, waving tickets and spitting complaints at the two harassed agents. The stewardesses, who had been hoping for a half-full plane, knew immediately that the plane would go out loaded. Often in weather like this passengers cancelled their reservations, but tonight was different. When the snow stopped, many people decided to go ahead with their plans, and by 7:10 that night, one hour and twenty minutes before the delayed departure of 15, twelve wait-listed passengers had already shown up at the gate. The agents were praying the computer wouldn't back up; if the flight was oversold, the passengers' wrath would be taken out on them.

Pat arrived in the gate area and stood just outside the railing; there were no seats left inside the enclosure but Mike had told her she could probably board early. She felt deliciously happy. There was no question in her mind that Mike had licked his drinking problem, and since Jean had agreed to a divorce, her own future appeared rosy indeed. Pat studied the clusters of anxious people: two nuns mingling in the crowd, a little girl, perhaps five or six, clutching a doll as well as her mother, four or five deeply tanned, flashy-looking television or movie executives. Finally, Brenda Moore, a TV talk-show personality, in mink coat and dark glasses, approached the gate flanked by two well-groomed men, probably agents or publicity people. They were accompanied by IA's passenger service representative.

Pat glanced down the concourse again and she saw Larry and Mike coming with their heavy black flight bags; their confident air and slight swagger told everyone that these were high-time veterans; men who handled giant aircraft with agility and experience, unafraid of nights like this when the wind lashed the large wraparound windows of the gate area with freezing rain.

"Hi," Mike said, "we'll put you on now."

Mike introduced Larry Zanoff, who went on ahead as they stepped over to the agent.

"This is a very good friend of mine, Miss Simpson. All right if we board her early?"

"Yes, Sir, as soon as the girls are ready."

"Full tonight?"

"Captain, I could take a hundred more if we had the space. Number 1 went out light."

Mike walked down the loading ramp, the spooker in his left pocket hidden by the overcoat that he dropped over his arm. Upon entering the aircraft, Mike went to the first lavatory and stored his thermos and looked at himself in the mirror. Not bad, he thought. His face had lost much of the old puffiness, especially around the eyes, and the telltale rivulets on his left side seemed lighter, almost blending into the apple red of his cheek. It was nearly eight hours since he downed the three-ouncer in White Plains and the pilot felt extremely well; the nap had helped and he said a short prayer of thanksgiving. He was over the worst of his problems, and surprisingly, Jean had been reasonable and understanding. He could now be with Pat. Even though he had not made up his mind about his future work he believed there was much opportunity for a qualified high-time, versatile pilot. He was adaptable and could handle anything that went up in the air.

Mike was happy. Much of his self-respect and pride had returned.

When he entered the cockpit he noticed the force with which the hail was hitting the front windshield.

"Christ, what's the runway visual range?" Mike asked as he slipped into the left seat.

"Three thousand. Doesn't look it, does it?"

"Sure as hell doesn't," Mike said, peering about; he could hardly see the line of red lights on top of the terminal.

As the two pilots were going through their paperwork, George Gibbons was moving around underneath the giant transport. The hail was blasting him in the face as he circled the main undercarriage. Everything on the visual walk-around satisfied his cautious eye. George did not linger at each inspection station; he spent just enough time to convince himself that N4962C passed her test.

The swelling passengers, standbys, and visitors filled the lounge area and overflowed into the concourse to the next gate. From where she stood, Pat could see the giant tail of the DC-8 through the beaded window; finally, a group was led toward her—the small blond child with her mother, two nuns, Brenda Moore, and a very elderly gentleman—the preboards. The agent told Pat to follow.

They walked down the loading ramp toward the plane. Inside the first-class cabin they felt the blast of cold air rushing in through the open galley door where the stewardesses, still in their overcoats, were taking in the last of the catering supplies. Seeing the group, Louise stepped out of the galley. "Ladies and gentlemen," she said, "until we close this door, I think you'll be more comfortable in the back of the plane." And she led the preboards to the first few rows of the coach section.

Pat noticed the little girl was starting to cry at the inevitable separation from her mother.

"Now, it'll be a wonderful trip and your Aunt Flo will be on the other end when you arrive."

The mother smiled at Pat Simpson, who exchanged a sympathetic glance. Pat got up and sat beside the youngster.

"Why don't we make friends," Pat said to the child. "We'll sit together. I'm going to Los Angeles, too."

"This is Marsha's first flight. My sister will be meeting her on the other end. I hope she'll be all right."

One of the girls in the rear of the plane came up and gave the child some Junior Stewardess Wings, but she still whimpered.

"Honey," Pat said, "I know the captain. Would you like to meet him?"

The small girl stopped sniffling and a slight smile crossed her curled-up lips. Pat took the child by the hand and the mother followed as they walked through the chilly blue and white first-class cabin toward the flight deck.

"I'm a friend of Captain Hagen," Pat told Louise. "I thought she would like to meet the pilot."

The stewardess nodded and they moved forward.

"This is called the cockpit, and there's the man who is going to fly us all the way to California."

Mike turned around and saw the small girl holding a doll, and he motioned her toward him. "Come into my office," he said with a big smile.

The little girl walked forward and Mike took the child on his lap.

"See all those instruments? They're going to tell us where we are."

"I hope she won't be too much trouble," the mother said.

"We have children all the time. They settle down very quickly. The stewardess will take good care of her," Mike said, handing the child back to the mother.

"Tell the captain 'thank you.' "

The girl was shy and she simply smiled and the mother led her back to the cabin.

Pat lingered for a minute. "What a night," she said.

"Bad down here, but the upper air is forecasted to be fairly smooth. We'll be out of this stuff soon after takeoff."

The flight engineer entered the cockpit and Pat returned to her seat. By this time the galley door had been shut and the first cabin was warming up.

"Let's see, Sister, you're in 3-C and D. Would you like something hot before we take off—a cup of tea, chocolate, or coffee?" Louise asked.

"That would be nice if you have time."

At 8:15 that evening the catering vans were backed from N4962C; the galley doors were secured, and the fuel truck had also drawn away from the aircraft. The elderly scientist was taken to seat 30-A near the Jetescape door, or exit 9, on the left side of the coach cabin. The other preboards were located in the first-class section: Pat in 1-A, the first seat on the plane's left side facing the small first-class lounge; the little girl who had taken a liking to Pat sat next to her, and her mother had left the plane feeling some relief. Two rows behind, Brenda Moore sprawled in a window seat reading *Variety,* and across from her on the right side, the nuns sipped hot chocolate.

At row seven were the Jetescape doors, one on each side of the first-class cabin; they looked like emergency window exits; however, upon pulling the red handle, a whole section of the fuselage came out and a pneumatic slide appeared from under the bottom door plate. There were no seats in the way of these Jetescapes, marked on the emergency information cards as exits 3 and 4. The main cabin entry door was labeled exit 1, the door serving the first-class galley, 2. There were four over the wing window exits on the DC-8, two on each side, and halfway between the trailing edge of the wing and the last exits were two additional Jetescapes for the coach passengers; and far to the rear, serving the two left and right galleys, were the last escape doors, exits 11 and 12.

If one stands back from the DC-8-61, quite far back, and sizes up the aircraft, a thought instantly comes to mind: something's wrong; the plane is too long, too skinny. Unlike the 707, the DC-8 can be stretched and little by little the plane has grown and become a very profitable airliner because of its increased seating capacity and range.

Mike Hagen was slow in adapting to these changes. Like other "seat-of-the-panters" on the IA line, he initially thought the Stretch 8 was too long. He had trouble adjusting to the tricycle landing gear, believing that a plane should have the little wheel in back and perch on an angle like a bird; in fact, he often said planes should have their wings on top, too. His flying instincts were *quite* basic.

After a while, a long while, Mike got used to the Stretch 8 and he accepted it as a fine aircraft, but his admiration never extended to the 747. That ship was just too big for Mike Hagen.

On the far end of JFK—along the easterly border —is runway 22-Left located about 6,700 feet from the control tower. On the night of the 20th, runway visual range (RVR) was measured at 4,600 feet. "RVR" is the most important indicator for a landing. On nights like this, when the runway visual range was constantly changing, it was very carefully monitored by the JFK control tower via a complicated set of instrumentation on the end of each runway, consisting of a projector, detector, meter, and remote recorder. The meter measures the light being transmitted through the atmosphere; the determined value is translated into feet and relayed to the tower. Runway 22-Left is equipped with RVR apparatus, but 22-Right has an older, less accurate device, "RVV" (runway visibility value), which measures the visibility in miles, not feet, like the newer instruments.

On the night of the hailstorm the JFK controller could not see his active runways. The visual range was changing rapidly; at one point, it dropped to 3,500 feet and the controller could just make out the center section of 22-Right and a light smudge of ghostly yellow —the high intensities at the far end. The snow committee was in the vicinity of runways 22-Left and 22-Right visually inspecting the surfaces, monitoring the traction reports from arrived aircraft, and generally supervising the trucks working up and down the runways, trying to stay ahead of the rapidly forming and reforming ice.

The boarding passengers moved through the endless cabin slowly, stopping to put their coats in the overhead rack, looking for seat numbers—the usual confusion of a fully booked departure. Two television executives slid in behind the nuns, shoving leather cases under their seats, and chatting casually as they eyed the others who were settling down in first-class. Suddenly one of them spotted Brenda Moore.

"Brenda, darling!" the plumpish, balding man said.

He climbed out of his seat. The TV star smiled, recognizing Kurt McGovern, the executive vice-president and prime time program director of a major network.

"How are you, Brenda?" he said, leaning over a man dozing in aisle seat 3-B.

"Kurt, love. I didn't know you were in New York."

"Just a little pow-wow. Signed a marvelous nighttime adventure series. Why don't we get together after the trip?"

Louise approached, telling the executive he would have to return to his seat because he was blocking the aisle; the last of the passengers were still filtering through the first-class cabin to the rear of the plane.

The agent came onboard with the final dispatch papers and finally the heavy door of the DC-8 was swung closed. George Gibbons came out of the cockpit to make his check of the exits, and he stopped and smiled at Pat and her now-cheerful partner. Then there was a tug on the plane and slowly the aircraft was backed from the gate.

Mike was to fly the plane this night and Larry set up 120.05 on one of the radios and called clearance delivery.

"IA 15, do you have our clearance?"

"You're cleared as filed. Report leaving 3,000."

"Report leaving 3,000. IA 15."

Larry snapped the frequency selector knob over to Kennedy ground control, 121.9.

"IA 15 holding terminal area. Ready to taxi."

After a pause, the busy ground controller rattled off ground directions to runway 22-Left. He advised the aircraft there would be some departure delays because of weather conditions.

The long plane started away from the gate area as Mike nudged the thrust levers ahead. Those with their faces pressed to the glass in the terminal saw the strobe lights on the DC-8 and the buttery flow from the long line of windows, but the faces inside were only smears, obscured by the sleet and rain. The people waved as if those aboard could see them huddled at the window. As soon as the Stretch 8 was away from the partly shielded terminal area, the full extent of the night noise could be heard: the hail rattled against the plane and the little girl next to Pat looked a little scared as she tried to peer out.

"Would you like to sit by the window, dear? Then, your doll could see, too." When the child agreed, they exchanged seats.

The outside noises—wind, sleet, and the powerful Pratt and Whitneys hanging below each wing—completely drowned any cabin conversation. Most of the passengers were quiet; a few read papers. The old biophysicist in seat 30-A closed his eyes wearily and leaned back. The TV executives were silent and the nuns held onto their prayer books and looked out the dark windows on the right side. The colliding noises were new and strange to some of the passengers and they were tense. The flight attendants, who were still hanging coats and moving about the cabin, noticed the apprehension.

Besides those on the flight deck, there was one other pilot on board, Carl Smith, sitting in the coach section. He flew for American Airlines and he could relax. He knew that the hail pounding on the DC-8 wasn't a problem; the wings had been de-iced, and once they were airborne, the internal heaters would take over.

The bell rang in the cockpit and the flight engineer picked up the phone. It was Louise. "We've got a few nervous ones out here. Perhaps the captain could make a PA when he gets time."

A moment later Mike's voice came booming over the loudspeaker.

"Good evening, ladies and gentlemen, this is Captain Hagen. The noise you're hearing is, of course, hailstones. While it's annoying, it doesn't hurt the plane. Our runway visual range is now 4,500 feet, quite a bit over minimums, and the weather upstairs— about 10,000—is forecasted to be smooth. This is a frontal situation and once we're clear of the area, we can expect a good flight all the way. There'll be some takeoff delays, but I'll report the situation as we near the runway and get a look at our sequencing. So sit back and relax and we hope you enjoy your flight with us tonight. If it's any consolation, the terminal weather in Los Angeles is now 64 degrees with scattered clouds at 7,000. Thank you."

JFK's runway 22-Left begins approximately 1,200 feet from New Rockaway Boulevard, Queens, a heavily traveled street bordering the north side of the airport. Inbound flights for 22 come over a low marsh on the left side of the road where the ILS lights are set on "T" stanchions; once across the road, the planes are usually down to about 150 feet as they approach the threshold. On the airport side of New Rockaway Boulevard, some 325 feet to the west, is a creek called Thurston Basin, which is used principally for drainage, as much of JFK was constructed on filled-in tidal marsh. Approximately 690 feet on the far side of Thurston Basin begins the hard surface of runway 22-Left, 150 feet wide, 8,400 feet long.

Off to the right side of runway 22-Left and in

line with the adjacent tangential runway, 31-Right, are the projector and RVR detector, the localizer and ILS glide slope equipment; otherwise, there are no buildings or obstructions near the border of 22-Left until the very end where another localizer, projector, and detector are situated.

On the far side of 22 is Jamaica Bay, which starts 590 feet past the threshold; approach lights are mounted on pilings running about 2,800 feet into the bay. (From the other end, runway 22 becomes runway 4-Right, a bearing of 40 degrees magnetic.)

Thurston Basin enters Jamaica Bay half a mile from 22's threshold at a distance of 4,120 feet from the runway border. Along the edge is a bulkhead set upon deep driven pilings to retard the water from encroaching the airport's landfill. From the junction where the creek enters the bay, the bulkhead edges closer and closer to the runway, its nearest point being less than 400 feet. The slope from 22-Left to the bay runs on an incline of about four degrees; on the night of February 20, it was under twenty-two inches of snow packed solid and coated with ice. The bulkhead was only two feet out of the water as the tide was high and waves were breaking against the barrier, sending up sheets of icy water curling about forty feet back up the incline toward runway 22-Left.

Because of the recurrent snow storms the previous week piles of snow measuring seven feet in height had accumulated, but these hard clumps were far enough from the runway so as not to interfere with aircraft operations.

When they reached the taxiway adjacent to 22-Left, Mike counted elven planes in front of them. It would be over half an hour before IA's 15 could be airborne. From the windshield he could see down the runway; there was a 747 taking off and he noticed her tail strobe light as she rotated somewhere around 6,000 feet into the murky storm.

"I think the visual range is better," Mike said.

"Yeah, it is," Larry noted. "Wish the damned sleet would quit—godawful racket."

Mike switched over to the tower frequency and told the controller they were ready in sequence. At that moment the runway visual range was 7,000 feet and the control tower could see the Stretch 8 move into position. The time was 8:45. It had been nine hours since Mike had his last drink and he felt fine, but he knew it would be a long night and he wondered if he would be visiting the first lavatory. He decided not to think about it. He picked up the PA.

"Ladies and gentlemen, Captain Hagen again. We're near the runway for takeoff and there are about eleven planes in front of us, so we'll be delayed up to half an hour. The runway visual range is improving so we might pick up some time. While we're waiting, I'm going to turn off the No Smoking sign, but before we go, please make sure all cigarettes are out. Also, I think we'll open up the bar for a little refreshment. Again, before we takeoff, all tray tables must be secured and the seats brought to upright positions. I would also recommend that your seat belts be securely fastened for your comfort and safety. Thank you."

The stewardesses who were seated on the jump seats shook their heads. The coach passengers wouldn't order too many drinks since they had to pay for them, but there'd be a lot of action in first-class where the drinks were free. On a night like this probably everybody would want a couple. One of the girls working coach came forward to help out and she took a tray of glasses and filled them with ice as Louise and the second stewardess moved down the aisle taking orders.

The TV men asked Louise if they could sit in the lounge and they signaled Brenda Moore and all moved forward.

"Would you like a Coke, Marsha?" Pat asked.

"I guess so," the child said, yawning.

"We'll have three vodka martinis, sweetheart, and some nuts if you have 'em," Kurt said, as Louise passed.

She ignored his rude manner and told them to fasten their seat belts.

"Did you get the drink order, honey?"

"Yes, Sir, I did!" Louise said snappily.

"Those little characters think they own the airline," Brenda Moore said, settling down in the lounge, bringing her skirt just high enough for Kurt and his writer friend to see her extremely well-shaped long legs.

The two nuns ordered tomato juice and far back in the coach section a lady sitting on the aisle next to the elderly scientist said, "Would you like me to order something for you?"

"Perhaps a brandy. That would be kind."

The DC-8-61 moved slowly toward its turn for takeoff. It was now 9:00 and there were still six planes in front of them. Mike rang the stewardess and asked for coffee as he brought the Stretch 8 closer and closer to the runway for takeoff.

When they were number two in position, Mike made another PA.

"We are next in line for takeoff, folks. We apologize once more for the delay. I'm going to turn the No Smoking sign back on. Please be sure all cigarettes are extinguished, tray tables are up and fastened, and your seats are in the full upright position."

The stewardesses quickly secured the galley; Louise and her assistant made a visual check of first-class while the four other flight attendants carefully went through the coach section, seeing that everyone was belted in and all tables stored. When they were satisfied, they sat down, the male attendant, Billy Joe, and one of the girls on the left side of the galley door near exit 11, the other two stewardesses on the right side of the galley adjacent to exit 12.

The second stewardess belted herself in on the jump seat that unfolded from the forward bulkhead near the main entrance door. The TV personality and her two male friends insisted on remaining in the lounge. They sat facing Pat and the little girl, who was nodding by now. As Louise went forward to take her seat, she noticed that Kurt's belt was hanging loosely around his middle.

"Would you tighten your seat belt, please, Mr. McGovern."

"Of course, dear."

She sat down on the jump seat with the second stewardess and took out a Gothic paperback.

The aircraft directly in front of IA 15, S.A.S.'s nightly Scandinavian service, was a DC-8-63, a long-range version of Mike's plane. The DC-8-63 swung on-to 22-Left and held for about ten seconds as the forward traffic cleared. The wind was gusting, holding from the southwest and whipping across the field just a bit from the left side. The before-takeoff checklist was read, each man contributing to the challenges and responses, and as the S.A.S. flight started her takeoff run, the control tower notified IA 15 to taxi into position and hold. Mike curled his hands around the throttles, brought them forward, and steered the "big 8" onto the runway. He lined her up with the white center stripe; he saw almost all the way down the runway. He called the tower.

"Say wind again."

"Thirty knots, gusting forty, 200 degrees," came the word back from the controller.

"Hurricane," Larry commented.

They remained at the threshold for about twenty seconds; the controller could not see the runway but he was monitoring the departures via his ground surveillance radar.

"What's he waiting for?" Mike asked.

Finally, at 9:19:30, the tower controller said, "IA 15, you're cleared for takeoff."

"IA 15."

Mike took his feet off the brakes and eased the thrust levers slowly up to forward position. (This was a full-thrust takeoff.) The plane directly behind them was a United 747, and the copilot who was watching the IA takeoff thought that the jet was *not* gathering speed as quickly as it should have. The turbines roared out their full thrust, 63,500 pounds, and again the noise was deafening. The TV group in the first-class lounge continued to talk about the season's ratings and the nuns in first-class curled their hands around the arms of their seats. Marsha pressed her nose to the window of the DC-8 watching the landing lights on her side flash by. Ten seconds into the takeoff run, the plane was only up to thirty knots and by 9:19:40 had covered 450 feet of the iced runway. Carl Smith, who was sitting at a window seat in coach, noticed how slowly the white runway lights were passing; the co-pilot of the United 747 saw the DC-8 move gradually into the slashing rain.

At precisely 18 seconds into the takeoff run, the RVR again changed from 6,500 to 3,100 feet, obscuring for Mike and Larry the extreme end of the runway. As the copilot in the waiting 747 saw the tail of the Stretch 8 disappear into the rain- and hail-soaked shroud, he continued to feel that the acceleration was slow.

Mike shared the same thought.

At 9:19:58, the airspeed indicator wriggled into the 80-knot range and they had covered 1,125 feet.

(On this night, V-1, the decision speed, was calculated according to gross weight at 141 knots with rotation, or reference, coming at 153.)

Mike could see a yellow smudge at the terminal end of 22-Left, the strobes disappearing into the blackness of Jamaica Bay. He sensed that something was wrong.

What? The headwind? To the pilot's sensitive ear, the high-pitched roar of the turbines sounded okay.

"George, are those turbines up there?" he asked with a loud snap to his voice.

"Yes, Sir! Fine."

The white airspeed needle struggled up into the 90-knot area sluggishly and painfully. For a fraction of a second, Mike didn't believe the needle. Shit, he said to himself, it could be at 120. Maybe the ice had frozen a pitot tube. No, the air intake was electrically heated. Innumerable thoughts raced through his mind; they came in microseconds; 26,000 flight hours were on the line. They entered the final stretch at 9:20:05; 4,000 feet were behind them, half the runway.

"Airspeed, Larry?"

"110."

Carl Smith in the coach section pressed his face closer and closer to the window. Why hadn't they rotated? The runway lights were passing too slowly. He listened. No change in the turbines; pitch, whine continuous—100 percent output.

The time was 9:20:10; they had been in the takeoff run 40 seconds. The strobes at the pier end of the runway were more defined now, coming up like the entrance lights to hell.

Although Louise sat with her eyes fastened on the pages of the Gothic novel, she suddenly realized the plane was taking a long time to get off. She had been flying for six years and was aware unconsciously of changes in the sound of the plane.

The nuns sat staring out the window. It was their first flight and they had no idea whether the takeoff should last forty-five seconds (the right timeframe for a gross weight DC-8-61) or five minutes. Others scattered about the plane thought that, perhaps, the takeoff was lasting longer than it should have, but there were no different sounds or signals. The group in the first-class lounge was completely oblivious to what was happening. They simply assumed that the pilot of the heavily laden jet knew exactly what he was doing. After all, that's what they paid for: safe, efficient transportation in soft seats and pretty girls to serve them big drinks.

"I don't like it, Larry!"

"Me neither!"

"Abort!" Mike screamed.

At that precise moment the DC-8-61 was

4,900 feet down the runway; the airspeed needle was vibrating in the 121 range, still under V-1. The spoilers were extended. Mike yanked his four throttles back; his hand flipped on top to four smaller throttles and he pulled them back, reversing the thrust of the turbines. He touched the brakes as he yanked on the reverse throttles.

Nothing.

But he already knew that the runway was slick and for an instant, between the time the forward thrust was wrenched back and the reverse direction pushed forward, the roar of the turbines went dead and only the bawling wind could be heard.

An eerie stillness.

The pilot in coach said to himself, "The best sound in the world, the silence of an abort." He had waited a long time for the pilot to pull it and the TV group suddenly stopped in mid-sentence; Brenda Moore shook her head, another delay.

Pat grabbed Marsha. She knew something was wrong. The nuns thought the plane was in the air. Of the six cabin attendants, only Louise had experienced an aborted takeoff; she threw her paperback down. She knew what was coming: the extreme higher pitch of the turbines in reversing thrust; the accelerated forces pushing people about. She hoped they hadn't missed any seat belts; it was too late now. Among the passengers, only a few apprehended the danger, but all realized that something had gone wrong.

Then they heard the higher pitched scream of the reversed turbine pushing out thousands and thousands of pounds of hot, compressed air. Three seconds had gone by. The plane traveled another 528 feet and the needle encased in the airspeed indicator dropped back into the 110 range.

At the controller's side in the tower is the surface detection equipment. He had watched the progress of flight 15 down 22-Left, its image the form of a small airplane moving on his "bright" scope. The controller also thought that the aircraft was proceeding sluggishly. After watching hundreds of departures in low-visibility conditions, he knew about how long it took for a jet to disappear from his scope and now, instead of accelerating toward rotation speed, the small airplane was actually slowing. The controller realized an abort was taking place.

"IA 15, are you aborting?" he asked.

Silence. They were too busy in the cockpit to answer.

"IA 15, do you read me?"

The wind was now cutting across the runway at an 18-degree angle and at the far end it was still gusting 40 knots. The plane wanted to move her nose into the high wind that blew from the left side of the runway. It began slowly.

As soon as he realized he had lost directional control, Mike took out his thrust, putting it back to forward idle. Then he used the only thing he had going for him at that point: the rudder. He jammed his foot in to straighten out the plane and for a moment she seemed to swerve just a bit toward the center of the runway.

"Goddamnit! Do something, rudder!" Mike shouted. "What the fuck's the matter here?"

"Let me try my side," Larry yelled.

Nothing.

Seeing the ice wall coming up, Mike used a touch of reverse thrust on the far side hoping that the asymmetrical thrust would bring them around. The jet was now in a beeline for the ice piles on the side of the runway.

The jumble of sounds: engines screaming forward; others thrashing out air in the opposite direction set up a chain of instant fear throughout the cabin. Pat gripped Marsha tightly. Far back in the coach section, Carl Smith sensed they had lost directional control; the lights to the side of the runway were coming up closer at an oblique angle. The nuns' hands were fastened around their rosary beads. And Brenda Moore froze in her seat, head bent as she tried to look out to see what was wrong.

The airspeed needle was wobbling around 80 and dropping off. Worse than the medley of turbine sounds evoking alarm along the plane's 127 feet of cabin was the swaying, surging motion set up by the opposite thrusts from each side of the wings. In its giant arch away from the ice piles, the DC-8 began an insidious side-to-side motion that accelerated, rocking the passengers faster and faster. They knew something dreadful was about to happen, and fear and panic showed in their faces. There were shouts of "What's wrong?" Carl Smith thought he knew; he quickly put his head down on his knees and called to the other passengers to do likewise. The kaleidoscope of noises and motions changed in fractions of seconds.

Mike was helpless. He saw the snow pile coming up and then after a painful few seconds, the plane began a sluggish turn away from the left side of the runway. The nose swung to the right; they were looking at the runway lights on the opposite side and Mike retarded the full thrust on the left wing.

At that precise moment, 9:21:14, the left wing of the N4962C was 37 feet over the side of runway 22 and completing the second half of its rapidly turning arc. The DC-8 wing rises on an angle of 6.5 degrees from the root, the point at which it meets the fuselage, to the outboard tip. At each end of the 148-foot wing spar, the tips are 17 feet 3 inches off the ground and there was over a 7-foot clearance between the piled snow and the underside of the wing.

No problem.

But 27 feet in from the wing tip hung the outboard Pratt and Whitney turbine on its pylon; there was less than 6 feet clearance between the bottom of the engine and the piled snow. A crucial obstruction.

The turbine smashed into the packed icy snow.

The collision speed was 78 knots; the exerted local forces about 3 positive, 2 negative. The brittle ice crushed the titanium fan blades in the turbine and the nose bullet settled far into the barrier, up to the integral gearbox on the bottom, the oil cooler on top.

Louise realized that something had gone wrong with the abort. She thought they had shattered the outboard, although much of the shock was absorbed, the force of the impact being dissipated as it traveled in along the wing. The stewardess beside her said something that she couldn't hear; the girl's face was white.

George Gibbons saw it first—a flashing fire warning light from the outboard turbine. Had the jet been moving faster when the engine glanced off the icy pile, it might have been deflected like a fast-driven billiard ball and the Stretch 8 would have continued its right turn. But the collision speed had just the right amount of inertia to rip the turbine from its pylon and it fell away, hanging on for a split second by shredded pieces of innards before belching out raw kerosene and black smoke. The grinding tear had ruptured the wing's inner spar torsion box that formed the outboard fuel tank and the distillate spurted up and out, covering the left wing.

Mike felt the plane's motion halt slightly. Everybody did. The seat belts were already digging into the passengers' stomachs as the negative decelerating forces took effect. The violent swaying movement, the sickening rolling sensation assaulted the frightened passengers with one wave after another. The cabin was a blur and the lights flickered.

"Fuck it! Fuck it! Fuck it!" Mike said.

His feet fought vainly with the limp rudder pedals, and as his hand reached over to retard all power and the plane swung in, he already could see that the turbine was gone. For a fraction of a second, as the turbine intake vanes were burying themselves in the ice and just before the engine ripped away, the force acted like a pivot plunged into the ground; it shifted the plane's direction, spinning it directly toward the snow pile. The acute change in the jet's course rocked everyone inside. Pat held tightly onto the shrieking child. The nuns were praying. Brenda Moore wailed.

The radar scanner hit the wall of snow first and it pushed the whole unit back against the pressure bulkhead. The controls came back in Mike's hands and his knees were jammed up into his stomach. The jet hit at 73 knots and it broke through the top of the ice pile, hurling jagged pieces high into the air. Mike felt the first "G" forces, then the windshield was blocked by a million bits of flying ice. Fifteen feet in from the front of the plane the nose gear smashed into the heaped snow and ice and the whole underside of the DC-8 began to peel away; the clawed chunks of ice cut the skin of the jet, opening it up as easily as a surgeon's knife cuts into a fleshy stomach.

The crash was deafening. Longitudinal and transverse floor beams directly under the first-class cabin were ground and meshed together. On the lower sides the air-conditioning ducts were twisting, shredding, and ripping.

As the wing and the three remaining engines hit the snow bank, the first galvanic shock was felt. The passengers' heads bounded forward. Most of them struck the semi-padded seat in front. Teeth sunk into lips and cut the soft inner flesh of the mouths. Jaws were smashed and noses gushed blood. There was a moment of stunned silence, then everyone seemed to cry out at once. It was a nightmare as the lights flickered and went out, leaving them in blackness.

Louise felt the shock and her head snapped back against the bulkhead and stars flashed before her eyes for a minute; then her body went the other way. She felt a pain in her stomach as the seat belt settled further down into her gut. But it held. The second stewardess was not as lucky; her seat belt came loose when her pelvis responded in the negative "G" force reaction to the crash. She spilled out and was thrown aft, her head glancing off the back of the first-class lounge. The girl crumpled up in the darkness.

Just at that point, about a hundred feet past the ice wall, the forward galley became a hot pressure chamber. It did not come apart; it disintegrated, more like an explosion of grenades, spitting out bits of lethal shrapnel: trays, bottles, glasses, loose silver, oven doors, and, finally, splashes of hot coffee that hit the second stewardess on her legs. The barrage hit the TV group as their heads snapped back. The seat belts held but their heads became targets for the exploding galley. They all fell forward uttering loud agonizing screams.

Outside the Pratt and Whitneys were stripped from their pylons and the left wing opened at the integral root that formed part of the center fuel tank. As the wing section went over the snow wall, two longitudinal floor beams under seats 14, 15, 16, and 17-D burst, thrusting the jagged, raw aluminum up through the cabin floor. Kerosene began to gush out, forming a small geyser in the coach section. The stench of the distillate spread immediately. Passengers started gagging and someone shouted there'd be a fire.

Once over the banked ice and snow, the plane began to decelerate rapidly as it slid down the incline toward the turbulent bay. The beautiful DC-8 was nothing but a long tube now, one wing partly attached and dragging. The other parts—the turbines, horizontal stabilizer, and the left wing—were scattered about the icy wall, spewing out gallons of volatile fuel. The windshield was clear of ice again and Mike could see the bay in front of him, the waves curling and breaking into long froths in the black night. Cakes of ice were piled and jammed against the three-foot-high bulkhead. The nose of the Stretch 8 reached the edge. The plane sliding down the ice on its ripped up belly was still under forward momentum, and the nose continued over the water. N4962C would have plunged into the frigid waters of Jamaica Bay had not the longitudinal beams under seats 6, 7, and 8 in first-class cracked and burst. The shock wave opened the fuselage 26 feet aft of the nose. The front part dipped into the black waters. Like a knife, it dug into the soft, slimy mud seven feet down; the left front windshield popped out and icy, sewage-filled water burst into the cockpit. What was left of the nose slid along the mud for a few feet, then bounded up from the bottom breaking the surface once again like a whale coming up for air. The 820-foot slide of the long DC-8-61 finally came to an end.

It had taken only eleven seconds for the huge airliner to complete her torturous plunge into the soft bottom of the bay after she began her final, uncontrolled swerve.

The controller monitoring the bright scope could not believe what he was seeing. Not only did the little airplane on his scope begin to slow down, it went crazy, zigzagging across the runway until it left the strip on an erratic route toward Thurston Basin.

"Holy shit!" he screamed out loud.

Each of the tower's four controllers jerked up.

"She just went off the runway," he said in awe. Instinctively, the controller pushed the crash alarm.

"IA 15, do you read?"

At that moment three members of the snow committee were standing in the lee of the blast fence located to the west of runway 22-Left. They were watching the sanders move down the parallel runway; hearing the change in the sound of the DC-8, they knew that something had gone wrong on the active. The men hurried to the far side of the fence just at the moment the Stretch 8 went over the ice pile and down the incline. They ran to their car that was parked to the side of taxiway zebra and one of them switched to the tower frequency.

"There's an abort on 22-Left! The plane's off the runway."

"Was there an explosion?"

"No."

A string of carefully planned operations was put into effect at once. The controller handling traffic immediately pushed a button on the 301 system, an instant inter-phone communication with hangar 11, the common IFR room.

"We've had an abort on 22-Left," he told the departure controller, who had not seen the flight come up on his scope.

Then he turned to the man next to him, the local control coordinator, one of the four positions in JFK's tower. "Close 22-Left down."

Another button was pushed and the coordinator informed approach control of the situation; it meant that JFK immediately ceased all operations as the other runway, 22-Right, was still being sanded.

Fourteen miles away in the dark rainy skies over Long Island a Lufthansa 747 jet, the nightly arrival from Frankfort, was on a heading toward the outer marker for runway 22-Left. Approach control instructed the flight to execute a missed approach; gear and flaps came up as the pilot in command moved his thrust levers forward.

On the ground equipment began moving toward the accident site. There had been a slight delay; the controller, in his haste, had neglected to tell the emergency equipment units housed in two locations at JFK the position of the accident and they called back on the inter-phone.

"Did you hit it by mistake?"

"Shit, no! We have an abort."

"Where?"

"Two-two left, a DC-8 in the infield about three-quarters of the way down. The guys on snow detail say there's no fire but get out there!"

The accident was reported to the New York City Fire Department's dispatcher and equipment from several Queens companies rolled toward JFK. Men on these trucks would render what initial assistance they could and, at the same time, evaluate the situation, ordering additional support equipment if necessary.

Throughout his 26,800 "good hours," Mike never thought it would happen like this. On the night of February 20, the obscene occurred. Mike's crash, the only one of his life, took place before flight. A lousy ground crash. Most appalling of all, it had happened after an abort with two high-time captains in the cockpit. There were over 52,000 combined flight hours between Mike Hagen and Larry Zanoff, and yet their expertly maintained DC-8-61 was in pieces, the front half resting on the bottom of Jamaica Bay. An abortive crash before reaching V-1 speed is one of the rarest of all accidents, accounting for only nine fatalities in the history of U.S. civil aviation.

Mike had never figured it this way and it so shocked him that he didn't feel the frigid water pouring through the shattered cockpit windows. The crash had been swifter than he imagined, far noisier as the galleys and bulkheads burst open behind them, but the acceleratory forces, the shock of the crash, were less than he visualized. The shoulder harness dug into his chest. It held: his head hadn't crashed through the windshield; his ribs weren't enmeshed in the control wheel, and his neck hadn't snapped back.

What were the exculpatory forces: What had gone wrong? How did they lose it? Was it the brakes? Why had the DC-8 not reached her V-1 speed in time? George had said the turbines were functioning. When Mike pressed the rudder pedals, nothing happened. Even Larry tried. What had the rudder pedals to do with the lag in acceleration? The pilot's mind was fuzzy with questions.

He became aware of the cold bay water creeping up around and released his belt. He heard nothing, nothing but wind and the slap of waves upon the bulkhead behind them.

It was pitch black.

His cock was hurting. It was the first pain he felt.

The sharp slices of icy water surrounding his genitals propelled him out of his seat; he didn't know how long he had sat there thinking. Perhaps only a second. He had lost track of time.

"Christ, Mike, we're not polar bears," Larry said as he snapped up from his right seat position. "Let's get the hell out and help those passengers."

Both men stood. The water was up to their waists and cascading in. George Gibbons sat dazed at his board. His head was bowed and he was close to tears.

"The turbines were okay," he cried. "Okay. *Nothing* was wrong!"

"Come on, buddy," Mike said. "Out! We're sinking in this fucking cesspool and there's people back there."

They pulled George from his seat and could feel his shoulders shaking. Mike groped for the flashlight mounted on the bulkhead wall. When he found it, he flashed it on the engineer's panel and found the DC emergency lighting switch. Mike threw the lever.

Not even a flicker.

The ice had cut the cables smashing the power packs. The vital light units were gone. Mike cut off the fuel control levers and pulled the fire control levers that disconnected fluids to the engines. By now Larry had reached the cockpit door. He jerked on it. But in the glare of Mike's light, he could see that the bulkhead was twisted by the torsional racking of their crash and the long slide over ice.

The three men trapped in the front did not know what was on the other side of the door. Larry thought the cockpit had been severed from the rest of the plane and was sinking to the bottom of the bay. There were no screams from outside. All they could hear were the high whistle of the wind and the pounding of powerful waves. They had no idea that the forward section of the plane was resting on the bottom of Jamaica Bay. The water continued to pour in and they all thought they were going down. George leaped up on the seat trying to pull open the emergency top hatch while Mike and Larry yanked at the jammed door, curling their fingers around the bend in the top half.

"The ax!" Larry yelled.

Mike took it down and began to hack through the door which was constructed of five dual layers of almost impregnable Formica and plywood. It was designed to keep out hijackers; in 1967, it had replaced the original light cockpit door that came with the plane.

For some seconds after the plane came to rest, there was complete silence in the cabin, the stillness of shock. The passengers stared around them, unable to see anything in the dark; then, there were sobs, some mounting into cries and screams of panic as the water level began to rise in first-class, and the smell and shower of kerosene from the belly tank rose in the coach section.

The sudden sounds from the other side of the cockpit told the flight deck crew that the front end of the plane was still attached to the main body of the fuselage, and they chopped furiously at the door, all the while expecting a delayed distillate explosion. That was their main fear, not drowning, but burning to death.

Several conditions must be exactly right for Jet 1-A to explode; the flashpoint must be attained and the fuel ignited. On this night as the jet sailed over the ice into Jamaica Bay, the conditions were not met, but distillate ignition is not an exact science, and the cockpit crew and the American pilot in the coach section knew the plane could turn into a ball of fire at any time.

Billy Joe had always wondered how he would act in an inevitable crash situation. He had memorized safety procedures and undergone the hours of simulation and training that were drummed into everyone. Neither he nor the other attendants in the coach sec-

tion were apprehensive in the beginning. Two of the
girls had been with the company five years, as signi-
fied by the gold wings they wore, and were fairly blasé
about the delay and the problems that night. The other girl, a small, pretty brunette, was very junior. She
had been pulled off reserve to fill in for a sick stewardess. Billy Joe himself had been with IA only a year.

When the plane began to swerve and rock violently, Billy Joe knew they weren't going to get off the
ground and immediately started thinking about emergency procedures. Remain calm, of course, wait until
the plane came to a complete stop, open galley door,
activate the slide, and command the passengers in an
orderly evacuation.

It didn't work that way.

The aft right galley came apart, shifting back-
ward on the negative "G" cycle, squashing the galley
bulkhead and unleashing the entire equipment, almost
crushing the two senior stewardesses who were strapped
in the jump seats. Billy Joe heard the Formica tear
away from the bottom longitudinal floor beams. The
girls across from him screamed, but at that moment
the lights went out. His head snapped back against the
bulkhead. He expected the wall to collapse and dug his
feet in to brace himself, but the bulkhead held.

In the blackness just after the jet came to a stop
and before the frenzied shouting began, Billy Joe un-
strapped himself and started toward the emergency
flashlight located behind 37-D, but he fell over something and tumbled into the aisle. When he got up, he
was turned around and didn't know which side was left
or right. His orientation returned and he located the
flashlight and removed it from its mounting.

In the beam of the powerful light, he saw the
destruction.

Seats had ripped loose from their supports and
were resting upside down. Passengers with loose seat
belts still dangling around them had been flung out; he
could see arms and legs twisted together in what had
been the center aisle. Mixed in with the crumpled

passengers were coats, pillows, blankets, attaché cases and overhead hat racks that had fallen down. Slowly, people began to move and moan and when the shrieks of panic returned, Billy Joe knew that most of them had survived or were mobile enough to get out of the aircraft. His light beam swung back and forth, and he picked up the splintered bulkhead and twisted metal of what had been the right galley. He quickly went over and peeled back the bulkhead parts, flinging the food-stuffed trays wherever he could, and dug the stewardesses out. They were dazed but didn't seem to be seriously injured.

They crawled to their feet. One of them had a swollen eye and a gash on her cheek. The other stewardess was holding her arm carefully and seemed uncertain as to what had happened. Their hair and uniforms were soggy with debris from the galley. The young junior girl who had been on one of the fold-up jump seats had banged her head when she was bounced up in the air, but otherwise she seemed unhurt and had already positioned herself at the left galley exit, 11, and was wrestling with the door. Billy Joe stumbled over coffee pots and hot cups to help her, and they yanked up the handle and the door opened; a gust of icy wind and rain entered the dark cabin. It was about a seven-foot drop to the ground below, and Billy Joe let out the chute which inflated and flopped on the ice until it was picked up by the wind and flung around.

The two older stewardesses found flashlights and moved forward to assist in evacuation from the Jet-escape doors, exits 9 and 10. The right rear door was inoperable; the deluge from the galley had completely blocked the exit.

The flow of kerosene into the coach section was strong and someone yelled, "This plane's going to blow up!"

"Explosion, let's get out!"

This started a stampede. Carl Smith, who had been sitting close to Jetescape 9 on the left side, was uninjured in the crash and already had the door open. He shouted, "Take it easy everyone. This way, don't panic."

The slide was inflated and he began pushing the people out, yelling at them to get away from the plane. The girl who had been struggling with the Jetescape door on the right side couldn't get it open and Carl went over to help her. The exit seemed to be jammed and he told the passengers who were crowding around to use the rear doors and wing exits.

The stewardess shouted to be heard, "Don't try to take your personal belongings. Leave everything and get off the plane."

The first people to reach the crash site were the members of the snow committee, a TWA pilot, and two Port Authority employees. They stood on top of the icy bank looking down.

"Christ, it's sinking in the bay!" the pilot yelled.

"We better try to help," one of the men said.

"She could go any time. Wait, the trucks will be here in a minute."

The black water was pouring into the first-class cabin when the flight crew broke through the cockpit door. The first thing Mike saw was Pat's bloody face. She was sitting dazed in a litter of spilled galley trays still holding the hysterical child. He pushed through the rubbish and unbuckled her.

"Are you hurt, darling?"

"No, I'm okay. What happened?" she asked.

"Don't know, we lost directional control somehow."

Mike noticed the water streaming up through the floor. The nuns were petrified, their lips still moving in prayer. Louise had a flashlight out by this time and she was shouting at the scrambling passengers.

"Stay calm, don't panic, you'll all get out!"

No one listened and Mike knew about passengers in a crash. They are not rational; only the emotions rule and young men ran over women in their fight to reach the open wing sections. The forward entrance and galley doors were completely useless and Mike pushed his way through the water and pulled at the Jetescape. It opened and he felt the blast of frigid air as he looked below; there was slick ice leading directly down to the bay, and the pilot realized that any passengers using this exit would probably slide straight into the water.

"They'll have to exit over the wings! Use the right side," Mike yelled.

He climbed over broken seats again, seeing the bruised faces of those moving along what had been the aisle now filled almost to seat level with litter. The water was up to row four, then five. Larry and George were working through the partly submerged rubble of the first-class lounge. The couch was ripped off its deck supports and the galley across from the TV executives had plunged on top of them; Brenda Moore was in the heap someplace. Icy water swirled in around them. The crew dug frantically into the pile of debris and reached the three people. Brenda Moore was unconscious and the others were spitting out blood. Rolls and salads bobbed around in the bay water, which now reeked of garbage and kerosene.

Mike and Louise had the wing exits open; they threw the windows out and yanked on the nylon ropes. The people would need them when they got out on the slippery wing. One of the passengers helped lift the injured second stewardess over the sill. Louise hurried back to get the two trembling nuns.

The group in the lounge was freed and the TV star was dragged out by two of the men. Mike picked up Marsha and led Pat to exit 6, where she and the child stood in line to follow the coughing, frightened passengers onto the wing.

Outside, Pat felt the bite of the wind, the blast of cold air against her shivering body. She and the child were completely soaked, and they smelled of kerosene. She handed the little girl to one of the men passengers

and slid down the trailing surface of the cold metal.
The people had tried to form a human chain along the
wing and up the slight incline. They fought just to
stand up against the pressure of the wind and slippery
surface. Pat grabbed Marsha and made her way over
the trailing edge of the wing; several times her feet
went out from under her. All she could think of was
getting the child away from the plane, and Mike—she
didn't want to leave him there.

On the outboard side of the wing she slipped
again in a gushing pool of kerosene. The main fuel
tanks under the plane's center fuselage section had
burst high on the hill, just in back of the ice wall, and
the entire surface was coated with the lethal liquid that
streamed into Jamaica Bay. Those who were out of the
plane started clawing their way up the slithery kerosene hill, groaning as the wind tore into them.

The three members of the snow committee scrambled down the distillate-covered slope to meet the passengers and help them up. The TWA pilot continued
on to the DC-8. The smell of raw kerosene was everywhere. Survivors were still spilling from the plane and
the pilot fought his way past several people and
climbed aboard; he saw Mike and Larry trying to carry
out a man still strapped to his seat. It was the elderly
scientist. He looked as if his neck was broken. There
were only a few left inside who could walk; the others
were unconscious in their seats or lying about the
aisle.

"We heard the accident and reported it to the
tower," the TWA pilot told them. "Crash equipment
should be here soon."

"Thanks," Mike said.

The TWA pilot waded into the murky water,
pointing his flashlight at the seats.

"Careful up front," Larry called. "I think she's
going down."

Crews from the quick-dash vehicles arrived on
the scene and immediately began to assist in the evacuation; they directed the passengers away from the

kerosene outflow, bringing them up the far side of the incline. Within a matter of minutes the major crash equipment was there and the hoses were unrolled from the 3,000 gallons-per-minute pumpers, and a mixture of water and foam was quickly sprayed on the distillate fuel to seal it. Two ambulances arrived, followed by the "Triage" unit, a bus-like vehicle, into which the passengers were placed to protect them from the weather and evaluate their physical conditions.

Pat and Marsha had been assisted to the top of the hill where they were placed in the Triage.

"How did it happen? Do you know?" one of the attendants asked.

"The Captain said they lost direction control," Pat replied.

"Thank God there wasn't a fire."

Mike worked frantically with the other crew members to evacuate the passengers. It took just six minutes to clear the plane, but nobody was sure the aircraft would not blow up; sometimes there are delayed detonations when kerosene is pouring out at high rates. Finally satisfied that everyone was out of the wreckage, Mike climbed the hill to find Pat. She was in the Triage unit and had a gash over her left eye; other than that, she appeared to be all right.

"Mike, I didn't know what happened to you!"

"How do you feel?"

"A little lightheaded, that's all."

"Darling, I have to go back and help," he said to her. Then to the driver, "Where will she be taken?"

"Jamaica Hospital, Captain."

Mike kissed Pat and climbed over the snow pile again. Most of the passengers had been brought up; there were a few stretchers being maneuvered slowly to the top.

The spooker!

Mike suddenly realized he would have to board the plane again.

The F.A.A. would tear the aircraft apart, inch by inch, and the spooker would certainly be found. It would have a devastating effect on the whole industry; Mike didn't care very much about IA, but he didn't want to do this to Joe Barnes. He looked over at the nose of the DC-8 and saw it was lower in the water; the plane was settling in the mud. My God, the tide was coming up. He grabbed a flashlight and climbed on the wing.

Larry struggled up the hill with the last of the injured passengers. He looked around for Mike and didn't see him; puzzled, he approached one of the rescue workers.

"Have you seen the captain?"

The man jerked his head toward the dark hulk below. "Went back onboard."

"He's on the plane?" Larry said incredulously. "Why the hell didn't you stop him! It's sinking!"

He turned without waiting for an answer, and stumbled down the hill again toward the DC-8.

Far down the aisle of the mutilated plane, Mike was struggling to open the door to the first lavatory, which was wrenched and twisted. The water slapped at his chest and dragged heavily on his legs, which were numb from the cold. But he had to get the door open and remove the spooker before it was too late. He yanked on the handle, but the door wouldn't budge and the rising water made the job difficult. He felt around for the fire ax and found it near the first-class lounge; he began to chop through the barrier. When he had enough of the door open he wedged his large body inside. The disposal bin had been canted as the bulkhead between the cockpit and lavatory was thrust back at a thirty-degree angle. Mike stuck a numbed hand inside.

The spooker was gone.

"Goddamnit!" he said out loud.

It had, obviously, become loose in the crash and was now somewhere under the water with the litter. He grasped the ax again and began to hack away at the top of the Formica counter. Between his furious smashes, he suddenly heard a loud wrenching sound.

It came from behind him. The plane was moving forward!

The water rose another few inches; Mike pounded desperately at the counter. It finally split open and he reached into the black water feeling for his spooker. He found it almost at once.

The water rose again. The added weight of the rising tide was dragging the shattered DC-8 deeper and deeper into the bay. Mike stared out of the head but the opening was smaller now; the water pressure had built up. At that moment, Mike realized he was trapped in the sinking jet. Goddamnit, he thought, this is the ultimate irony. Hagen, you're going to drown in an airplane. He couldn't believe what was happening to him and gazed at the spooker in his hand, seeing the dim outline of the thermos that had almost ruined him and now was finally taking his life.

"You little bastard!" he screamed. "You're *not* doing this!"

The front section of the plane lurched sickeningly on the ice. Mike sucked in a deep breath and with all the power left within him, he crashed his big body against the lavatory door. It moved slightly. He hit it again and the door gave a little more but the water was rising rapidly. He only had enough strength for one more heave; this time, the door cracked enough to let him through.

Suddenly, there was a sharp, crunching sound beneath him; the front part of the DC-8 was breaking away, sliding into the bay and Mike was going with it; he frantically grasped the back of a seat fastened to the deck and jerked himself toward the rear with the water already up to his neck. The stench made him gag and his muscles ached with the strain; he pulled away to safety just as the plane separated and the cockpit disappeared beneath the bay. He was standing there looking at the black, gaping hole, still clutching his spooker when Larry found him.

"Are you crazy! What the hell are you doing here!" Larry shouted.

Mike said nothing. He turned stiffly and looked at Larry, and then the check pilot saw the thermos in Mike's hand; he grabbed it, looking at the shot glass fastened to it. Larry screwed open the top and sniffed the bourbon. He knew why Mike Hagen had to return to the sinking jet.

"You goddamn SOB. How the hell did you hide that?"

"It was glued to the disposal bin."

"Christ, I looked there."

"Pushed way back. Joe Barnes knew something, didn't he?"

"Yeah, a couple of girls got suspicious when they saw you going in and out of the head so much, and Joe asked me to check it out."

"You're going to tell him?"

"You know I have to—you can't drink on the goddamned airplane! He can handle it any way he sees fit but for now, I'm chucking this thing in the bay. That's all we need on top of everything else. Someone to spot the pilots running around with shot glasses and booze on 'em."

"Larry, I've been off the stuff," Mike cried. "I was almost off!"

"Then why was this aboard? You're a damned fool, Hagen!"

"Protection, that's all. I had withdrawal jitters once, but I'm down to four ounces now. Here. I've got a book, I can show you."

"Book? What the hell are you talking about?" Larry said impatiently.

"This fuck-up tonight had nothing to do with it, Larry. You felt those rudder pedals!" Mike was wild.

"I honestly don't know what happened tonight, but one thing's for sure, fellow, it's all over for you."

"It *wasn't* my fault!" Mike bawled.

"Maybe not. Maybe you're just an unlucky bastard. Come on, let's get the hell out of here."

They stood at the edge of the bay and Larry was

about to throw the thermos into the churning waters when Mike reached for it.

"Let me," he said.

Mike looked around, making sure he wasn't seen by the crash crews busy in the rear of the aircraft, and he tossed his spooker out into the black water. He watched it sink below the surface.

"You little shit."

They huddled there for a moment in the wintry air, then made their way up the incline.

Thirteen

When Joe Barnes was informed by night operations that 15 had crashed after an abort, he rushed from Englewood to Teterboro and chartered a helicopter. It took him half an hour to fly through the bad weather to a clearance area just outside IA's operational entrance. The station manager and night operational chief had kept the F.A.A. from talking to the crew until the company could agree on a joint statement.

By the time Joe Barnes landed, it was fifty minutes after the crash; the time was 10:12. It had been over ten hours since Mike Hagen had a drink, and he sat with Larry and George Gibbons in the night operational manager's office at the direction of Mr. Fitzsimmons who, along with Cliff McCullen and Peter Hanscom, was on his way to the airport.

As soon as Joe entered Operations, the night manager came over and handed the chief pilot the casualty list. No fatalities. There was one broken back, two suspected broken necks, five broken collarbones, three fractured jaws, three concussions, and a collection of other internal injuries plus lacerations. Twenty-six passengers from the flight refused treatment and they signed the carrier's standard release form; the others were taken to Jamaica Hospital for treatment and observation. Joe walked into the office where the flight crew lounged on chairs with blankets over them.

"You guys okay?" Joe asked.

They nodded.

"Have you spoken to the F.A.A.—anybody?"

"No," Larry answered.

"Brass is on the way. Let's get the stories straight. What happened out there? They tell me the plane is totaled."

"Very totaled," Mike said.

"We're lucky there're not too many injuries, but enough to make this damned serious. What happened?"

"Go ahead, Mike," Larry Zanoff said. "You were flying."

Mike got up and walked around the room. "Well," he began, "conditions were bad—not below-minimums, but goddamned windy with some freezing rain. We started down the runway, but the plane wasn't coming up to speed."

"Brake handle off?"

"Yes, I checked that."

"So did I," Larry added.

"Go on," Joe said, lighting his cigar.

"It felt like we were dragging something."

"What about the turbines?" Joe asked the flight engineer.

"Nothing wrong, Captain Barnes. Every engine was up to full takeoff thrust."

"Maybe your brakes locked," Joe said.

"Just the frictional heat would have melted that," Larry interjected.

Joe motioned Mike to continue.

"Well, I just said to hell with it, I didn't like it. So, we aborted. We had her in reverse thrust and she started to weathercock. I pushed in right rudder to compensate, but nothing happened. Then Larry tried it."

"Larry?"

"Nothing there, Joe. Absolutely nothing."

"No steering control?" Joe asked.

"None," Mike said.

"Then what?"

"We put her in asymmetrical thrust and the plane started to swing back to the other side of the runway. The outboard engine struck an iced-over snowpile. This wrenched us around and we crossed the runway at right angles, hit the ice pile at about 75 knots, I guess. The left wing and engines came off and the plane continued down the slope and crashed. The cockpit and part of the first-class section are in Jamaica Bay."

"Sweet Jesus!" Joe said, rubbing his head. "Why didn't you guys abort sooner?"

"We still would've lost direction control. We couldn't brake her on that ice. We aborted long before V-1."

"What was your V-1?"

"141," the flight engineer said.

"What was your speed when you yanked it?"

"I don't think it was even 121," Larry said.

"But you were far down the runway."

"That's true, but nothing seemed to be wrong," Mike said.

"Nothing wrong, except the plane didn't want to accelerate! Shit, of course, there was something wrong —*had* to be," Joe said.

"Joe, can we speak to you alone for a minute."

"Okay. Gibbons, leave us," Joe said, "and don't say anything to anybody until I tell you."

"Captain Barnes, I just wanted to stress again that my board was all right, and I inspected that undercarriage thoroughly . . ." George's voice trailed off plaintively as he gave a hoarse cough.

"I understand. Go call your wife and tell her you'll be here all night. We'll get you some rooms at the International. And ask Medical to give you something for that cold. Sounds terrible."

When the flight engineer had left the room, Joe turned back toward the two senior captains. "Is that what really happened?" he said under his breath, puffing hard on the cigar.

Larry pointed towards Mike, "Do you want to tell him, or should I?"

"Look, you two, let's get the story straight. What the fuck went wrong out there?"

"There's something I didn't want George to hear," Larry said. "Mike?"

"Go ahead, it doesn't matter anymore. Tell him everything."

"What!" Joe blasted. "Tell me what? Come on, don't play games. The F.A.A. and the execs will be here in a minute."

"Mike went back onboard at the last minute," Larry said. "It was a crazy thing to do, he almost got trapped in there. But he had a thermos in the head, Joe. The booze was there all along in the trash bin. Glued in."

Joe Barnes's face became beet-red with rage as he peered alternately at Mike Hagen, then Larry Zanoff.

"Is that true, Mike?"

"Yes, it's true," Mike said with a kind of marked despair. "I was drinking on the plane a while back, but I was almost off the stuff."

"What did you do with the fucking thermos?" Joe said.

"Threw it in the bay."

Joe's heart was racing and he sat down by the desk and buried his face in his hands. He drew in a few breaths and tried to calm himself. It was lucky they had retrieved the thermos because Joe was sure the F.A.A. investigators would have found it. Just the appearance of booze hidden in the lavatory would have cast a tremendous doubt over the whole accident investigation, no matter what had gone wrong with the equipment—if that, indeed, was not the causative factor.

Mike crossed over to Joe and put his hand on the chief pilot's shoulder. "Joe, believe me, I had it under control. I wasn't endangering anyone."

"Did Cochran know?"

"Yes," Mike said.

"Shit, why didn't *you* tell me? I would have understood. I could have helped."

"I'm sorry, Joe, I should have."

"Mike, we're going over to the hospital to take some blood tests. I want to know if there's any booze in your system."

At IA, as at most of the large carriers, it was routine procedure to examine the flight crew following any accident, and the three pilots went over to Jamaica Hospital. After his blood sample was taken, Mike went down to see Pat. Her head was bandaged but X-rays revealed no skull damage. The little girl had been placed in the pediatric section, and her mother was already there. The nuns had lacerations; their teeth were knocked out. Brenda Moore's skull was fractured and the TV executives suffered internal injuries. Of the 203 passengers aboard flight 15 that night, 61 remained at the hospital for treatment. Ten were listed as serious, one critical.

Just after midnight, the lab technician called Joe, "We have the blood and urine analyses, Captain Barnes."

"Give me Hagen first."

"Well, hemoglobin, 13.6, white blood cells, 7,600; rapid plasma—"

Joe broke in, "Was there any measurable alcohol in his bloodstream?"

"Alcohol? No, Sir."

Mike's lunchtime drink had been totally absorbed. Joe walked into the small solarium where Mike sat dozing after he called his wife and spoke to her and the children.

Joe shook him. "Okay, Mike, there was no booze. Let's go over and make out the accident report."

"What happens to me, Joe?"

"I'm so pissed off I can't think straight. We'll talk tomorrow."

"I'm sorry I let you down, Joe. I want to say good-night to Pat and call the doctor to tell him I'm okay."

Mike went into the darkened room and he kissed Pat good-night. "They didn't find any booze in me," he whispered.

"What now?"

"I don't know. Barnes's really mad, but it's a goddamned irony. The only crash of my life and I was cold sober."

The Port Authority ordered runway 22-Left to remain closed until the N.T.S.B. investigation team could reach the scene; that would not be until morning as they had to come up from Washington.

After Joe Barnes had explained the accident to Fitz and the others, the IA group took a company station wagon and, led by a Port Authority official driving a car with a strobe light, the group proceeded to the crash site. The rain had let up by this time but the wind still blew hard from the southwest. As soon as they reached the threshold of 22-Left, Joe noticed something odd. In the far distance he could see the spotlights of the crash equipment trained on the highrise tail of the Stretch 8, but all along the runway there were groups of men in storm parkas laying down small cinder-blocks.

The two cars moved up the runway and about 3,000 feet from the threshold, Joe Barnes ordered the driver to stop.

"Want to see what this is all about," he said.

Joe climbed out and walked across the still slick surface to a group of men huddled around the blocks. He dropped his eyes and saw a piece of rubber being held down and protected by the heavy block.

"Don't touch it!" one of them said. "F.A.A. said to mark each one."

"What the hell is it?"

"That's worn-down rubber from the Stretch 8."

"How many are there?" Joe asked.

"Ten, twelve, all along here. She blew her tires out long before the abort."

Joe stood rigid, paralyzed. The clues were devastating. The chief pilot had no idea what happened to 15, but one thing was certain: the DC-8 had proceeded down 22-Left losing rubber all the way—the wheels weren't turning! As Joe looked down again at the shredded tires, he could see that one side of the jagged rubber was black with heat friction.

He returned to the car and told the driver to proceed up the runway centerline to the next group.

"What was it?" Fitz asked.

"Rubber from our Stretch 8."

"What do you think happened?" Cliff McCullen asked the chief pilot.

"Wheels froze," Joe answered quickly.

"Brakes perhaps?" Cliff said.

"Don't know. Maybe the whole gear."

At the next stop on the runway, Joe saw more shredded bits of evidence: blackened pieces of undercarriage rubber. The plane was surrounded by mobs of people—F.A.A. and the Port Authority. They finally located the F.A.A. district branch chief, who told them that the entire area was roped off. Joe asked if he could inspect the gear, which was lying about.

"Sorry, N.T.S.B. says no. They'll be up on the first flight tomorrow. Port Authority wants the runway open by midmorning if possible. There *is* something you can see."

"The rubber?" Joe asked, pointing back toward the direction they came.

"No. Score marks. That plane was sliding on her rims."

The branch chief took the IA team down the runway about 1,850 feet from the point where the Stretch 8 hit the snow bank. In the glaze of the worklights, Joe could see the deep score marks in the ice, which had been painted with red dye in case the ice melted before the investigators arrived. Photographers had also been called in and movies and stills were recording the path of blackened marks—the trail of the final moments before N4962C lost directional control and plunged into Jamaica Bay.

Joe Barnes suddenly felt sick. He was perspiring in the cold night air as he gazed down on the evidentiary score marks, the long curve that ended on the snow banks where the gear collapsed, leaving the fuselage for its final belly slide into the water.

"Oh, Christ!" Joe said to himself.

What if the plane had taken off. What if Mike hadn't grabbed those throttles! In a frightening, paralyzing moment, Joe saw the rest of the flight. It would have been a normal takeoff. He was certain that with the accelerated headwind, the Stretch 8 would have rotated successfully, become airborne. The gear would have retracted as usual and the green lights on the panel would have turned amber, then gone out.

Joe continued his agonizing scenario: Flight 15 would have moved across country and on their long final into Los Angeles, the gear handle would have been pushed into the down position; the three green lights would have come up on the board indicating that the landing gear was down and locked.

Joe saw it in his mind: sparks kicked off by the tireless gear touching the runway surface, perhaps a swift bump felt in the cockpit. Mike and Larry would have known then that something was wrong, but it would have been too late. The whole assembly would have collapsed. At that speed, probably 130 knots, or so, there would have been structural failure, wings ripping off, a cascade of volatile Jet 1-A, sparks and the inevitable:

Explosion!

Joe's mind went blank and he stood there for a long time looking at the ash-black score marks.

"What are you thinking, Joe?" Cliff McCullen asked.

"I was saying a prayer."

"That they didn't take off?"

"Yeah, it would have been hell on the other end."

"Know what you mean. They're lucky people," the vice-president of the flight department said solemnly.

They were just about to enter the station wagon again when Mike Hagen arrived in a F.A.A. car. He got out and walked over.

"How do you feel, Captain Hagen?" Fitz asked.

"Not too bad. I didn't get hurt. The plane was fairly well decelerated by the time we hit the snow bank."

"Tell 'em what you told me about the accident, Mike."

The pilot related the events leading up to the abort, emphasizing how slowly the plane accelerated.

"Your whole undercarriage was locked, Mike," Joe said.

Mike turned toward Joe Barnes and then he exchanged looks with McCullen and Fitz. The pilot said nothing for a minute.

Joe continued, "All the tires were blown out. By the time you reached the halfway mark, you were sliding over the ice on your rims. There are chunks of rubber all down the runway—score marks where the rims cut the ice."

"Holy shit!" Mike said, realizing what would have happened had the flight taken off.

"When you aborted, you lost directional control. There were no tires on the nose wheel."

"Did this occur to you, Captain?" Fitz asked.

"No."

"Were there any indications of brake problems?" Cliff asked.

"No, while Larry was copying the ATC clearance, I took her away from the gate and let go the brake handle, testing them lightly with my feet. Even though there was ice, the brakes worked at that point."

"Something must have happened between the gate and the runway," Joe said. "We'll know in the morning. It's an investigator's dream. Everything is still intact."

Joe realized now that his pilots had done all they could. He turned to Mike and said, "Beautiful work, Captain Hagen, once again."

There had been nothing on the board or in the

book that indicated anything was wrong with the DC-8. As she raced down the runway on bare rims, it was calculated that the jet would have reached rotation speed about 1,820 feet before the end of runway 22. Joe Barnes knew there were many pilots who would have pulled back on that yoke and taken off. Mike Hagen wasn't one of them.

They climbed into the station wagon and drove away from 22-Left.

In pilot's language, the abort on 22-Left was a rejected takeoff. The Snow Committee, the first ones on the scene, called it a bad crash and that description was re-disseminated from the tower to the police and fire departments and from there to the news media. The press, especially TV, quarries this sort of story; it's big, hard, local news, always visual.

The words "bad crash" coming on such a bitter night resounded throughout the city newsrooms. They rolled quickly. In every station wagon jammed with equipment, newsmen, and technicians the same silence prevailed.

In a city like New York news people are hardened to disasters; that's their work. But an air crash with its own emphatic, grisly horror touched their nerves, and when they arrived on 22-Left after a slow drive along ice-covered approach roads, the newsmen's image of the bad crash was realized. Before them on the icy, foam-soaked infield was the hideous sight.

The harsh emergency lights, the layers of mucky CO_2, the shredded ends of the fuselage resting by the bay with the nose submerged in the black water, heaps of twisted, gnarled wings, tail and engine pieces flung about, the stench of raw kerosene, oil, and other liquids oozing out made the accident appear much worse than it was. The fire trucks, the foam, the tangle of dripping hose lines, the hordes of emergency workers sloshing through the litter with axes and poles evoked the impression that there had been a terrible fire or explosion.

A minute after the press arrived, the IA public relations man who was on the scene quickly told them what had happened.

"You mean everyone walked away from that?" the CBS newsman asked.

"There were a few injuries, but no one was killed."

"Christ, I can't believe it. How did the pilot save everyone?"

Laced into that question was the story. For a change they had a news break, a serious airline crash, where the angle was pilot heroism and skill, not death.

Nineteen N.T.S.B. experts arrived at runway 22-Left the morning after the crash precisely at dawn, 7:10. The evidence was clearly on the runway and when they had charted and measured the bits of rubber and the score marks, they moved to the location of the undercarriage gear scattered near the melted snow bank. Each piece of the plane's undercarriage was marked, charted, and removed, the pieces filling a large F.A.A. stake truck that had been brought to the crash area. Just before 8:00, a portable crane was rolled down 22-Left and each of the Pratt and Whitney power plants, after being marked for location, were lifted onto two more flatbed trucks. A bulldozer pushed past the snow bank and with the crane in position, it pulled the Stretch 8 free of the ice-caked bay. The right wing was cut away from the root after each of the nonruptured Jet 1-A tanks had been drained and a barge crane lifted the forward section out of the water.

When the fuselage was nothing more than a long cylinder, powerful hydraulic jacks were placed against the belly and it was jacked high enough to slip heavy-duty wheeled dollies beneath. By 9:00, what remained of N4962C was being slowly hauled back to IA's hangar number one for reassembly; the various N.T.S.B. teams would begin to sift, study, identify, inspect, and pull out every clue that might tell them what went wrong on the evening of February 20th, why rubber peeled off the rims.

By 10:00 A.M., after the Port Authority had inspected the runway, it was again open to traffic. The ice had melted and the score marks were gone forever; the only hints that there had been an acute abort the evening before were the dark places on the side of 22-Left and the thousands of footprints in the snow.

Joe Barnes called Jim Cochran the morning after the crash. "Get over to my office at La Guardia right away."

"What's wrong?"

"Fifteen cracked up at JFK last night. A friend of yours was in the left seat. No one was killed."

Joe didn't have to say anything more and within an hour the copilot walked into the flight office.

"Jim, let's get this straight from the start. We know all about Mike's drinking, the thermos in the trash bin. I want you just to sit there, relax, and tell me everything. Leave *nothing* out."

Jim related the whole story, how the drinking started, the painful details of the Philadelphia incident.

"Did the flight engineers ever know? Anyone else?"

"No, sir. I was the only one."

"You're absolutely sure?"

"Yes."

"Didn't it occur to you that your duty was to come to me?"

"It did, but Mike said he was going to a doctor and, besides, he was such a damned fine pilot."

"Damned fine pilot," Joe laughed mockingly. "That's beautiful. You just confirmed that he snuck drinks in the head and almost piled up the plane in Philadelphia. Is that a damned fine pilot, Mr. Cochran? If it is, then you and I have some problems."

"I didn't mean it that way. When we were coming into Philly that night, Mike knew he was high and hot, but he simply stuck it on like it was a piece of bacon. Then he made a casual PA explaining that we needed extra airspeed and that's why the landing was so hard. He was very calm."

What rattled Joe's mind was the cluster of approbations surrounding Mike Hagen. Hinged to Jim Cochran's appalling story of the Philadelphia landing was his praise of how the pilot had stuck it on. What a terribly mixed sense of values, Joe thought.

The legend of Mike Hagen became even more entrenched when the New York *Daily News* printed a picture of the wreckage on the front page with a thick black headline: PILOT SAVES 213 LIVES IN JFK CRASH.

If they only knew, Joe thought.

Joe was still trying to put things in order when Mike walked into the office. They talked for quite a while. It was a friendly and candid conversation and, in the end, Mike said he was quitting the airline.

"Why did you dislike IA?" Joe finally asked.

"It wasn't IA, the whole business—I just wasn't right for the job. But there are a few things I can point to."

"Like last night?"

"Yeah. Take super-spy Zanoff . . ."

"I had to do something, Mike."

"Fine, but Zanoff, the perfect IA skipper, the great check pilot and numbers man, sat there last night like a lump. You heard the tape. Did he say anything about that takeoff?"

"No, he didn't."

"*I* was the *one* who rejected it!"

"You were the captain."

"Sure, but if Zanoff suspected something, why didn't he speak up?"

"He didn't suspect anything. Larry told me."

"I didn't think so. There was a similar crash with an 'Eight' up in Alaska. That guy tried to take off and forty-seven were killed. Whatever else you may think of me, Joe, you make damned sure you remember that I saved lives."

Joe agreed with part of Mike's rationalization: it

was true the pilot could do things with planes that few, if any, other captains at IA could match. But Mike's whole magnificent inventory of contact flying skills, the acrobatics, the precise knowledge of how to lay down insecticides on a field whose division lines were high tension wires, and everything else Mike knew or thought he knew had very *little* to do with the job of handling the big jets in an age of computers and specialization. That was the particular tragedy of Mike Hagen. When Mike finally admitted he wasn't right for the airline job, Joe knew that the pilot had come to terms with himself. He was far better off spraying a soybean field.

There remained a large question: were Mike's twenty-one years in the airline business a total wasteland?

The answer was "no." Mike Hagen was an anachronism. He had just been born too late. Though he disregarded many rules and did things his own way, he nevertheless had an uncanny air sense, a quick and frequent smile, and he was one of the few men on the IA line who personally greeted the passengers. Yes, he had just been born too late, for the days of seat-of-the-pants flying had long been over. But Joe realized that, perhaps, there should be just a touch of Mike Hagen in every airline pilot.

"What are you going to do now?" he asked.

"I don't know."

They talked a little while longer, and then said good-bye. As Mike walked down the hall, Joe saw a magazine sticking out from his side pocket—*Ag Flyer,* it said.

Joe leaned against the doorjamb. Mike stopped, waved at him, and then disappeared into the stairwell. The clacks of his heavy footsteps on the metal stairs were wiped out by the roar of a jet taking off.

"Mike," Joe said, though there was nobody there to hear him, "good-bye and thanks for not taking off last night." He looked down the long hall. The empti-

ness of the corridor seemed to mirror the hollow cre-
ated by the departure of Mike, the last of the contact
men. The chief pilot returned to his office and closed
the door.

Note

Eighteen weeks later the N.T.S.B entered its final report on IA 15's attempted takeoff from runway 22-Left, John F. Kennedy International Airport, at approximately 9:20 on the evening of February 20, 1975:

The National Transportation Safety Board determines that the cause of this accident was the failure of the aircraft to attain the necessary airspeed within the determined time frame and runway distance, thus effecting an abortive procedure.

The absence of proper acceleration, undetected by the flight crew until the aircraft reached 121 knots, was the result of extreme frictional drag caused by the failure of all main landing gear wheels to rotate. Due to the iced runway conditions at the time of the attempted takeoff, the aircraft proceeded down the runway over a highly glazed surface until a sufficient heat build up caused detonation and extrusion of the aircraft's eight tires. The remaining ground run of the aircraft was upon the bare rims over an iced surface.

It is further determined that the entire brake system had failed. Investigation revealed that a back pressure of undetermined origin built up in the hydraulic system oil reservoir, which delivers pressure to the brake pads at the time the pilot released his foot brakes. While the accident resulted in several

serious injuries, there was no loss of life. Normal
directional control was lost after the abortive
procedure.

The aircraft impacted an iced-over snow bank to
the left side of runway 22, sending it off the runway.
The forward section of the aircraft came to rest in
Jamaica Bay, the waterway 600 feet southeast of
runway 22. There was no fire or explosion upon
impact.

ABOUT THE AUTHOR

ROBERT P. DAVIS, originally an art director of movies, is now a writer of movies. He will again take on his role of art director when *The Pilot* becomes a film, as well as coproducer and adapter. In 1961 he won an Oscar for his short, *Day of the Painter*. His previous books are *Apes on a Tissue Paper Bridge*, *Good-bye, Bates McGee*, *The Dingle War* and *Cock-A-Doodle Dew*.